MW00883693

WAITING
FOR THE
SUN

ISBN-13: 978-1981946020
ISBN-10: 1981946020

WAITING FOR THE SUN

xoxo
RHill

ROBIN HILL

DEDICATION

To Stephan,
For reading this over and over and over.
For believing in me when I couldn't.
For giving me courage and when that failed, cognac.

PLAYLIST

"Circles" by machineheart

"Touch Me" by The Doors

"La Vie en Rose" by Edith Piaf

"Ain't Never Been Cool" by Ellen Cherry

"Promises" by Ryn Weaver

"This Isn't Everything You Are" by Snow Patrol

"El Perdón" by Nicky Jam & Enrique Iglesias

"Back Door Man" by The Doors

"Watercolors" by machineheart

"Parade" by Meg Myers

"Wrecking Ball" by Miley Cyrus

"It's Over" by Civil Twilight

"White Blank Page" by Mumford & Sons

"Love Her Madly" by The Doors

"Flight" by Lifehouse

"Forever for Now" by LP

AUTHOR'S NOTE

The South by Southwest Music Festival, abbreviated SXSW, is the largest event of its kind in the world and takes place every March in Austin, Texas. It grows and changes annually, so while I tried to keep its treatment as authentic as possible, things that are probable one year are likely improbable the next. Therefore, I took some liberties, combining some likelihoods and omitting others, to enhance the story. Locals refer to the festival simply as South By, which is how it will appear in this book. If you're ever in Central Texas during early spring, I hope you check it out.

Can you feel it,
Now that spring has come?
That it's time to live in the scattered sun.

—The Doors, "Waiting for the Sun"

PROLOGUE

Not To Touch The Earth

Darian

"Darian, come on. Call him back when we get to our gate. I need to get Annie settled and I want to check flight times."

I trail a few feet behind my wife, head down, eyes fixed on my phone. "You can't check them here? There are monitors everywhere, Jules."

I stop abruptly when she does, biting back my smile at the sight of her glare. For the most part, my wife's a pretty understanding woman. She understands why I have to cancel on her because the band got a gig. She understands why I have to take business calls during dinner. Hell, she even understands why I'm a little too polite to the fucking groupies.

Unless she's traveling.

The woman is not a traveler.

"I'm serious, babe. He's called three times in five minutes. I need to take—dammit, Julia, will you wait up?"

I say, watching her tightly wrapped bun bob up and down as she marches off.

I toss my head back and look up as if asking God to please help a guy out.

My dad chuckles behind me.

"Fine," I say to her back as the distance grows between us. "I'll walk and talk."

She turns around and glares at me again. I smile because it makes our little girl giggle.

"You know she's mad at you, Daddy."

"I know, baby."

My mom catches up to me and squeezes my shoulder. "Julia's kaput," she says.

"Kaput? Is that your new word this week?"

Her face lights up. "Yes, it is. What do you think? It's a great word, but no one ever uses it."

"It's lovely, Mom, but Julia can't be kaput. We just got here."

"Cut her some slack. She's a nervous traveler; you know this."

"You're right," I say over the lump of guilt forming in my throat. "And she'll be fine as soon as I get a glass of wine in her."

"Take your call, sweetheart," Mom says, stretching tall to ruffle my hair. "Your dad and I will find her a decent chardonnay." She smiles down at Annie. "Anabel can come with us."

"Yay," Annie says as she tugs on Mom's skirt. She pulls a PEZ candy from her Minnie Mouse dispenser and pops it into her mouth. "What do I get?"

"Anabel, chew first, please," Mom says.

Dad grabs Annie from behind and lifts her over his head until she squeals. "You get milk, small fry," he tells her.

She scrunches up her nose. "Milk? Yuck."

Dad laughs as he puts her down. "No milk, huh? What about a milk*shake*?"

Annie squeals again as she runs ahead to Julia. Prattling about milkshakes, she grabs her mom's hand and bounces up and down, jerking her back and forth like a yoyo. Julia's long, dark hair tumbles to her shoulders, and she stops, right there, in the middle of the busy concourse. Although I can't see her face, I'd bet money her eyes are squeezed shut and she's counting to ten, willing herself not to snap. She looks back at me, and there it is. Glare number three.

God, I love her. She's so fucking cute when she's mad.

"Thanks, guys," I say to my parents. "Make it a big chardonnay."

Dad gives me a thumbs-up as they walk ahead.

I dial my manager back, and he picks up on the first ring.

"Sorry, Rick," I say as I slow my pace. "Trying to navigate an airport with the fam. Not an easy feat. What's up?"

"Thank God I caught you. Have you boarded yet?"

"No. Why?"

"You need to postpone your trip a day," he says.

I stop. "What the hell for? Is this about Bearfield? He's your problem, not mine."

Rick laughs. "No, my boy, this is about Global Records. They have a guy in town. Today only. He heard your demo and wants a meeting."

My heart stops. "Holy shit."

"Holy shit is right."

Adrenaline races through my veins. I grip the back of my neck and shake my head as a foolish grin spreads wide across my face.

No fucking way.

"Darian?"

This could be it.

"Jules is going to be pissed," I say, my smile firm despite my words.

"Jules will get over it when you take her to the Four Seasons in Bora Bora instead of a piece-of-shit all-inclusive in the Bahamas."

"Please. My mom is going," I say. "It's a really nice piece-of-shit all-inclusive."

Rick scoffs. "Whatever you say, man. Look, Darian, I don't have to tell you, Global is the big time. And *they're* asking *you* for a meeting."

Holy shiiiiiiit.

I clear my throat. "What time?"

"Five sharp. Be there at four."

"Have you talked to the guys?"

"Not yet. I wanted to tell you first. I'll call them as soon as we hang up." Rick blows out an exaggerated sigh. "I know this means I'll be out of a job soon, but I'm excited for you. I really am. I'll text you the address."

I find my family in a small café across from our gate. Annie's managed to cover both herself and Minnie Mouse in chocolate, and I laugh at Mom's vain attempt to clean them up. She brightens when she sees me, her eyes meeting mine with a mix of love and amusement as she motions toward an austere-faced Julia and mouths the word, *Kaput.*

Dad gives me his trademark my-life-couldn't-be-better smile as he passes Mom a stack of napkins. I nod and then lower my gaze to my wife. Her hair's been re-piled on top of her head in what can only be described as a bird's nest, and she has more mascara beneath her lashes than on them.

So fucking cute.

It's all I can do to bridle my own my-life-couldn't-be-better smile.

"Daddy!" Annie's high-pitched shriek nearly launches Julia from her chair.

"Hey, little one. Is that good?"

Annie nods and hands me her milkshake. A whiff of chocolate invades my nose as I take a long pull from her straw.

She arches her eyebrows as her little hand reaches for the cup. "Just a sip, Daddy."

"You're right. That *is* good," I tell her.

She smiles.

I sit in the chair beside Julia and carefully pry her fingers from the stem of her glass. "Hey, babe, we need to talk for a second. That was Rick."

Her eyes slowly lift to mine. "Is everything okay?" she asks.

But she knows it is. My grin gives me away.

"Global wants to meet with me. Tonight."

My mother gasps. I turn my smile toward her and her cheeks flush pink.

"Sorry, dear," she says. "You were talking to Julia. I'll try not to eavesdrop." She scoots her chair closer to Annie. "Anabel...oh, honey, look at this mess."

My focus returns to my wife. Her eyes are stretched wide and her grin mirrors my own.

"So, I'm going to meet you guys in Nassau," I say.

I brush the loose pieces of her hair behind her ear. She shakes her head, and more strands fall.

"No way." She pushes back from the table and begins to collect her things. "Are you kidding? We're coming with you."

"No, Jules. You guys go. I'll fly out tomorrow."

"Darian, this is huge."

"I know, baby. That is precisely why I need to do this by myself. I need to focus. And it will be a lot easier to change one flight than five, not to mention the hotel and the car."

Her eyes begin to water and it almost breaks my resolve.

"You'll be fine. It's the Bahamas, for crying out loud. Look, I'll take the red-eye. I'll be there when you wake up in the morning." I hold my hand to her cheek and brush my thumb across her bottom lip. "We'll leave Annie with my parents tomorrow night and I'll take you out to celebrate."

"Darian, come on. We'll wait. We can all go tomorrow. I'll take care of everything."

I reach for her hand and thread our fingers. "I'm sorry, Jules, but no. Mom and Dad live over an hour away, and Annie will be crushed. Can you just work with me on this?"

"Your parents can stay with us, and Annie is spoiled rotten," she says. Her mouth curves into an adorable pout. "It won't kill her to wait one day."

The airline announces preboarding.

I look at my watch. "You need to go."

I lift her hand to my lips and kiss her palm. She pulls it back.

"Look, baby, you're already here. I know you hate to travel, especially out of the country, but they speak English. It's not like you're going to Budapest. And my parents will be with you. I'll be there first thing tomorrow. I promise." I sit back in my chair. "I really need you to do this for me."

She grabs a napkin off the table and dabs the corners of her eyes. "Annie, come spend a few minutes with

8

Daddy. He's going to have to meet us in the morning."

Once I pay the tab, I take Annie's hand and we cross the concourse to our gate. The plane is boarding.

I tell my parents goodbye. I tell them I love them. They each hug me and tell me how proud they are. Mom promises to look after Annie. She says Julia will be fine.

I pick up my baby girl. "Bye, Annie, honey. You be a good girl for Mommy, okay?"

"I will, Daddy."

She hands me her PEZ dispenser, and I smile at the tiny chocolate fingerprints on the stem.

"What's this?" I ask her.

Her little brows furrow in confusion. "It's Minnie."

"I know, sweetie, but why are you giving her to me?"

"I want her to stay with you so you won't be lonely." Her arms circle my neck and a mop of springy curls brushes my cheek. "Now you give me something," she whispers in my ear, "so I won't be lonely."

"I have just the thing," I say, reaching in my pocket for the green piece of plastic I'm never without. "This is my lucky pick. Take good care of it, okay? I need it to play my guitar."

Her body jerks back with a gasp. "It's lucky?" she asks, grinning as if I'd given her a pony. "I promise. I'll take the best care of it ever."

The line begins to dwindle, and I see Julia walking toward us. The look on her face tells me I have some kissing up to do.

Not a problem, I think, glancing down at my carry-on. *When she sees her new ring...*

"Mommy!"

"Oh, Annie. Ouch. You'll make your old man go deaf."

She giggles.

"Think that's funny, do you?" I say, tickling her. "It's time to go." I give her a huge kiss on her cheek and squeeze her tight. "I love you more than anything."

"I love you too, Daddy."

I put my daughter down and turn to the love of my life. "I'll be there tomorrow, Jules. First thing."

She glares at me.

I shrug.

What can I do?

CHAPTER 1

My Eyes Have Seen You

Ten Years Later

> Drew: Having a good time?
>
> Darian: Grr.
>
> Drew: I'll take that as a yes.
>
> Darian: You're a shit friend. You should've come with me.
>
> Drew: You'll thank me when you don't wake up with a hangover tomorrow.
>
> Darian: Whatever.

Frankie

"Hold that thought," Jane says as I turn the corner onto Cesar Chavez.

I've been rambling for the last hour about our five-day South by Southwest adventure in Austin. We haven't missed the music festival in three years, and no way Jose are we breaking tradition and missing it this year. I tell myself this, but the regretful look on my best friend's face tells me something entirely different.

She sets her phone in her lap and sighs. "I can't go."

"What do you mean you can't go? We're already here," I say, talking over machineheart blasting through the speakers. Maybe if I play "Circles" for a third time, she'll reconsider. I know what's coming next, and I mentally kick myself for being so selfish.

"Then I can't *stay*. Mom just texted me. Jacob's miserable. I thought my little guy was feeling better, but she can't even get him to eat ice cream."

Jane holds the title of World's Best Mom, so it surprised me she hadn't canceled the trip at his first sneeze.

"I'm so sorry," she says.

You've failed me, machineheart. I should have stuck with Morrison.

I'm pulling into the IHOP parking lot to turn around when Jane reaches across the console and grabs my arm.

"Did you bring a book?" she asks.

"Of course I brought a book. Why?"

She waits until I stop the car to answer. Good foresight on her part. The only thing that would suck more than the demise of our getaway would be slamming into the Mercedes we were trailing.

"Because you're staying. And without my engaging company, you'll need one."

"Jane, it's okay. I understand."

She turns in her seat to face me. She sucks in a deep breath and pushes up her sleeves. "No, Frankie, you're not canceling. You're—just no."

No? I give her a defiant stare.

"You never do anything unless it's with me." She crosses her arms. "Live a little, will you?"

"You sound like my dad."

"There you go," she says, seeming pleased with herself. "You promised him you'd come out of your shell. Here's your chance."

"I was thinking more along the lines of going to a movie by myself, not taking a vacation." I roll the window down a couple of inches. The cool March air rushes inside, carrying with it the scent of day-old grease and stale festival beer. I roll the window back up. "I don't know."

"Frankie, you need this. Ever since your dad passed away, the only time you leave your house is to go to work. You're not coming out of your shell; you're not doing anything. It's been six months. I know you're grieving, but it's time to join the land of the living." Her worried gaze falls on me as I swallow the uncomfortable lump rising in my throat. "I know you're scared, but you'll be okay. I promise."

"I'm not scared."

"I think you know what I mean." She smiles. "And besides, this is perfect for you. Think of all those music-industry geeks who go by themselves. It won't be weird at all that you're alone. Just hit some day parties and catch a few live bands. Pretend you're taking notes. They'll think you're a scout."

"A music scout without a badge? Really?"

"A hot young blonde with a clipboard? Please. No one will even notice you don't have a badge."

I don't have a clipboard either.

I sit quietly in the parking lot and watch hordes of people stream down Cesar Chavez in both directions.

"Look at all of them, Frankie. Only a handful are in

pairs. Most of them are by themselves."

She has a point.

"There are advantages to going without me, you know."

I quirk a brow. "Such as?"

"You won't have to eat a single thing from a food truck."

Jane taps her fingers against her chin as if she's trying to come up with another one. I'm quite sold on the first one.

"Oh, I won't drag you all over the city looking for free drinks."

"You mean I can actually go to a music festival for the music? People do that?" Before she can answer, I grab her hand. "Wait. We're in your car. How will I get home?"

We always take her little red Chevy Cruze in case she ever needs to get back to Jacob—kind of like right now. Plus, the sound system is killer. Especially when compared to the nonexistent one I enjoy in my old 1965 Chevy pickup.

"I'll come back," she says. "Early if I can."

Maybe Jane's right. Maybe I *do* need this. If it wasn't for the diner where I work, I could easily go weeks without seeing another human. I'm not what you'd call a social butterfly. I'm more of an antisocial caterpillar who's yet to don a pair of wings. It's not that I'm shy; I'm just...

Stuck in my ways. An introvert. A loner.

Jane nudges my arm. "What do you say?"

Boring.

"Earth to Frankie."

A faint smile peeks through my scowl, but I quickly squash it. I'll admit, the idea intrigues me, but there's no way I'm letting that little fact slip to Ms. Flutterby over there, or next thing I know I'll be booked alone on a cruise.

Wait. What am I thinking?

"Jane, this is crazy. We could book a cruise for what we're paying for our room."

Her brows pinch together. "Frankie, it's South By. The cancelation ship sailed a week ago."

"Ugh. I forgot about that."

"No, not *ugh*," she says. "This could be really good for you. I think Jacob's timing might be perfect."

I think Jacob's timing might be planned.

I heave a defeated sigh. "You swear you'll try to come back early?"

"Cross my heart."

"Because the main ingredient in a girls' trip is *girls*. Plural."

"Can't argue with that."

"Okay."

"Okay?" She squeezes my hand. "Just think, Frankie. This would make the best book: Single girl *finds herself* at the world's largest music festival." She lifts her backpack from the floorboard and starts rummaging through it. "Find a guy too, and I'll make it a romance."

Jane considers herself an aspiring writer, but I consider her an aspiring *finisher*. She writes all the time; she just never *finishes* anything.

"Why not focus on one of the dozens of books you've already started?"

"This is better."

I shift the car into reverse. I'm pulling out of our parking space when she slaps a colossal box of Trojans on the console. I slam my foot on the brakes. "You bought me condoms?"

"Don't be ridiculous. I brought them for me. I'm a

15

single mom living with *my* mom. I was hoping to get laid."

My mouth falls open. From the size of the box, it appears I would've been flying solo anyway.

"Don't judge," she says. "Vibrators are great, but they're no substitute for the real thing."

I love that she's not even remotely offended I'm gawking at her.

"And at least I date occasionally," she continues. "If anyone in this car needs to get laid, it's you."

Jane only dates *occasionally* because of Jacob. Back in high school, she could have had a different date every night of the week if she wanted. My best friend is stunning—hazel eyes, honey-brown hair, and skin that tans so effortlessly during the summer she looks like a walking advertisement for Hawaiian Tropic. I, on the other hand, look like a walking advertisement for aloe.

I release the brakes. "You're certifiable. You know that, right?"

She shrugs, and I shake my head.

"I said I would stay," I tell her. "But you can keep your family-size pack of condoms."

"Suit yourself."

It's just after seven o'clock on Monday evening when I pull up to the Four Seasons. Two valets are on us instantly, and Jane laughs as they open our doors.

"What's so funny?"

"No one ever does this at our usual hotel," she says, stepping out of the car.

"Motel. And if we were booked there this year, I'd be going home with you." I climb out of the driver's side and leave the door cracked. "Think you'll be able to find your way back to San Antonio?"

Jane pops the trunk and grabs my duffel as I make my

way around the car. "Crazier things have happened."

I smile. "Just promise me you'll use your GPS and not your instinct, okay?" Jane's the only person I know who can get lost in her own driveway, which is why I usually drive.

"Yes, Mom," she says, buckling herself into the driver's seat.

With my bag slung over my shoulder, I lean in and hug her goodbye. "I won't talk to strangers. I'll eat my vegetables and drink plenty of water. I'll get eight hours of sleep—"

"Good God, Frankie. You're going to put *me* to sleep. And I thought you were dull last year."

"Hey, I wasn't dull. I was just worried I'd get carded and they'd kick us *both* out."

She closes her door, her eyes fixing on mine as she rolls down her window. "You're twenty-one this year. I expect you to act like it."

"Then I'll drink all the free vodka I can find while having wild sex with strange men. Better?"

"There's my little romance novel heroine. I love you," she says. "And if Jacob gets better, I'll come back, but in the meantime, try to have some fun." She puts the car in drive and slowly rolls past me. "You'll thank me for this one day."

"Or kill you."

A rush of cool air kisses my cheeks as I step inside the Four Seasons lobby. *Wow. This is different.* Dark wood-beamed ceilings. Polished marble floors. Intricately carved mahogany walls. And cowhide. Lots of cowhide. If I had to sum it up, I'd say rich-people rustic, and I am not rich people.

I have a small party-planning business I started in college. It does okay, but it's inconsistent. To make up the difference, I wait tables. When my dad passed away, he left me a nice little nest egg by way of his life insurance policy, but I haven't touched it—not even to pay my half of this ridiculously expensive hotel. As soon as Jane and I scored the room, I began pulling doubles at the restaurant. I'm a work-first, play-later kind of girl.

"Checking in," I say when I reach the front desk. "Francesca Valentine." I take out my ID and credit card as the clerk consults his computer for my reservation.

"Is it possible the room is booked under a different name, Ms. Valentine?"

"Try Jane Townsend."

Jane Town…send, the clerk mouths as he returns to his computer. A slight frown pulls at his lips as his fingers click against the keyboard.

My stomach growls, and he glances at me over the rim of his glasses.

"I'm sorry this is taking so long. Is it Town*send* or Town*sand*?"

"Town*send*."

He shakes his head. "I'm sorry, ma'am. We don't have a reservation under either name. Do you have your confirmation?"

The blood drains from my face. Jane made the reservation; she has the confirmation.

"No. Yes. Hold on a sec." I dial Jane's number, but the call goes straight to voice mail. "Jane, please tell me you have—you know what? Never mind. I'll call you back."

If we don't have a room, we don't have to pay for a room. *That's good, right? Because there's no guarantee she'll even be able to make it back, and I don't* really *want to stay by myself, do I?*

You promised him, Frankie.

My stomach clenches. If I go home, I'll spend another six months eating frozen dinners and binge-watching Netflix. I'll *want* to change. I'll *want* to live a little, but I won't actually do it because brooding is way too easy.

Can a person brood to death?

Breathing an uneasy sigh, I lift my gaze to the clerk. "I have to have a room; my life kind of depends on it. Okay, that may be a tad dramatic. It's just…I promised my dad and—oh forget it." I throw my head back, my lips pinched in a frustrated smile. "I'm sorry. It's been kind of a long day and a really long year and *I. Am. Kaput!*" The last three words ring loudly, giving us both a start. I lower my voice. "I don't have my confirmation, not with me anyway. Look, I've never had this problem with your hotel before, Mr."—I stand high and mighty on my tiptoes, stretching to read his name tag— "Hernandez." *I've never had this problem before because I've never stayed here before.* "May I speak to the manager?"

"Of course, Ms. Valentine," he says, sounding a little too eager to be rid of me. "One moment."

I move off to the side and check my watch. It's almost seven thirty. I guess I could *try* to get a cab or an Uber, but the idea makes me laugh out loud. A ride after seven at South By is harder to come by than a golden ticket in a Wonka Bar.

Ugh. On a scale of one to ten, this has a suckage factor of eleven.

I dial Jane again and get her voice mail…again. "Jane, I hate to do this to you, but I think they lost our reservation. You might have to turn around. Call me."

Okay, don't panic. You're stranded in Austin, not Tokyo.

Mr. Hernandez reappears with his manager, and it's painfully obvious I'm not getting a room.

"Ms. Valentine, I'm Brad Harper. I apologize for this inconvenience."

Inconvenience? An inconvenience is taking too long with room service or forgetting to replace my towels. This is a little more than an inconvenience.

"We're calling a few neighboring hotels and the festival lodging committee," he says. "We're trying our best to remedy this situation."

Mr. Harper's eyes are kind and his smile is warm, but his words are crap.

This situation cannot be remedied with another hotel. Finding one will be impossible. There are never available rooms in this part of Austin once South By kicks off. The festival's so big, most downtown hotels only accept reservations from badge-holders, and we aren't, nor have we ever been, badge-holders. It was a fluke we were able to reserve this room.

From the looks of it, you weren't able to reserve this room.

"I appreciate it," I say, sagging against the counter, "but I think we both know I'm SOL."

Mr. Harper gives me a rueful smile. "Probably, but let's give it a shot anyway. I'll be right back."

The second he steps away from the desk, a chill sweeps up my spine, making every little hair on the back of my neck stand beneath my sweater. It's that feeling you get when you know someone's watching you, but it's more intense—like they're not just watching, they're *staring*. I slowly, discreetly, turn my head until my eyes land on the source of my suspicion.

Who is that?

My breath catches at the sight of him—tall and uncommonly handsome. *Hollywood handsome*, as Jane would say. I drop my gaze to his fingers, casually unfastening the button on his suit jacket, then to his

20

hands as they disappear inside the pockets of his slacks. He rocks back on his heels and a slow, sexy smile spreads over his lips, turning my knees to water. *Swoon.* I stand up straight and grip the counter for support. The way he's looking at me…it's deliciously unsettling. It's like he *knows* me, but I'm certain he doesn't.

A girl wouldn't forget a face like that.

Mr. Harper clears his throat, and I jerk my head in his direction.

"Unfortunately, you appear to be right," he says, reaching across the counter with my ID and credit card. "I do apologize, Ms.—"

"Actually…" I take a deep breath and try to stand taller than my five-and-a-half-foot frame. "I understand these things happen, but without a room I'll miss the festival. Is there anything you can do to make this right?"

Is there anything you can do to make me look like less of an idiot in front of Mr. Beautiful over there?

"Make this…" His words trail off, and a smile so small I almost miss it flashes on his face. "Ahh, Mr. Fox."

CHAPTER 2

Twentieth Century Fox

Drew: It's a good thing you're handsome or that panel you just gave would've been a real snoozer.

> Darian: It's already uploaded? And why are you stalking me?

Drew: Slow day.

> Darian: Obviously.

Drew: BTW no chance in hell you're getting laid in that tie bro.

Frankie

"Mr. who?" I turn my head to find *him* standing right beside me.

"Might I suggest a comparable room, courtesy of your upstanding hotel, on a weekend of her choosing?" *he* says to the manager before glancing down at me. "Would that satisfy you?" His voice is as satiny and rich as cream cheese frosting on a red velvet cupcake.

I'm sure this is where I should say something, but I'm too preoccupied with his last sentence to form one of my own…until I realize both men are staring at me.

"Oh, um…yes, it would satisfy me."

Jane and I can have a do-over!

Mr. Harper narrows his eyes at my new advocate and then smiles down at me. "Ms. Valentine, I think that can be arranged. I'm generating a two-night voucher for a complimentary guest room as well as restaurant credits for both days of your visit—for you and a guest, of course," he says, casting a glance at *him.*

The thought instantly propels me into fantasyland, and poor Jane is forgotten.

He stuffs the voucher in an envelope and hands it to me. "Just have your original confirmation number available when you make your reservation."

"Thank you," I say, tucking the envelope in the front pocket of my duffel.

"Thank *him,*" Mr. Harper says, his lips curling in amusement as he backs away from the desk, "and make sure he knows he owes me one."

As soon as he's gone, the man beside me offers me his hand. "Darian Fox."

I'm mesmerized by how soft yet strong it is. Tanned and lightly dusted with hair.

"Ms. Valentine?"

And so large it practically swallows mine.

"It is Valentine, right?" he says, giving my hand a squeeze.

My eyes snap to his. "Oh, sorry. Yes, Francesca Valentine."

Now, let go of the nice man's hand, Frankie.

Darian Fox *is* beautiful. Too beautiful. I want to run my fingers through his tousled chestnut hair but think better of it.

Thank you for your help. Do you mind if I touch your hair?

His skin is sun-kissed, a stark contrast to mine. And he's tall. He towers over me by at least seven or eight inches—and that's with my boots on. He's dressed in a black fitted pin-striped suit, a crisp white shirt, and a quirky necktie patterned with little multicolored Flying V guitars.

That *didn't come from Men's Wearhouse.*

My eyes climb from his tie to his upturned lips and continue their ascent until they're captured by his olive-green stare. My cheeks warm at the intensity, and I quickly lower my gaze back to his hand and to his long, slender fingers gripping and tapping the counter in front of us.

"It's nice to meet you, Mr. Fox, and thank you," I say once I've pulled myself together. "I'm pretty sure I was on my way to twenty percent off my next visit before you showed up."

"You're welcome. And it's Darian."

My lips curve into a smile. "It's nice to meet you, *Darian.*"

The growing crowd drives us from the front desk to the lobby where we sit opposite each other on matching navy suede love seats. I watch Darian curiously as he takes off his suit jacket and loosens his tie. He's silent for a minute while he fusses with the jacket and then looks over at me.

"I have a proposition for you," he says.

I arch my brows. "A proposition?"

Darian laughs, and the most adorable dimple appears on his left cheek. "Okay, maybe that wasn't the best word choice."

"You've certainly got my attention," I say, smiling.

He returns my smile as he leans forward, his elbows resting on his knees, his long fingers linked together. "I'm staying at The Mendón on Sixth. I booked the entire top floor for myself, which leaves three available rooms. You can have one if you want it."

Oh. My. God. Mr. Beautiful just offered me a room. The best romantic comedies start this way. But…so do the best horror movies. And probably the best porn.

"Why?" I ask.

"Why am I offering you a room?"

"Why did you book the entire floor?"

"So I could proposition you—clearly."

Laughter bubbles out of me, but I dial it back.

"I'm kidding," he says. "I'm here on business. I never know if I'll need the extra space."

"What happens if you *do* need the extra space?"

"I'll see that I don't."

A tingling sensation creeps up my neck and settles in my cheeks, sending my gaze to my lap. "I appreciate it," I say, suddenly fascinated with the frayed fabric on my duffel strap. "But my friend will pick me up."

Darian sinks into the love seat and brings his ankle to his knee, one arm draped over the armrest, the other stretched across the back. "I'm not sure where your friend is coming from, but are you familiar with Austin traffic?" He checks his watch. "It's nearly eight. This place is about to be a madhouse, and God knows how long it will be before your ride gets here. The room is just sitting there, vacant."

I scan the bustling lobby, which is filling up fast. I'll be waiting here for hours.

He smiles. "It's a really nice room."

Hmm…go with this stranger who could potentially be a serial killer or take my chances in the Four Seasons lobby? Live a little,

26

huh? The man is seriously hot.

Have you ever watched an episode of *The Fall* and thought, *Yeah, I'd let him murder me?* Well, here we are.

"What's the other *why?*" I ask. "Why are you offering me a room?"

"I told you, it's not being..." His expression turns pensive. "You mean, why do I care that you take it?"

I shrug. "Now that you mention it."

His eyes glaze over with a faraway look. "Because you're *kaput*, and it would disappoint my mother if I abandoned you in your state of kaput-ness."

Heat colors my cheeks. "You heard that, did you?"

"It's a great word, but no one ever uses it." He's quiet for a moment, then clears his throat as his focus returns to me. "Anyway, where were we?"

"The room." I sit back and drag my fingers over the smooth suede of the armrest. "Can I at least reimburse you for the night?"

Darian pushes off the love seat and stands. "That's not necessary, Ms. Valentine," he says formally as he drapes his coat over his arm. "It's already paid for. Company perk." He nods toward the window behind me. "If you want it, it's yours, but we should probably get going before it gets too crazy out there."

"Please, call me Frankie."

He takes a few steps toward the door. I start to follow him and then stop and drop my duffel.

His smile is sincere when he turns around. "Francesca, I promise, you're safe with me."

The use of my given name is not lost on me. My instinct is to correct him, but I don't.

It isn't often I hear it, and when I do, it's by doctors or bank tellers or the little old lady who delivers my mail. They draw it out in clunky syllables—*Fran-chess-ka*—as if saying it takes effort.

"Francesca?"

But the way Darian says it, it's like warm caramel melting on the tongue. Rich and smooth. Effortless.

I shake my head to clear it. "I should let Jane know."

"Jane?"

"My friend, and…" My words fall away when I notice Darian's picture displayed prominently on the far side of the lobby. "Wait, *who* are you?"

"I hosted a small business panel here earlier," he says.

"And you're friends with the manager?"

"I had drinks with him last night. I wouldn't call us friends."

"You're telling me I owe my free weekend at the Four Seasons to a couple of cocktails?"

His lips stretch in a grin and he holds out his hand. "Can I see your phone?"

"Sure, uh…hold on a sec." I bend to rummage through my bag, digging through a week's worth of clothes as shoes, socks, and bras spill over the side. "I know I…" I pat my sweater, even though it doesn't have any pockets, and then my jeans. "Voila," I say, handing it over.

Darian laughs. He snaps a photo of his driver's license, then hands it back. "Text that to your friend. If you go missing, she'll know where to look."

"Thank you," I say as I slide my phone in my pocket.

He zips my duffel and throws it over his shoulder. "Shall we?"

Darian's driver—company perk number two—delivers us to The Mendón. We go straight to the front desk where Darian gets me checked in, swapping my name for his on the reservation.

"Thanks again," I say once we're inside the elevator. "This is generous. More than generous."

He adjusts my bag on his shoulder. "It's no trouble."

The door opens to a wide corridor that serves as a vestibule of sorts for the four suites that make up the top floor. He stops at the first set of double doors on the right.

"So, I was thinking." He sets my duffel at my feet. "I'm going to have dinner delivered to my room. Would you like to come over? I mean…would you like to have dinner in my room? *Are you hungry?*"

I giggle as he stumbles over his words.

"Wow," he says, a scarlet flush sweeping across his cheeks. "That sounded much better in my head. Hey, would you like to come to my hotel room *alone* and '*have dinner*'?" He emphasizes that last part with air quotes, and I burst with laughter. "God, listen to me. Let's try this again. Would you like to join me downstairs in the very public hotel restaurant?"

"I'd love to join you for dinner," I say, "but the very public hotel restaurant had a very long line reaching into the lobby, and I'm starving. Room service sounds perfect. Just promise you won't kill me until after I've eaten."

He crosses his heart with both hands as a smile slides over his face. "You have my word."

"Whoa."

Darian wasn't kidding; this is a *really nice room*. I walk through the foyer to the living area and lean against the honey-colored leather chaise lounge. Plush white carpet, royal-blue damask wallpaper, two massive crystal chandeliers. I could stay here for weeks and never set foot outside the door.

I pick up the remote on the end table and press the button labeled Divider.

No way!

The entire white-paneled wall in front of me lifts to the lofty two-story ceiling, revealing the bedroom hidden behind. Make that *three* massive crystal chandeliers. The oversized bed, dressed in white down bedding, has so many pillows I make a mental note to allot myself time to remove them before climbing in. The master bath is just as grand with a marble tub so deep I could snorkel in it.

If Jane could see me now.

Oh crap, Jane…

My phone vibrates in my hand the second I take it out of my pocket.

"Frankie! Finally!" she screams in my ear. "My phone must have died as soon as I left Austin. Are you okay? What happened? And why did you text me some hot guy's driver's license? Is this a new drunken scavenger hunt you're trying without me? Because I'd rather you wait—"

"So I assume you're home? You're not on your way back to Austin, are you?"

"Not yet, but I'm walking out the door right now."

"Don't bother," I say, failing to curb the smile in my voice. "I'm good for tonight."

"Good for to—" Jane stops mid-sentence, and I can practically see her eyebrows rocket to her hairline. "Shit,

30

Frankie, did you meet someone…*already*? Is it driver's license guy? He's super yummy and *older*, though he certainly doesn't look it."

"He's not *that* much older." I bring up the image of his ID and try to do the math in my head.

"He's thirty-six, slowpoke," Jane says. "*Man-aged*. And he's from Miami. I've always wanted to go to Florida."

Me too.

"I think you're jumping the gun a little. He's just being nice." Slouching against the shower door, I give her the CliffsNotes version of the last two hours.

"He's being more than *nice*. Swoon. It's so romantic," she says, sighing. "Is there an adjoining door? Because I had this idea for our book—"

"Jane…" I step out of the bathroom and scan our adjoining wall. Sure enough, there's an adjoining door.

"Okay, fine," she says. "But just so you know, I stashed the box of condoms in your bag."

"Jesus, Jane. Whatever. How's my godson?"

"He's fine. He's five. Just missed his mommy." She relaxes her tone. Jane can be a little scattered, but nothing centers her quite like her son. "Go on now. Don't worry about us. I'll be here, Googling your mystery man," she says. "I'm proud of you, but—and please don't take this the wrong way—you're rusty."

"Thanks for the vote of confidence."

"I just mean…less is more. Don't talk too much. Avoid spaghetti. Actually, avoid anything with sauce."

"He hasn't run screaming yet." I take a deep breath. "The truth is, I'm a little nervous. It's been a while since I've…well, since I've done *anything*."

"You know I was teasing, right?"

I shrug, which she obviously can't see. "I didn't exactly think this through. I guess I kind of did—for all of five seconds—but not *really*. That's not like me, Jane."

"Nothing you've done today is like you. Maybe you've changed." She pauses and I hear Jacob's sleepy voice call to her in the background.

"You should go," I say. "Give Jacob a kiss for me."

"I will. And, Frankie, all jokes aside, you need to be careful. We don't *know* him. Stay alert, and don't drink too much. And make sure you take your Taser just in—"

"Yes, Mom."

We end our call, and I return to the bathroom to freshen up.

Should I change? No, this isn't a date. It's just dinner. In a stranger's hotel room.

I decide to stay in my cream cowl-neck sweater, black jeans, and black leather riding boots. I dab my favorite honeysuckle oil behind my ears. I check my nose. I brush my teeth. I twist my long hair into a bun and make up my face, so it looks like I didn't just make up my face. With my light-blonde hair, pale blue eyes, and super fair skin, it's a skill I've had to master over the years. But I have to be careful. There's a fine line between tramp and translucent, and my goal is to fall somewhere in between.

I open my adjoining door and only knock once before Darian opens his.

Well, hello there.

He's changed out of his suit and into a pair of distressed jeans, torn at the knees, and a slim-fit Grateful Dead T-shirt. His biceps press lightly against the sleeves, and I have to fight the urge to touch them.

"I'm glad you came," he says, closing the door behind me. "I was worried you might have come to your senses."

An arch smile plays on my lips. "Where's the fun in that?"

I drop my purse on the coffee table in the living area

and sit on the arm of the sofa. Then I feel stupid for not just sitting *on* the sofa, so I slide down the arm to the cushion, tipping over a little as I land.

That was graceful.

I try to recover by crossing one leg over the other while leaning against the back of the couch, but I'm not quite long enough to do both, so I kind of lie there, stretched over the cushion, like it's a perfectly normal way to sit.

Darian clears his throat. "Would you like a drink?"

Yes, several.

"Please. Whatever you're having."

Needing something to do with my hands, I reach for the remote control on the coffee table.

"Dirty martini?"

"Perfect."

Darian peers at me through the mirror hanging above the wet bar as he opens a bottle of Tito's and a jar of olives. "You can play something if you want."

The room floods with Kenny G as soon as I press the Music button, and I have to bite down on my lip to keep from laughing. "Easy listening, huh?" I lower the volume.

A grin spreads across Darian's face. He scoops ice from the ice bucket, and it clinks loudly as it tumbles into the glass shaker. He pours the vodka over the ice and shakes it. "It's not what you think."

"It's not my place to judge," I say, setting the remote beside me on the sofa.

His smile converts to a laugh as he divides the mixture between two glasses and garnishes them with olives. He brings me my drink and then nods toward the floor-to-ceiling windows showcasing a perfect view of the city. "Terrace?"

I follow him outside. He sets his glass on the patio

table and slips his hands in his pockets.

"So, what's your story, Francesca? How did you manage to get yourself stranded?"

"I'm not *that* stranded. I don't live far." I take a sip and struggle to keep a straight face. I think the dirty may be missing from the dirty martini. "I came with my friend, but as soon as we got here she had to leave. Her son's sick," I say, setting my glass beside his. "It's my own fault for not confirming the reservation, especially since I don't have a badge."

Darian's eyes widen. "You came to South By without a badge?"

"If you stick to the smaller day parties, they're not really necessary."

"But you miss the best parties, the best concerts."

"I suppose. But I've never had one, so I don't know what I'm missing."

Badges are expensive—like a thousand dollars expensive—and they *aren't* necessary. I'd much rather put that money toward our room. Or food. Or Barnes & Noble. Jane and I always skip the badge and attend just the free daytime events. But sometimes she gets a wild hair and attempts to sneak us into a badge-only evening showcase, like she did last year.

I pick up my drink and take another sip.

Darian crosses his arms over his chest and studies me. "Hmm…so your friend had to leave, and you decided to stay? By yourself?" He strokes his chin with his index finger and thumb. "That sounds like something I would do."

"Vacationing solo is new for me, but I'm a loner by nature so I thought I'd give it a shot."

Room service interrupts the silence that follows, and Darian excuses himself to let them in. I lean over the iron railing with my chest pressed against the beveled edge. Thick lines of people crowd the sidewalks and spill onto the street. It's dark, and I suspect the evening's showcases will begin soon.

As I turn to go inside, my phone buzzes a text from my back pocket.

Jane: How's it going? Mystery man behaving? What did you order?

Frankie: Totally awkward start but better now. Ordered ribs with extra sauce.

Jane: Calling BS on the ribs!

Frankie: Jacob asleep?

Jane: Of course not. We're about to start book #3.

Frankie: Don't keep him waiting. We'll talk later.

Jane: Be safe and text me before 12 or I'm calling 911.

Frankie: K. Love you.

Jane: U 2.

I look up as Darian steps onto the terrace.

"Hungry?" he asks. "I thought we'd eat inside." He juts his chin toward the street below. "It's getting pretty loud down there."

With the doors closed, the noise from outside is completely muted. Darian turns the easy-listening station on low, and "Careless Whisper" drifts through the speakers.

"You're not going to knock *this* one, are you?" he asks.

I shake my head. "*This* one doesn't count. Everyone loves George Michael."

"Everyone loves Kenny G," he says with conviction.

I give him a sideways glance, and he scoffs under his breath as he removes the lids from our plates. A thick wave of garlic hits me, and my stomach rumbles.

"This smells fantastic," I say of the Texas-size rib eyes he ordered. "And Kenny G doesn't even love Kenny G."

Another scoff.

We sit at one corner of the long dining table. Darian picks up a bottle of wine and immediately sets it down. "Shit. I didn't even think to ask if you were vegetarian."

"I live in Texas," I say. "I'm not sure that's even allowed."

"Good thing because I think those five green beans they stuck on our plates are meant for decoration." He pours the wine and hands me a glass. "Should we toast?"

"We should definitely toast."

"Okay, how about…" He purses his lips and then smiles. "To the Four Seasons?"

A warm, fuzzy feeling blooms in my chest. "To the Four Seasons."

He lifts his glass to his lips and lets it rest there for a second before taking a sip. "Huh. That's pretty good."

"You sound surprised." I taste it. It's better than good and nothing like the plum-heavy merlot I usually drink.

He turns the bottle until the label faces me. "It's a Texas cab. I wanted to try something local, but I'll be honest, I wasn't expecting much."

"Because you're in Texas?" I tease, cutting off a piece of my steak. I take a bite, closing my eyes as the crispy, salty crust touches my tongue.

Holy Moses, that's good.

"Well, yeah," he says. "But to be fair, Florida doesn't scream *fine wine* either."

"Touché." I twist the cap off a bottle of San Pellegrino, pour a little into my water glass, and pass him the rest. "So, what's *your* story?"

Darian straightens. "My story…"

"Just the basics. Are you from Miami, or are you a transplant? And what do you do that has you hosting panels at South By?" My hand flies up. "Wait, one more. If you weren't working this week, what band would you want to make a surprise appearance?"

His smile is hesitant. "Okay, I'm game," he says slowly as he cuts into his rib eye. He eats a small piece and then chases it with a sip of wine. "But you go first."

I lean forward, wrestling my chair closer to the table. "I live outside of a little town called Fisher Springs. I'm a party-planner"—*mostly*—"and if I were staying, I'd love to see Cross to Bear."

Darian relaxes in his seat with his elbows planted on the armrests. His gaze fixes on mine, and he grins as if he's going to tease me, as if I'd said One Direction, not CTB. It's an annoying assumption but one I'm used to. Their pretty-boy front man garners a hefty preteen following, which doesn't do their serious fans any favors.

"Your turn," I say, reaching across the table for the bread basket.

Darian's grin melts into a lazy smile. "I was born and raised in Miami, I own an independent record label, and I'd love to see The Doors."

My hand stalls over a dinner roll. "Shut up. Seriously? The Doors?"

"I know. I'm aging myself," he says with a laugh. "It's probably not likely. I hear their lead singer's a bit dead."

"No, it's not that." I grab his wrist, then quickly release it. "The Doors is my all-time favorite band. I'm borderline obsessed." I take a slow sip of my water, followed by an equally slow breath. "It was something I shared with my dad."

"Shared?"

"He passed away six months ago."

"I'm sorry." Darian's eyes grow dark and distant. His smile falters. "Were you close? Shit. Sorry, that was really—"

"It's okay," I say, keeping my voice steady. "We were very close. I'm an only child…or *was* an only child."

"Your mom?"

I shake my head, and he nods in understanding.

"What about you?" I ask.

"I *was* an only child too." He spears a green bean with his fork and moves it around his plate. After a few rotations, he sets the fork down and looks over at me. "So, Francesca, kindred only child, what's your favorite Doors album?"

I tap my finger against my chin. "Hard to say. It depends on my mood. Being a Texas girl, I favor the blues over the psychedelic stuff, but I love them all. I tend to waver between *Morrison Hotel* and *L.A. Woman.* What's your favorite?"

"Hands down, *Strange Days.*"

"Ahh…the melancholy album."

His brows knit together. "The melancholy album?"

"Just as *Waiting for the Sun* is the romantic album." I stab my fork in a piece of steak and dip it in butter. "Comparatively speaking, of course."

"Then I suppose you're right—comparatively speaking." He leans over the table, resting his chin on his palm. "So, you're a Cross to Bear fan too?"

"I guess I shouldn't be surprised you've heard of them considering your line of work, but they're not what you think. They're not some boy band." I take a bite of the buttery steak.

"I'm mildly familiar," he says, one corner of his

mouth lifting in a half-smile, "but I guess I'll have to pay more attention."

"Jane and I have been fans for years, but we've never seen them live. They never come to Texas. You should check them out. They're in Miami all the time."

He glances down as he takes a sip of water, his smile curving above the lip of his glass. "Maybe I will."

After dinner and a final glass of wine, Darian walks me to my room—the long way, all thirty seconds of it. "The suite's at your disposal all week, if you'd like to stay."

Thank you. I'd love to. The words itch to leave my lips. "Thank you, but no," I say instead. "Jane will be here tomorrow."

"I should warn you. I'm going to try to change your mind," he says, a twinkle of mischief in his eyes. "Just try not to leave *too* early?"

I pull my key card out of my purse. "I expect her around eleven. She'll want to avoid traffic."

"Eleven," he repeats. "I can work with that."

I can't quite figure him out. He refuses to call me Frankie, favoring Francesca for reasons unknown to me. He's bold *and* demure. Confident but not self-absorbed. And he's beautiful. Have I mentioned that yet? On the surface, it's his boyish features—his long, heavy lashes, the tiny dimple that only appears when he laughs, his smile.

But it's what's lingering beneath the surface I'm most attracted to. There's a vulnerability there, a sadness I can relate to. I feel it each time I look into his eyes. They contradict his youthfulness, like they've seen more than his years suggest. And, staring into them now, I get the strangest feeling something big happened tonight.

"Thank you for your company," Darian says after a

short span of silence.

"You're welcome. I mean, thank you." I feel my entire body blush, and I don't know if it's the wine or the confinement of the corridor or the fact that he's standing so close to me. Maybe it's all three. "I had a good time. I felt very *safe*."

He laughs, and his eyes hold mine for several seconds. "I hope I'm able to do it," he says. "I hope I change your mind." He slips his hands in his pockets and leans back against the wall by my door. "Besides, it would be a pity for you to waste a vacant suite and such *charming* company." His attempt at smug is foiled by reddening cheeks and a shy smile.

I close my fist tight around my key card as I fight the urge to cave. "So, I'll see you in the morning then?"

He shrugs. "If I succeed."

"Goodnight, Darian."

"Goodnight, Francesca."

My phone buzzes a text from Jane the second the door closes behind me. I check the time—eleven fifty. I have ten whole minutes before she calls in a SWAT team. I use half of them to brush my teeth and change into a nightshirt and the other half to clear my bed of pillows.

> Frankie: I'm home Mom. Had a good time. See you when you get here.

> Jane: Check your e-mail.

Jane isn't one to cut corners. Her e-mail resembles a modern-day *War and Peace* that includes hyperlinks, JPEGS, and a spreadsheet. It's flagged *urgent*, and the subject line reads, *OMG*.

Her flair for drama brings a smile to my face but does little for the tightness in my chest. I darken the screen, set my phone face-down on the nightstand, and climb into bed. I'm leaving tomorrow, and after that, I'll probably never see Darian again.

A heavy sigh fans the hair from my eyes.

I'd like to see him again.

I lie on my side, burrowed beneath a mountain of covers, and stare at the upside-down phone as if I expect it to do something. It just sits there, taunting me like it holds the secrets of the universe.

It holds a spreadsheet, Frankie.

Ten long minutes pass before it lights up and vibrates across the glass tabletop.

> Jane: Can you believe it?
>
> Jane: Wait, how far did you get?
>
> Jane: R U asleep?
>
> Frankie: I'm awake.
>
> Jane: Well?
>
> Frankie: A spreadsheet? Really?
>
> Jane: OMG just Google him then!

"Fine," I say, folding like a cheap suit. "I'll just Google him then."

My conscience weighs heavy on my shoulders as I open my browser. Typing Darian's name into a search engine just feels wrong.

Like you said, you'll probably never see him again.

And he owns a record label; surely, there's no harm in checking out his company. Pushing the guilty feeling aside, I scroll through the hits on my screen. There are more than I expected, and when my finger stills over an actual Wiki page, my curiosity gets the better of me. After that, I can't click through the pages fast enough.

> Darian Fox is founder and CEO of Fox Independent Artists, Inc., a thriving indie record label he launched in his late twenties. Prior to that, he was lead singer and guitar player in a moderately successful rock band based in Miami, called For Julia.

My face breaks into a grin. I was rescued by a rock star; no wonder Jane was so insistent.

There's a wealth of information on the label—bands signed, awards won, upcoming releases, upcoming tours. There's even an editorial in *Rolling Stone*. I browse through the bands on his website, and I recognize many of them, not the least of which is Cross to Bear.

I bark out a laugh. "'Mildly familiar,' my ass."

There's much less on For Julia. I find a feeble attempt at a fan site—iheartjuliaforever.com—with a few promo shots of the band. My gaze goes straight to Darian. Despite his boy-next-door features, he *looks* like a rock star. His presence is commanding, and it takes me a moment to realize he's joined by three other guys.

Cute and *sexy*, I think as I navigate the site. *Don't see that every day.*

> For Julia had a devoted regional following and was expected to skyrocket to stardom. They found success through a handful of national singles, but their breakout hit was "Halcyon Girl."

I wonder if I've heard it. Probably not, considering I was ten when it was released, and at ten, if it wasn't on *American Idol*, it wasn't on my radar.

I open another web page and search for the song, but I have no luck. I can't even find lyrics.

That's odd. How does a song just disappear?

I return to the fan site and learn For Julia disbanded following the death of the band's namesake—Darian's wife.

Holy shit.

My head starts to pound. I Google *For Julia* and *death* and...

> MIAMI-DADE COUNTY, FL (AP)—FOR JULIA FRONT MAN, DARIAN FOX, LOSES FAMILY IN MYSTERIOUS PLANE CRASH OFF THE COAST OF MIAMI
>
> Caribbean Air Flight 356, bound for Nassau, Bahamas, plunges into the Atlantic Ocean shortly after takeoff from Miami International Airport Sunday afternoon, killing all 88 passengers and crew. For Julia front man Darian Fox's wife, four-year-old daughter, and parents are among the casualties. The cause of the crash is unknown.

Is this...no, it can't be...

My stomach roils as I push up against the headboard. With a trembling finger, I scroll down to a picture of Darian and Julia, and then—*oh my God*—I inhale a sharp gasp as my eyes land on an image I know all too well.

"Anabel."

It is. This is that *crash.*

My mind jumps back almost ten years to that miserable Sunday in May, exactly one week after my twelfth birthday.

I was lying on the couch, half-reading Harry Potter, *half-listening to reruns of* Laguna Beach *on MTV, when the story broke. Dad sat in his recliner and turned up the volume, drawing my full attention to the television.*

MTV ran a clip of the Fox family at the beach. The heartbreaking sobs of a little girl with brunette ringlets and big brown eyes echoed loudly in our small living room. She was inconsolable after a large wave leveled her sand castle. Her mom giggled at her dad's desperate attempts to calm her.

"I'll build you a new one," he said. "Even bigger."

It didn't work; she only cried harder…

That night was the first time I dreamed of the sobbing little girl on the ill-fated plane as it spiraled out of the sky. No matter how hard I tried, I couldn't get the image out of my twelve-year-old head. The nightmares lasted for months and resulted in my fear of flying. I was in college before Jane convinced me to go to Cancun for spring break, and I only fly now with the help of Xanax or a cocktail or six. *How does Darian do it?*

How does Darian do anything?

My throat grows thick with tears. I had *time*. I *knew* my dad was sick. I *knew* the end was coming. Darian had no warning, no chance to say goodbye. They were all just…*gone.*

His entire family.

Dad was diagnosed with early-onset Alzheimer's at fifty-seven. I was only sixteen. We had four precious years together before his disease took me away from him. After the fifth, it took him away from me.

"Frankie, I want you to stop fussing over me and sit down. I have something I need to say to you before it's too late."

"You're being dramatic, Dad. You're fine. You had a bad spell, and now you have a prescription."

"Frankie, stop. It's Alzheimer's, not the flu. Yes, I'm fine now, but you heard the doctor. These 'spells' are going to keep happening, and they're going to get worse. Now, sit down."

His tone made me flinch. I moved to stand beside him at the table, but I couldn't bring myself to sit.

"One of these days, my mind will go, and when that happens, I don't want you spending every waking minute at my side. It won't do either of us any good."

"Dad—"

"Frankie..." His voice splintered around my name, causing the backs of my eyes to sting. "You are a bright, beautiful girl. You have your whole life ahead of you; don't waste it. Come out of your shell, conquer this flying thing, and see the world. Live a little."

He pushed back from the table, wildly flapping his arms, and I smiled through the ache in my chest.

"What have I always told you?"

"Be the butterfly."

"Yes. Be the butterfly, Frankie. Spread your wings and fly."

My phone buzzes in my hand, pulling me back to the present. I dry my eyes on my shirtsleeve and force a smile, determined to remember that day as a happy one.

Jane: You OK?

Frankie: It's so surreal.

Jane: Are you going to tell him?

Frankie: No way. That crash gave me nightmares but it destroyed his life.

Jane: I think it did a little more than give you nightmares.

Lying down once more, I draw the covers to my chin and open my browser. Anabel's smiling face stares back at me from the screen.

Julia was Darian's high school sweetheart. He married her right after graduating from the University of Miami, and their daughter, Anabel, came nine months later. After the accident, he dissolved the band and launched the record label.

There are several reports chronicling the crash as well as speculation on his subsequent inheritance. Nothing else personal has been reported since.

Frankie: She was his daughter. My nightmares were about her.

Jane: I know.

I imagine Darian in his twenties, happy and loved with a young family and a promising career. But in one disastrous moment, everything was ripped from him. The son, husband, and father became orphaned, widowed, and childless overnight.

Losing my dad was devastating, but it was inevitable. Children are supposed to bury their parents, not the other way around and not their whole family all at once. I can't begin to wrap my head around it.

Frankie: I feel connected to him somehow.

Jane: You are in a way.

Frankie: It's weird though. I felt it earlier, before I knew.

Jane: What are you going to do?

Frankie: He asked me to stay.

Jane: Just be careful.

Frankie: I have my Taser.

Jane: That's not what I mean.

I set my phone on the nightstand and turn off the lamp. My eyes burn the second I close them. My chest feels hollow. I was so young when it happened, so consumed with the cries of a four-year-old girl and the nightmares she gave me, I never once thought of her father.

Her *father.*

But he's all I can think of now, and as I drift into what will surely be a fitful sleep, my heart breaks.

CHAPTER 3

Touch Me

Drew: Sorry man. I was "tied up" when you called. ;-)

    Darian: Thanks for that visual.

Drew: You said you met a girl?

    Darian: No. I said I saved a girl. All knight in shining armor like.

Drew: Nice. Did you get laid?

    Darian: You're such an ass. Get this. Her favorite band is CTB.

Drew: Ahh…so you're going to get laid. You just haven't yet.

Frankie

I open my eyes and stare at the paneled ceiling in a weary fog. My thoughts pick up right where they left off last night, the sun-drenched morning doing little to dampen them.

Better snap out of it, Frankie. You can't be all doom and gloom in front of Darian.

I force a smile and chant through my teeth, "You're fine. Darian's fine. Everything's fine."

A knock at my door has my tangled feet warring with the covers. I jerk out of bed in a panic and breathe a sigh of relief when the words, "Room service," drift through my suite.

Room service?

I open the door to a stack of lidded plates. A heady bouquet of sage and maple syrup pushes into my room, followed by the server with his heavily stocked cart.

He stops in the foyer and straightens. "Ms. Valentine?"

I manage a nod.

"Inside or outside?" he asks.

"Um…inside's fine."

I stare, wide-eyed, as he transfers the plates to the dining table and begins removing the lids. I consider asking if there's been a mistake, but my rumbling stomach is quick to silence me. Pancakes, scrambled eggs, sausage *and* bacon, fruit, biscuits and gravy, orange juice, coffee, champagne…

Champagne?

A smile pushes through the morning's melancholy.

Darian, what are you up to?

The server's gaze bounces around my empty room before settling on me in my *I don't do mornings* nightshirt.

"I'm expecting guests," I blurt out. "Pajama breakfast."

He sets the stack of lids on his cart. "I apologize, ma'am. My ticket said one diner. I'll send up additional place settings."

"Thank you."

"How many?"

I glance at the table, which is completely covered with food. "Six. Yeah, I think that should do it."

"Yes, ma'am," he says, then presses his lips together as if to suppress a smile.

He holds up the bottle of bubbly, and I shake my head in a decisive no.

But if you have a Diet Coke on that cart somewhere...

"Very well," he says, placing it back on ice. "And I was instructed to give you this."

He hands me an envelope, and I wait anxiously as he packs up his cart and wheels it out of the room. The second the door closes behind him, I tear into it.

Inside, I find a flyer for Stoli and Seventh—otherwise known as *the* party. One of the only day parties you can't get into without a badge. You can't even sneak into it. I know; I've tried. At the bottom of the page there's a hand-drawn arrow in red marker. I flip it over.

A BADGE AWAITS YOU AT THE FESTIVAL REGISTRATION
BUILDING.

IT'S NONREFUNDABLE. I'D HATE TO SEE IT GO TO WASTE.

DF

A what *awaits me* where? *He got me a badge?*

Excitement swells like a balloon in my chest and then deflates at the thought of actually having to face him.

"But you're not facing *him*," I whisper. "Not really."

The Darian I met yesterday is not the Darian I Googled last night. The one I met laughs and jokes and smiles. The one I Googled wouldn't be capable of such things.

I hug the flyer to my chest.

51

You shouldn't know anyway. Just pretend you don't.

I round the corner onto Brushy Street wearing a pale pink sundress, a blue jean jacket, and a pair of black Converse sneakers that should probably be replaced. I spot Darian immediately. The patch of brick on the side of the warehouse housing the Stoli and Seventh party frames his silhouette as if he intentionally picked the spot. His charcoal suit and cream-colored oxford bear a striking contrast to the rustic wall behind him, and if I didn't know better, I'd think I was disrupting a photo shoot. Focused on his phone, he doesn't notice me until he hears the gravel crunch beneath my shoes. He looks up and smiles.

"Ms. Valentine, what a surprise," he says, slipping the phone inside his coat pocket. "I'm glad you decided to stay."

I lift the badge hanging from the lanyard around my neck. "This…" I say, shaking my head as my own smile emerges. "I did not see this coming. Thank you." I tap the words *Fox Independent* printed beneath my name. "So, I work for you now, I see."

He laughs. "I asked The Mendón to order your badge using your check-in information. I had to tell them something." His gaze lifts to mine. "So, are you staying?"

I purse my lips, pretending to mull it over. "For now."

"That's a start," he says, stepping toward me.

He offers me his arm, and I take it, linking my elbow with his as I look past him to the long line of people snaked through the parking lot.

"Does this badge have magical powers?"

"No, but I do," he says, jutting his chin toward the throng. "Come on. It's not as bad as it looks."

I follow close beside him, stepping in time to the dull thud of bass that serves as the heartbeat of the city during South By. As we reach the front of the building, we're met with an explosion of sound, and Darian tightens his hold.

I keep my head down, my eyes trained on my feet as he guides me through the crowd. We stop at the VIP entrance. A woman with short reddish hair pushed back by tortoise-shell glasses sits perched on a stool in the doorway. She flashes Darian a bright smile and waves him in.

"Thank you, Lisa," he says, stepping aside and bringing me forward. "But she probably needs a wristband?"

I dig my ID out of my pocket and hand it to her.

"Thanks, hon," she says, lowering her glasses. "Even badge-holders need wristbands for S&S this year." She holds my driver's license at arm's length and then brings it forward until it's in focus. "Unless, of course, you're him." She shoots Darian a playful glare.

"Riley inside?" he asks her.

Lisa snorts a laugh as she straps a bright yellow band to my wrist. "That boy is something else. Runnin' around here like a headless chicken."

Darian turns his attention to me. "Riley's my assistant. This is his first South By." He drags a finger across his bottom lip. "He's a…"

"An eager beaver," Lisa says. "Now, you two, move along." She gives me a wink. "You're holding up my line."

The place is packed, which surprises me, considering

the sheer size of the building and the hundreds of people still waiting outside. No wonder we couldn't talk our way in last year; badge-holders aren't even guaranteed entry. I get why this party's so popular. Not only does it showcase the most sought-after bands, but it's also decked out like a local county fair—complete with carnival games and all the popcorn, cotton candy, and caramel apples your inner child could possibly want.

"I think you forgot something," Darian says, my driver's license wedged between his fingers.

"Thanks. I guess I got a little excited." I slip my ID in my jacket pocket. "This is unreal."

"Pretty cool, huh?"

"I'm disappointed there's no Ferris wheel," I tease, "but other than that, yeah, I'd say it's pretty cool."

He laughs, his shoulders lifting in a shrug. "I hear there's an impressive lineup…and free drinks. I think we should start there."

I follow Darian to the bar for a couple Stoli cranberry lemonades and then to a small table he's reserved near the stage. We sit across from each other in bar-height chairs that are so close together, our knees almost touch.

I bend forward with my arms folded in my lap, my eyes narrowed. "I'm not even going to ask how you got this table."

Darian lowers his gaze to his cup, and a small smile creeps over his face as he lifts it to his lips. "Magic," he says and then takes a drink.

He slides out of his suit jacket, hangs it on the back of his chair, and leans against it. The new angle pushes his knees into mine.

"Magic." I shake my head. "Of course."

I turn in my seat to take in the party from my elevated position. In addition to the carnival games lining the perimeter, waiters dressed as carnival clowns wander through the dense crowd with trays of junk food.

"Want something?" Darian asks.

"No," I say, drawing out the word. My hand falls to my stomach. "I think it'll be a while before the pancakes wear off. Thank you, by the way, for breakfast."

He cocks his head. "I hope you had more than pancakes."

"I may never eat again."

The current band finishes their set and begins hauling their equipment offstage. I turn back to the table just as Darian does. His eyes hold mine for a beat before our faces split in a pair of smiles.

"So, you're—"

"They're really—" I laugh. "You go first."

He straightens in his chair. "So, you're twenty-one."

I'm not sure what to make of his question—if it is a question. I hold up my wrist. "I have the band to prove it."

He rests his elbows on the table, arms crossed. "No, I mean, you're *only* twenty-one."

"Almost twenty-two," I say, eyeing him skeptically. I take a sip of my drink. The cold, tart cranberry slides down my throat. "Is that a problem?"

"No, it's not. I'm just—I thought you were older. You look—you don't look twenty-one. And you love The Doors, *and* you drank a martini last night. What twenty-one-year-old drinks martinis?"

"I do, I guess." My chest tightens. I'm feeling as if my age is somehow something to be embarrassed about.

Darian's lips part like he's going to speak, and then they close over the rim of his cup as he takes a drink. The silence grows thick at our small table. I turn my attention to the stage where a new band is warming up. It's a punk band from Tampa—a *loud* punk band from Tampa—and I'm grateful for the distraction, however short.

When the set ends, I turn back to Darian, who's mindlessly thumbing over the condensation coating his cup.

"You're thirty-six," I say matter-of-factly. "Is our age difference making you uncomfortable?"

"Yes, I'm thirty-six, and no"—he looks up at me—"it's not that. It just surprised me; that's all. Twenty-one is really young to be someplace like this…alone. I mean, you're practically a…"

My body tenses. "A kid?"

"No. I'm—"

"I'm not a child," I say calmly, quietly, despite the heat rising up the back of my neck. "I can see how my recent decisions may argue that point, but I assure you, I'm not."

Clearly, I shouldn't have accepted his help last night, and dinner in his room wasn't my brightest idea ever, but Jane knew where I was. I watched him pour our martinis from the *same* shaker, our wine from the *same* bottle. And I carried a Taser.

He leans over the table. "You're misunderstanding—"

"It's okay—really." I nod toward the restroom line. "I just need to—excuse me." I slide off my chair, cringing at the unintentional creak it makes as it pushes against the concrete floor.

"Francesca, wait. Please."

"I thought you wanted me to stay because you liked me. I don't see what my age has to do with it." Then, just like a child, I toss back the last bit of my watered-down drink and duck away to the only semi-private corner in the warehouse to call Jane.

"Frankie, you didn't," she says once I've relayed the story to her.

"Didn't what? Did you hear the part where he said I was practically a kid? It's making it really hard to imagine him naked." Shame sets my cheeks on fire. "I shouldn't have said that. God, I'm such a jerk. After everything I learned last night…I shouldn't let something so stupid get to me."

"It's okay to feel what you feel," Jane says. "But I think you should cut the guy some slack. You said yourself how awkward he was last night. Is it possible he didn't mean anything by it?"

I'm pretty sure I said it was *me* bringing the awkward, but I decide not to correct her.

"I know," I say. "I'm sure he didn't. It's just…being treated like a child makes me crazy. I get it. Twenty-one *is* young, but I don't know. I really don't see myself as a typical twenty-one-year-old."

My dad's diagnosis came the same year Jane had Jacob. At fifteen, I was this happy-go-lucky kid who was obsessed with boys and nail polish. At seventeen, I was taking care of my dad and helping my best friend raise a baby.

"I'm *not* a typical twenty-one-year-old."

"You're not," Jane says, "but it sounds like you may be acting like one. He can't possibly know why that upsets you."

I swallow a large gulp of air, and it burns as it slides to the pit of my stomach. "I'm so embarrassed."

"Don't be embarrassed. You're human…and out of practice. And so is he."

"Which one? Human or out of practice?"

Jane laughs. "Probably both."

We end the call, and I'm headed back to the table

when I hear Darian shout my name. I find him sitting on a bench, partially obscured by the restroom line, his hand raised in a wave. I cross the crowded walkway and sit beside him.

"I'm sorry," I say, curling my legs beneath me. "I know you didn't mean anything by it."

"No, I promise, I didn't." He smiles. "I do like you, by the way." His fingertips brush against mine as he speaks, causing goose bumps to break out across my skin. "And I was going to say, practically a *target*, but I suppose someone who looks the way you do would be a target anywhere...with anyone."

My heart stutters. *Someone who looks the way I do?*

Darian stands from the bench, bringing my hand with him. My gaze falls to our laced fingers.

"Come on," he says. "The last band's about to start."

I unfold my legs and push to my feet. "The last band? Already?"

"You were a little late."

"Breakfast ran a little long."

Darian grins, and his grip on my hand tightens, sending a tiny jolt of electricity up my arm. Pulling me close behind him, we weave through the crowd to the front of the stage.

"It's going to get cramped up here," he says, "but I promise, I won't let you get trampled."

"Trampled? Who's playing?"

Before I get my answer, the lights in the warehouse dim and the voices around us fall silent. Then, from somewhere offstage, a violin begins to play.

Shut up!

I spin around. "Cross to Bear?"

"What are the chances?" Darian says, a wry smile etched on his face.

Yeah. What are the chances?

Darian's gaze slides past me, and I turn to the front just as the band emerges onstage. My lips lift in a grin. I'm high on adrenaline, lost to the beat, oblivious, as the crowd behind us surges forward. Darian's arms come up, caging me against the stage. Our bodies are unintentionally close. By the end of the third song, his elbows bend and his chest brushes my back. By the end of the fourth, I lean against him.

The band announces their final song, and I tilt my head, pressing my cheek against the cool cotton of his shirt. "This is my favorite part."

A light sheen of sweat blends with his spicy cologne and holds my nose hostage. It isn't until Cross to Bear breaks into their customary Doors cover that I'm able to pull away.

When the song ends, Darian bends to my ear. "Any interest in going backstage?"

His breath is warm and intoxicating and smells of cranberries. I momentarily lose my footing, and it has absolutely nothing to do with the fact that I'm about to meet my favorite band. Fortunately, Darian thinks it does, and he chuckles at my unsteady feet.

As we head backstage, it hits me—what a complete blockhead I am. The signs posted everywhere bear the Fox Independent logo. This is *his* party.

"That was surreal. I can't believe I got to see them live, much less meet them," I say as we exit the back of the warehouse onto Eighth Street. "I've never met anyone famous before. Cade Corban was so *nice*. I had it in my head all rock stars were assholes." The nippy air masks my blush as I glance back at Darian.

I guess not all *rock stars are assholes.*

"Cade…now, which one was he?"

My head whips around. "Very funny."

"Nice guys are a rare breed in this industry," Darian says, falling in step beside me. "I'm sorry it got cut short. They're on a tight schedule."

"No, it was great. Really, thank you." I make a face. "Jane's going to be so jealous. She's had a thing for Cade since he was just a kid playing with Urban Riot."

"Maybe wait to tell her, then."

"I plan to."

A brisk breeze rustles my hair, and I pull my jacket higher on my neck. Darian stops, slides out of his sport coat, and drapes it over my shoulders.

"I'm fine," he says when I look up at him.

He smiles, and then his hand moves to my lower back and we continue walking. A few blocks down, we stop at a crosswalk.

"Any chance you're hungry yet?" he asks.

"I am—surprisingly."

Darian takes me to a French restaurant near our hotel. It's charming, romantic, with Edith Piaf softly crooning beneath a cacophony of clattering plates and wine-warmed voices.

We make small talk as we wait for our food, but we barely speak as we eat. Dessert comes, and I realize, "This looks amazing," is the first thing I've said since, "I'm too full for dessert." I dip my spoon in my chocolate mousse and take a bite. When I look up, Darian's eyes are fixed on me.

I set my spoon on my plate. "What is it?"

"I have a confession," he says, a shy grin flitting on

his lips. "I hate South By—all the people, the *noise*. But it was my year to *take one for the team*." He says that last part with an eye roll, and it makes me laugh. "I was preparing myself for a week of hell when our paths crossed yesterday. I didn't expect you to stay, but after dinner last night…" His gaze falls to his finger drawing circles on the tablecloth. "I don't know. I just really wanted you to. I took advantage of your kindness by buying you the badge."

Realizing he's being sincere, I swallow back the sarcasm shaping on my tongue. "You bought me a platinum badge. I'd say it's *your* kindness in question here."

Darian lifts his head. "Except I didn't do it to be kind. I did it so you'd stay. I preyed on your guilt."

"My guilt?"

"You didn't seem like the kind of person who'd let a nonrefundable gift go to waste."

"I have a confession too," I say.

His grin widens to a full-fledged smile. "Oh yeah? What's that?"

"I'd already decided to stay." I lift my badge and hold it above the table. "So it looks like you wasted quite a bit of money."

"I disagree," he says and then pauses. "I think it was worth every penny."

I bury my gaze in my dessert as I take another bite, the warmth from his words spreading through me like a sudden fever.

"But as much as I'm enjoying your company," he continues, "I don't want you to feel like you have to hang out with me. Obviously I didn't think that part through."

"Are you kidding? After I made an ass out of myself earlier?" I blink. "I'm surprised you still want me around.

I overreacted. Sometimes I do that. I'm…"

Darian scoots his chair closer to mine. His gaze falls to my lips, and for just a moment, I think he's going to kiss me. I *want* him to kiss me. I lean in…

But he takes my hand instead.

Le sigh.

"You didn't overreact," he says, his thumb sweeping over my knuckles. "I thought about what I said. I get how it must have sounded." He steals his hand away and signals for the check. "Let's get out of here."

We end up at a small bar tucked away in the corner of downtown and sit at a table by an open window. Sipping on Lone Star longnecks, we talk and laugh as live blues filters in from a nearby showcase.

When the set ends, I excuse myself for the restroom, but the second I push out of my chair, I realize I'm a little bit drunk. Thankfully, the ladies' room isn't far from our table. Standing in front of the mirror, I dab cold water on my face with a paper towel and then pull my hair back in an elastic. My makeup is all but gone, and if it weren't for the alcohol coloring my cheeks, I'd look like a ghost.

"I should probably call it a night and get back to the hotel before I'm incapable," I say as I slide into my chair.

"I just ordered nachos," Darian says, sitting up. "But I can cancel—"

"Nachos?" My voice comes out high-pitched and loud. "I think I can make it a little longer."

I hope.

Darian smiles. "You're in my hands, Francesca. I promise to deliver you safe and sound to your room."

I'd like to be in your hands.

Ooo-kay. I may be more than a little bit drunk.

I flag down our waiter and order a bottle of water. He delivers it with the nachos just as a new band starts up. I drink half of it in one swallow.

"How am I still hungry?" I say, piling a chip high with jalapeños. "Great call."

I devour a third of the nachos before the heat from the peppers joins forces with the alcohol already in my system. My lungs constrict.

Oh no.

I suck in a deep breath, hold it, and then slowly let it out.

No way, Frankie. You are not *hiccupping.*

Darian leans back in his chair and rests his arm on the windowsill. "That poor guy must have been shunned by the Four Seasons too," he says, pointing to the twenty-something emo passed out on the sidewalk.

I follow the line of his finger. "Why don't you go rescue him?"

"I'm not *his* knight in shining armor, Francesca," he says, circling his thumb around the lip of his beer. "I'm yours."

The way he says "I'm yours" causes my belly to flutter.

"And I suppose, as such," he continues, "I *should* get you back to your room." He takes one last look out the window before pushing back in his chair, a dry smile tugging at his lips. "I'd hate for that to be you out there."

Yeah, me too.

By the time we reach our floor, my brain's turned to blissful mush. I think the water was too little, too late. My filter disappeared somewhere around Sixth and Brazos, and I'm feeling both bold and amorous—a dangerous combination.

Darian stops in front of my door and peers down at me with those arresting eyes of his. I swear this morning they were a light olive, and tonight they're a deep forest green. I don't know how long I stay lost in them before he whispers my name, releasing me from their hold.

"Where's your key?" he asks.

"Don't worry; I have it."

He laughs. "Well, I think we're gonna need it."

"We?" I say, my face brightening.

"You."

I frown. Quite possibly, I pout. "Thank you for tonight," I say, "and today. Both actually. You've been amazing."

"You're wel—"

"A perfect gentleman. And you said you liked me. You said I was worth all the pennies."

Darian stiffens beneath my fingers as they glide across his chest and down the line of buttons on his shirt.

"But you haven't made a pass at me," I say. "Well, except for that almost kiss at the restaurant. What *was* that anyway?" The memory makes me giggle. The giggling makes me sway.

He closes his hands over mine and holds them against his chest.

"Was it because we were in public? Because this isn't public. Well, *this* is," I say, peering down the corridor. I nod toward the door of my suite and smile. "But *that* isn't."

I don't think I'm slurring. I'm going to go on record

and just say I'm not. Probably. But I can hear the desperate words leaking from my mouth, and I'm helpless to stop them. And what fun would this humiliation be if I didn't at least try to make it worse? That's when I decide to lean in for a kiss.

Darian steps back, dropping my hands and cupping my shoulders. Holding me in place. Holding me away from him. "No, Francesca. I'm sorry. It's just—I can't. Let me see your key."

"I'm fine," I say, pulling the key from my jacket pocket. "I don't need to be tucked in."

I wake around three in the morning. I'm disoriented and my head is throbbing. What the hell did I drink last night that tastes like turpentine-flavored Kool-Aid?

I make a beeline for the bathroom and brush my teeth. Twice. Then I gargle Listerine until my mouth catches fire. *Much better.* Holding my hair back, I wash the lingering makeup from my face. It's then I notice the Doors vintage 1968 *Strange Days* concert T-shirt I'm wearing.

Strange indeed.

I contemplate how I wound up in Darian's shirt as I journey back to bed. I'm fairly certain nothing happened last night because A.) it's been an embarrassingly long time since I've had sex, and I'd probably be limping, and B.) so far, he's been a perfect—

Oh shit.

My body freezes in place as the memories piece themselves together. "No, no, no. Oh God, no—"

"Francesca?"

I look up. Our adjoining doors are wide open. I pad lightly across the carpet and reach for the handle.

I'm just a blubbering mess, wearing your T-shirt. Nothing to see here.

"I'm sorry I woke you," I say, pulling the door toward me.

"I wasn't asleep. Are you okay?"

"Yeah, I'm fine. Bad dream." I pull the door a few more inches and then stop. "I'm in your shirt."

"You couldn't find your bag and I didn't want to snoop, so I gave you a T-shirt. But you changed in the bathroom. Scout's honor."

"Thanks," I say, the memory returning.

"You're welcome."

"Well, goodnight."

"Wait, Francesca…come here. Please."

Reluctantly, I release the doorknob and walk toward him. He's wearing a pair of sexy-as-hell black-framed glasses and a white V-neck T-shirt that glows brightly beneath the light of his bedside lamp. He's leaning against the headboard with a tattered paperback perched in his hand. *Dune* by Frank Herbert. My dad had the very same book in hardcover; he read it all the time. Darian sets the book on the table, removes his glasses, and scoots to the center of the bed as I approach. I sit on the edge with my back to him.

"Are you okay?" he asks again.

My shoulders curled in, my spine bowed, I stare down at my feet. "I'm so sorry."

"Francesca—"

"I can't believe—I mean—I've never—I'm *so* embarrassed," I stammer, my fingers gripping the edge of his sheet. "I had way too much to drink—obviously. I got upset with you for making me feel like a child, and then I went out of my way to prove you right. I *am* young, and I *am* alone in the big, bad city. Not that it matters. I'm alone all the time. And I don't mind being alone, except being alone is so…*lonely*. Jane says all I need is a herd of cats—*and* now I can't stop talking. Oh God. Just kill me."

As I start to stand, Darian's fingers circle my wrist. "Don't go."

He draws the bedding back, making room for me. I hesitate.

"Just sleep," he says in a low voice.

I lie down beside him, my back to his chest.

He wraps his arm around me. "I'm familiar with lonely."

CHAPTER 4

Do It

Darian: You up?

> Drew: Yep. Can't sleep. Watching a Sex and the City marathon.

Darian: Just once can you lie and say you're watching Scarface or something?

> Drew: This is educational! Why can't you sleep?

Darian: That girl I told you about came on to me and I shot her down. I think I hurt her feelings.

> Drew: See? If you watched more chick shit you'd know it's OK to have a one night stand occasionally. Girls like one-night stands. Well, not Charlotte. Samantha though…

Darian: Been there, done that.

> Drew: That's why I said occasionally.

Frankie

Darian's chest rises and falls beneath my cheek. Our legs are tangled together. His arms are wrapped around me. I've never felt this content, this at peace. Lonely is so much lonelier when you realize what you're missing. And this is what I've been missing.

Come Sunday, I'll be missing it again.

I'm careful not to wake him as I unravel myself from his body. He moans softly as my toes touch the carpet. He rolls over as I pad back to my room.

Memories of my behavior last night come and go in flashes. I know weeks from now, Jane and I will have a big laugh over a giant vat of ice cream when I tell her all about how I threw myself at Darian like a lovesick teenager. But today, it isn't very funny. It's humiliating.

I don't want to venture out today. I think I'll skip the bands—and certainly the free drinks—and hide out here with room service and a book. Get lost in someone else's romantic woes for a while. Maybe reread *The Time Traveler's Wife*. Nothing's more woeful than a disappearing husband. I'm sure, at some point, Darian will come by, and I want to be here when he does.

So I can apologize—again.

But he doesn't come by.

He's here on business, Frankie. You keep forgetting that.

When the room darkens to match the sky, I close my book. I set it on the coffee table and stretch out along the sofa beneath the comforter from the bed. Just as I'm drifting off, I hear a loud commotion in the hallway, and even though I know I should mind my own business, I can't stop myself from opening the door.

Darian glances up at me with an apologetic grin. "I'm sorry. I hope I didn't disturb you," he says, stacking CDs in a beat-up cardboard box. He shrugs. "No one listens to these things anymore."

"I do…sometimes," I say, bending down to help him. My fingers brush against his, and there's a staticky crackle, like a sheet from the dryer without softener.

He gestures to the CD I'm holding. "Help yourself then."

I pick up a few more, quickly scanning the covers. "Oh, I'm not really familiar, but…maybe you can introduce me"—heat crawls up my neck the second the words leave my lips—"sometime?"

Darian lowers his gaze to the mess on the floor, and mine falls to the white cotton shirt stretching across his back. He's wearing dark navy slacks and polished brown dress shoes. His matching suit coat and a lavender tie are stuffed in the crook of his arm.

"Sure. Sometime." He gathers the last of the discs and stands with the box. He smiles tightly. "Thanks for—"

"Darian, about last—"

He lifts a hand to my face and holds his thumb over my lips. "Have a good night," he says and then disappears into his room.

Isn't it funny how guilt and embarrassment feel so similar? Physically, I mean. A hollow feeling that can only be filled by reassurances like, *It's okay; I forgive you*, or, *You have absolutely no reason to be embarrassed.*

I felt bad before, but after that awkward exchange last night, I feel terrible today. And the truth is, I don't even know why I feel this way. *Is it because I keep making a fool of myself or because I was rejected?*

I consider taking the easy way out—packing my bag and slinking home—but knowing what Darian spent on my badge, that would be a pretty shitty thing to do. So I decide to stay even though I avoid the parties that would require me to use it—the parties where I might run into him—and I slum it with the rest of the non-badge-holders at an unofficial showcase. I make it a whole two hours before I give up and go back to my room.

For the rest of the day and well into the evening, I stay curled up in bed with my book, reading until the lines blur together on the page. I wake with it tented over my face, my nose wedged in the binding, to Darian's soft tapping on the door between our rooms. I fly out of bed and send the book skating across the floor.

"Hey," Darian says, holding a bottle of Bordeaux and two glasses. His gaze travels my body before settling on my eyes. His lips lift in a grin. "I took a chance you'd be here."

I glance down at my attire and turn as red as the wine. I'm in my underwear and, as if that isn't bad enough, Darian's Doors T-shirt. "Oh no. Hold that thought. I'll be right back. I mean, come in."

I rush to the bathroom and pull on my sweatpants, and just as I'm about to walk out the door, I grab my bottle of honeysuckle oil and dab some on my neck.

Well, that was stupid.

I saunter into the sitting area in my shabby sweats with my head held high, like it's perfectly normal to smell like a flowering vine while dressed for the gym.

Darian's amused grin returns and he holds up the bottle of Bordeaux. "Nightcap?"

I sit beside him on the sofa. He's dressed casually in worn jeans and a Jethro Tull T-shirt. His tanned feet are bare. He hands me a small pour of wine, and I relax as the first sip slides down my throat. It's warm, soothing, and tastes like tart cherries. I set my glass on the coffee table in front of us. Now unsure of what to do with my hands, I pick at the edge of the cushion and then finally place them in my lap with my fingers linked together.

"I haven't seen you much in the last day or so," I say. "Any more cardboard box malfunctions?"

Cardboard box malfunctions? My God, Frankie, stop talking.

Darian smiles. "Nope. Malfunction free." He slides his hand in his back pocket. "I stopped by for a reason actually," he says, pulling out a single ticket and handing it to me. "Glass Surface has a show tomorrow."

"Glass Surface?"

"One of the bands from last night. You know, that I had CDs for? The ones with the weird-looking solar system on the insert?"

"I remember," I say, looking at the ticket. "VIP?"

"Yeah, killer seats, backstage access…" He takes a sip of his wine. "I thought maybe you'd like to check them out…with me."

Is he asking me out? Is this an actual date?

"I'm on a tight schedule tomorrow, so I'll have to meet you there," he says. "I mean, you know…if you want to go."

Maybe not.

I hold the ticket between my fingertips, mindlessly thumbing the surface as I reach across the sofa to set it on the end table. "Sure. Thanks. Sounds like fun."

"And I was thinking maybe we could grab a late dinner after."

Maybe so.

I turn my head toward him. His gaze is trained on his glass, on the tip of his middle finger absently sliding up and down the stem. Long, silent seconds pass. Then he tosses back the rest of his wine and sets his glass on the table.

"So, what do you think about the Bordeaux?" he asks, looking over at me. "I picked it up at that French restaurant we went to. The sommelier recommended it."

He reaches for the bottle, and I quickly place my hand over my glass.

"I love it but no more for me." I smile nervously. "I'm taking it easy. I don't think my ego can handle two rejections from you this week."

He sets the bottle back on the table without pouring any. "Do you really think that? That I rejected you?"

I tilt my head from side to side with my nose scrunched. "I know I wasn't the epitome of sexpot, all wobbly and slurry, but—"

"Francesca…you're…well, you're you. And I'm…I'm thirty-six. I'm closer to forty than you are to thirty. And you were—it was the alcohol talking, not you. I wasn't about to take advantage, which is exactly what I would have been doing."

"It's fine—really," I say, waving off his explanation. "I was in no condition to be doing anything anyway. I didn't even need to be upright at that point. Not that I'm saying I needed to be horizontal. Well, I did need to be horizontal but not horizontal like that. Oh dear God, what am I saying?"

A slow smile builds on Darian's face, and I take a very unladylike gulp of wine.

"I get and appreciate why you didn't stay. But yes, I thought it was me. I thought you were rejecting me, even before the embarrassing display."

"I wanted to kiss you," he says. "I *almost* kissed you."

"You did? I was beginning to think I'd imagined that."

"Jesus, Francesca." He takes my glass and places it on the coffee table next to his. "Get up."

My toes barely touch the carpet before he's dragging me into the bathroom. "What are you doing?"

"Showing you what an idiot you are."

Oh, I'm fully aware.

Darian stands behind me and our eyes lock in the mirror.

"Is this where you tell me how beautiful I am and how any man would be lucky to have me?" I ask. "Or is this about you? Because you're so old and gangly?"

"Are those my only two choices?"

I shrug.

"I didn't *want* to say no to you the other night, Francesca." He pulls my hair away from my neck and skims his fingertips down the side of my face. "It took every ounce of self-control I had."

A charged silence fills the bathroom. I feel the warmth of his hands as they close over mine, and despite the butterfly Olympics his touch sets off in my stomach, I feel brave...*ish*.

A long swallow rolls down my throat, followed by a steadying breath. "Darian, the alcohol didn't make me want you. It just gave me the nerve to tell you."

His gaze falls to his feet and I cast a nervous smile which he fails to see with his head down.

"So I guess what I want to know is, if I threw myself at you again, right now, would you shoot me down?"

A quiet laugh escapes him. I turn around and push myself onto the counter.

"Francesca, I—"

"Darian, I like you. I think you're pretty hot—in spite of your AARP eligibility. I'm not looking for a two-carat ring and a white picket fence. I'm on vacation. I'm trying to *live a little*." Sitting between his outstretched arms, my eyes holding his, I lift my T-shirt—his T-shirt—over my head. "It's just sex, Darian," I say with this newfound bravery. His five o'clock stubble tickles my hands as I bring his face closer. I gently brush my lips against his. "No strings."

Stepping between my legs, he pulls my hips forward. Finally, he kisses me. *Really* kisses me. He holds my head still as his soft lips press against mine. He parts them, sweeping his wine-laced tongue into my mouth. I kiss him back and an unfamiliar tingle spreads through me, circling my heart and whirring in my stomach.

Is he feeling what I'm feeling? This overwhelming sensation so strong, it reaches all the way to my dangling toes?

It's just a kiss, Frankie.

Then why is the room spinning? Spinning and…moving.

Darian carries me across the suite to the edge of the bed, finally releasing my swollen lips as he lowers me to the floor. He pulls the drawstring on my sweats, and his gaze travels my body as I wiggle out of them. He removes his shirt and then my bra. Diffidence and desire swirl in my stomach as I watch him watch me. Holding my breasts in his hands, he drags his tongue across a nipple. It hardens, and he draws circles around it. Then he takes it between his teeth and sucks it between his lips.

"I do want you." He feathers my skin with kisses, working his way down my body until he's on his knees, staring up at me. "Don't think I don't."

His words swell in my brain until I can't think at all. Raspy moans spill from my lips as he pulls my panties down.

"Lift," he says simply.

I pick up one foot, then the other, and a bright pink scrap of lace tumbles from my toes. My breath leaves my body and my heart bounces in the void like a ping-pong ball. I'm nervous. I'm excited. I'm...

"Ohh..."

Darian touches me. Slowly. Softly. I arch my back and push against his hand, against the teasing kiss of his fingers. My legs struggle beneath me and I grab his shoulders.

"Darian, I need..."

"Tell me what you need."

It's strange—this mix of bravery and fear. It's...*exhilarating.*

"Your mouth. I need your mouth on me. Please."

With a deep, throaty groan, Darian takes hold of my hips, then touches his lips to my lower abdomen and works his mouth south.

"Spread your legs, Francesca."

"Oh God. Okay."

He tortures me with long, slow pulls of his tongue. I shove my hands in his hair, twisting the strands around my fingers, tighter and tighter, pulling him forward until his mouth is pressed against me.

"Darian..."

"Francesca."

"You're gonna—I'm gonna..."

Tilting his head back, he peers up at me with those big olive eyes. How innocent they look beneath that dense shelf of lashes. How deceiving they really are. Amusement flickers behind them, and he smiles. "That's the idea."

With a final stroke of his tongue, Darian stands and guides me backward onto the bed. "Are you sure?"

I nod with fervor. "I'm sure. I'm sure."

His smile brightens, and the butterflies from earlier take flight through my body. Kneeling between my legs, he watches me as he reaches inside his pocket and fishes out a condom. I fixate on the small foil square dropped beside us on the bed until the metallic slide of his zipper brings me back to him. My gaze climbs to his eyes and then rolls down his body, down his golden and sinewy chest, to that sacred patch of skin peeking through his unfastened jeans. He pushes them down and kicks out of them, then slips his thumbs inside the waistband of his rubber-ducky boxers. I bite back a grin. *That has to be the cutest fucking thing I've ever seen.*

But then the boxers come off.

There is nothing cute about that.

Darian crawls up my body, and my skin blazes beneath him. His hands cradle my face. His eyes bore into mine.

"I imagined this," he says, his fingers brushing the hair from my face. "I think, last night, I dreamed it."

His words pull me from the pillow like a magnet, and I lift my head and kiss him with every bit of the fire I feel burning in my veins—eager and impatient, tongues sliding together, stroking, twisting. Wanting. *Needing.* The force of it pushes me back against the pillow, the fluffy down rising above my ears with the weight of his lips. His scratchy stubble grazes my skin as his mouth moves over mine, and his fingers curl in my hair. He grips and tugs the strands, working me like a marionette. Every pull causing me to move. Every move causing me to moan.

I smooth my hands down the soft, velvety skin of his back and dig my fingers into his hips, pulling him closer. His erection strains against me, and as he grinds down, a long, broken sigh tears from his throat.

Peeling himself off of me, he sits back on his heels, shakes his head, and smiles. "God, you're beautiful."

A man telling you you're beautiful might not hold

much weight when you're naked beneath him, but Darian isn't looking at my body. He's looking at my face, staring into my eyes. He sits still for a moment just watching me, and then his gaze falls to the bed, the sheets tugging and pulling beneath us as he rifles through them for the condom. The wait is agony. My legs twitch and my knees draw up. My hands grab for his thighs. His eyes darken to a deep forest green as he rolls on the condom, and I become captive to them. Leaning forward, he eases my ache with a pass of his fingers, and the last of my inhibitions melts away as he pushes into me.

"God, it's so…" I slide my arms around his neck, my hands dangling over his back. "Darian…you feel…this feels…"

My words crumble to nothing, and Darian grins against my lips.

"So fucking good," he whispers, his large hand consuming my body as it trails down my side. It disappears between the back of my thigh and the bed, drawing my leg forward.

His rhythm is slow and steady, lulling the butterflies in my stomach. My eyes close. I feel his lips first, then his tongue, and the butterflies awaken.

Our hearts beat faster as Darian pushes harder. His pace quickens. A glowing, hot ball of intensity builds inside me, expanding with every thrust. I hold onto him tightly, belting my legs around his waist and my arms around his neck. Tremors assault my body, and I clench around him, drawing out his release. I cry out…

The room quiets. Our short, labored breaths and the ruffling of sheets are the only sounds between us. Darian kisses my forehead, and his lips linger for a moment on my skin.

Then he pulls out of me, climbs off me, climbs off

the bed. He doesn't say a word as he picks up his boxers and disappears into the bathroom. I sit up against the headboard with the sheets pulled high around my chest, wondering if that was code for, *Thanks and goodnight.* An empty feeling settles in the pit of my stomach and I have to remind myself that I wanted this.

But he surprises me. He comes back to bed.

I wake with last night's grin still plastered on my face, but it quickly fades. The sheets on Darian's side of the bed are pulled neatly to the headboard, and they're cool to the touch. It hardly looks like he slept here, much less slept *with me* here.

And I'm not sure how I feel about that.

No strings, Frankie. Your words, remember?

I should call Jane, right? Or is this the kind of thing you tell your best friend in person?

Hey, so guess what? You know how I said I was going to sleep with strange men? Well, I did! It took two tries, but I finally talked him into it!

Oh God. I'm a slut. I'm a slut who had to beg for sex.

Maybe I should just text—

My hand flies to the nightstand, knocking over the lamp. It tumbles off the table and lands on the floor, but I don't give it a second thought as I grab my phone and power it on.

No texts. No messages. None. Zip.

Damn. He really didn't tell you goodbye.

I'm not sure how I feel about that either.

Frankie: So…I got laid last night.

Jane: I'm calling you. Pick up.

"Hi, Ja—"

"Oh no. Are you okay? How long have you been analyzing?"

"I'm not analyzing. I'm—he left before I woke up. Is that normal? And does that make me a slut?"

Jane laughs so loud, I have to hold the phone away from my ear.

"No, Frankie. It's the one-night stand that makes you a slut."

"Yeah, well, there's that."

"Frankie, I'm kidding. He probably just had things to do and didn't want to wake you. It's almost noon. Did you expect him to wait?"

"No. Yes." I swing my legs around and perch myself on the edge of the bed. "I don't know. What if I was terrible? It's been a while, Jane. Oh no. What if he had to wait until I fell asleep to coyote-ugly his way out of my bed?"

"Do you hear yourself?"

"I'm trying not to listen."

"Do you have plans to see him again?" she asks.

Duh. He didn't need to tell you goodbye. You'll see him in a few hours.

I heave a sigh of relief. "Yes. Tonight. He gave me tickets...a ticket. Tonight."

"Then stop panicking. You'll see him tonight."

When I bend over to pick up the lamp, I find a note—Darian's note—which simply fell to the floor.

SORRY I HAD TO RUSH OFF. EARLY MEETING.

DF

Despite my excitement, or maybe because of it, the afternoon drags. I don't have enough time to venture out, so I stay in, get ready at a leisurely pace, and then page through my book. After a while, I give up on trying to read and opt for pacing back and forth in front of the balcony door. It looks as gloomy outside as AccuWeather predicted.

When the clock strikes seven, I grab my purse and bolt from the room. Yesterday I didn't want to leave it; today I can't bear to be in it.

I glance at my reflection in a shop window on my way to the show. Several pieces of hair have escaped my elastic and are blowing in my face. The wind is biting and ruthless, and I'm happy I had the good sense to wear my hair up. My fifties-style dress, on the other hand, wasn't well planned. The sleeves are short, and the skirt is full, catching the wind like a kite.

I scan the crowd for Darian as I near the building, but the lines are long and congested and it's impossible to make anyone out. I battle with my dress as I search for him, more hair falling loose from my ponytail and masking my eyes. I must be a sight. With my purse clutched between my knees, I attempt to fix my hair and smooth out my skirt. If Jane were here, she'd fuss over me, probably going as far as spitting in her hand to flatten my flyaways. Luckily Jane isn't here, and my disheveled appearance does little to affect my mood. Darian doesn't strike me as the kind of guy who cares about unruly hair. He strikes me as the kind of guy who causes it.

I follow the signs to the Special Guests entrance around the corner, my stomach twisting tighter and tighter with each step. By the time I reach the door, I have full-on pretzel tummy. My heart is in my throat, my hands are clammy, and I'm beginning to wonder if Jane's spit isn't such a bad idea. First-date jitters. Even though this isn't a first and may or may not be a date.

Darian isn't waiting for me like I hoped he'd be, and although I know he's working, my heart sinks a little. I give it a few more minutes, but after my hair falls a third time, I shake it out, slide the elastic around my wrist, and hand the door attendant my ticket.

The Stoli and Seventh party was the first time I'd ever been backstage, and it was just a roped-off area in the back of a warehouse with a few benches and a keg. This is much different. For one, it's packed. Wall-to-wall, body-to-body packed. I don't think I've ever seen so many people crammed into such a small space. It's a madhouse of photographers, journalists, roadies, and fans, and everyone seems so tall. At five and a half feet I'm considered average, but sardined between so many people, I feel pretty short.

I make my way to the bar and pull out my phone. I have two texts from Jane and one from my boss with next week's schedule. Nothing from Darian. I shoot a quick reply to Jane and message Darian to let him know I'm here. The bartender hands me a beer, and I move to the side, turning to face the mass of people while I consider my options. But my only option, it seems, is to get to my seat and hope Darian's there waiting for me.

I find an usher and show him my badge. He smiles brightly when he reads my name. He either really loves his job or he was expecting me. As I follow him onto the stage, I quickly learn it was the latter.

"There are only two chairs," I say, craning my neck to look past him. "This has to be a mistake. I'm supposed to be in the VIP section. Where are all the VIPs?"

He turns toward the people filing into the front row. "There's your VIP section. Think of this as the VIP of VIP. These seats are special."

The usher winks at me before walking away, and I sink into my chair, an uneasy feeling sitting like rocks in the pit of my stomach. Darian should be here by now.

I pull out my phone and check my texts again. I have one from Jane—*I expect details*, it reads—but nothing else. I slide my phone back in my purse as I scan the audience. Hundreds of eyes, all of which seem to be set on me. I can't blame them. Besides myself and the drum set, there's nothing else up here to look at.

Or they're shooting daggers at you for being the special girl in the special seat.

Maybe if the chair beside me wasn't so painfully empty, I'd feel special. But right now, I just feel exposed. I check my phone again, shaking my head when I realize only a minute has passed. I silence it this time and then put it away. Darian never said this was a date. Something probably came up. Some South By emergency only he could handle. *Maybe he'll still make it. Maybe he's just…*

Doubt pushes forcefully against the wall of my chest. *He would have texted you, Frankie.*

I don't want to be here, and I really don't want to be *up* here. I consider making a run for it, but before I can even stand from my chair, the lights flicker and everyone is asked to take their seats.

Darkness swallows the music hall as the concert begins, and I try to relax into it, hoping to disappear. But three songs in, my invisibility is cut short when the lead singer begins to serenade me. When the song ends, he asks how I scored the lucky seat.

Jane would eat this up, and as much as I'd like to be

more like her, as much as I'd like to *come out of my shell*, this is too much. I'm in the spotlight—literally. It's on me and only me, heavy and blistering as it circles my lonely chair. My heart thunders in my ears and my eyes burn.

Wearing a forced grin between my burning cheeks, I choke out a single word, "Contest."

The singer smiles. The crowd cheers. The spotlight returns to its star.

And I'm back to being blissfully forgotten.

The March Austin air was chilly before the concert, but it's freezing now. It was foolish of me to dress for a guy, and the fact that I'm standing at Third and Nueces by myself really drives that point home.

I rummage through my bag for my phone and turn it back on. My heart plunges deep in my chest. Still nothing.

Well, Frankie, I think it's safe to say he's not coming.

This is exactly how I felt the first and only time I slept with Chad Abrams. On prom night. Incidentally, it was also the first time I'd slept with anyone ever, and he never spoke to me again.

After Chad, I only had sex within the confines of committed relationships, of which I had exactly two—both in college and both incredibly short.

Darian Fox is my first no-strings sexual encounter.

No strings? You're freezing to death on a street corner at eleven thirty at night, pondering your sexual history. There're so many strings you could knit a sweater.

I hop on a pedicab and brave the icy wind as we pedal our way back to the hotel. The cold is numbing and I consider asking the driver to circle a few more blocks before dropping me off. I don't though, and all too soon, we come to a stop.

I'm both grateful and disappointed I don't run into Darian on the way to my suite. Once inside, I toss my bag on the chaise and kick out of my shoes. I sigh in resignation as I walk to the adjoining door and hold my ear against it. Darian's there. I hear him talking, but I can't make out what he's saying. I raise my hand to knock, then drop it to my side. *What would be the point?*

I slide down the door, draw my knees to my chest, and close my eyes. It isn't long before his muffled voice lures me to sleep.

Even on the unforgiving floor, I don't wake until the sun rises. It casts a warm glow on the little patch of carpet I'm curled up on. My head aches and my neck's sore, but my heart's okay.

I'm okay.

I pack quickly and throw on a clean set of clothes. I sit down at the oversized mahogany desk and pull out a single piece of the hotel's stationery.

DARIAN,

THANK YOU SO MUCH FOR EVERYTHING THIS WEEK.

HAVE A WONDERFUL FINAL NIGHT AND A SAFE TRIP BACK TO MIAMI.

GRATEFULLY YOURS,

FV

P.S. I HAVE YOUR T-SHIRT. I'LL MAIL IT TO YOUR OFFICE.

I grab my bag and quietly sneak into the hall. I'm careful to avoid him, tiptoeing soundlessly to the bank of elevators. When I reach the lobby, I drop the letter off at the front desk and hail a cab home.

CHAPTER 5

Been Down So Long

Drew: Do you ever pick up your phone? I've been calling all day.

Drew: Hello?

Drew: If I don't hear from you soon I'm calling Riley.

> Darian: Duck off man. Busy. Thugs to do.

Drew: Duck off? Thugs? Are you drunk?

Drew: You alive?

> Darian: No.

Drew: What happened last night?

> Darian: Didn't Riley tell you?

Drew: I'm asking you.

> Darian: I stood the girl up and got shit

faced with Riley.

Drew: Fuck Dare. Is this about Jules?

Darian: No it's not about Jules. Not everything is about my dead wife.

Darian: I'm sorry. I'm just tired and feeling like a jackass.

Drew: You like this girl.

Darian: I stood her up.

Drew: Yeah, but first you asked her out. :-)

Frankie

My little cabin in the woods is mocking me. My once peaceful and secluded haven is now painfully silent. A week ago, I loved the solitude. Now, I think I hate it.

Frankie: I'm home.

Jane: Thought you were coming home tomorrow.

Frankie: Changed my mind.

Jane: Everything OK?

Frankie: Everything's fine.

Jane: How was date night?

Frankie: It wasn't a date. He got tied up. Couldn't make it.

Jane: Did you go?

Frankie: Yeah, it was awesome.

Jane: You sure you're OK?

Frankie: Jane...

I ditch my duffel on the kitchen table and pad

through my lifeless living room. Everything is still. Too still. Even the dust caught in the midmorning sunlight is unaffected by my return.

Welcome home, Frankie.

I collect the mail scattered on the floor by my front door, flipping through it as a courtesy before tossing it in the waste bin on my way to the bathroom. The notion of a long, hot bath reels me in like a fish on a hook. The headache I woke with is getting angrier by the second and my chest burns like someone punched me.

The hotel had a perfectly good bed, Frankie. You should have used it.

I turn on the faucet in my claw-foot tub, toss back a couple ibuprofen, and peel out of my clothes. The temperature is just north of scalding. I carefully sit down, watching my skin go from white to pink as the tub fills around me. I pour in a few drops of honeysuckle oil and rest my head against the porcelain, but just as I begin to relax, the air thickens to a sugary-sweet fog so rich it turns my stomach.

Ugh!

I'm an achy, nauseated, miserable mess and it's all Darian's fault…except it isn't.

God, how could I have been so stupid?

I spent the entire ride home trying to come to terms with whatever the hell it is I'm feeling. I survived two breakups—however minor—without so much as a bowl of Rocky Road. *So why am I so hung up on a guy I don't know? A guy who doesn't live here? A guy I knew I'd never see again?*

You'll be fine, Frankie. You just have a bruised ego.

This feels a little worse than a bruise.

With my shoulders underwater, my saturated hair pulls at my scalp, making my already throbbing head that much worse. I wring it out and twist it in a knot behind me. Then I close my eyes and focus on the water rushing out of the faucet.

You're in a Costa Rican rain forest, floating in a pool of blue beneath a thundering waterfall. The sun is directly overhead, its warm rays shining down on you. And you're naked.

With Darian.

My eyes snap open. "No, not naked. And *not* with Darian."

Wow, Frankie. What the hell is wrong with you?

I miss him. I know it's crazy. It's been, what? Five days? I've had zits last longer than that. But those five days made me feel alive. Now I just feel...*blah.* Maybe it isn't him.

Of course it isn't him.

I'm just missing...*something.* I just want...*something.*

I extend my leg toward the faucet and toe it off. My small box of a bathroom is swallowed by the same silence that greeted me when I walked inside my cabin. I slide deeper into the water until my head is completely submerged and blow out a breath, transfixed on the bubbles rising to the surface.

I want something...*more.*

Loud knocks at my front door jerk me from my thoughts. I sit up and pull my knees to my chest, tucking my face in the hollow of my folded arms.

Go away.

The knocking stops, only to be replaced by the sound of heavy footsteps on creaking floorboards, back and forth across my small porch.

Silence. Then the knocking resumes, louder this time. Determined.

Seriously?

I get out of the tub and slip into my robe, not bothering with the sash or a towel. I trudge through the house, soaking wet, leaving a trail of water behind me.

"Be nice, Frankie," I whisper to myself before yanking the door open. "Can I help—*Darian*? What are you…"

The words die on my lips at the sight of him. I take in his wild hair, the bags under his eyes, and the Misfits T-shirt he quite possibly slept in. He's a mess, and he still looks like a *Rolling Stone* centerfold.

I tighten my grip on my robe. "What are you doing here?"

"Francesca…" My name crawls off his tongue in a sultry, breathy growl.

He takes a step toward me and my thoughts become fuzzy.

Stay strong, Frankie. Resist! Re—

I jump at the sound of the door closing behind him.

He pins me against the wall, his darkening olive eyes boring into mine. "I needed to see you," he says as he works his fingers through my soaking wet hair.

Water rains down my body, awakening every nerve ending in its path.

I open my mouth to speak, but he covers it with his lips, fills it with his tongue. He kisses me as if last night never happened, and I do nothing to stop him. If anything, I encourage him by stretching as tall as I can to give him a better angle.

My pulse races out of control, and I wonder if he can feel it as his fingers trail down my face and neck. He slips them just inside the opening of my robe and continues down my chest, between my breasts, until our hands touch. He pries the terry cloth from my grip and pushes the fabric off my body. The cold air bites my skin, but I only notice it for a second before my attention is drawn to his T-shirt as he tugs it over his head. My gaze moves from his eyes to his chest and rolls down his stomach to the low-hanging waistband of his jeans. I unfasten the button and pull down the zipper. My name, a chant on his lips, almost inaudible over my thundering heart and spastic breathing, stops abruptly when I slip my hand inside his boxers and wrap my fingers around him.

"Hold on. Wait…wait. Fuck," he says, cupping my jaw. He blinks slowly and breathes a long sigh, fanning the loose strands of hair away from my face. "I don't have a condom."

"Oh God." I close my eyes and press my forehead against his chest while I catch my breath.

His cock shifts in my hand.

Time to let go of his dick, Frankie.

"This is awkward," I say, removing my hand from his shorts. "And a little embarrassing."

"Please don't be embarrassed. This was all me. I swear to you, I had a whole speech planned, and none of it involved getting you naked."

"Oh shit, I'm naked."

A nervous laugh echoes above me. Darian touches his lips to the top of my head before turning around and refastening his jeans. "Sorry. I thought you knew."

"I was a little distracted," I say, picking up my robe and sliding into it. This time, I tie the sash. "What are you doing here, Darian?"

He grabs his T-shirt off the console table and paces several strides with it before pulling it on. "I'm sorry," he says quietly, interlocking his fingers behind his head and turning away from me.

"It's not like I was resisting. I practically—"

"No, I mean, I'm sorry about last night. Not showing up." He hesitates. "Not calling."

Oh yeah. That.

My body tenses at the reminder.

We step around the corner and into my living room. Darian sits on the sofa and I sit across from him on the edge of the coffee table. Our knees touch, and I swear a thousand volts of electricity pass between us. It's like some unexplainable pull that's always there. I felt it in the Four Seasons lobby, and I feel it now. I stand up from the table and move to the other side.

"I'm sorry," Darian says again.

"What happened? Were you working?"

"No, I wasn't."

"Oh." I busy myself with my robe, pulling the sash tighter, knotting it.

"I just...I couldn't. I don't want you to...I mean...*dammit*. None of this is coming out right," he says, raking a hand through his hair. His voice softens. "I fucked up."

"You fucked *me*," I say, my eyes hard on him, "and then you disappeared. We had seats on the stage, in front of everyone, and you never showed. Do you have any idea how embarrassing that was?"

Darian flinches. "They put us on the stage?"

"No, they put *me* on the stage."

"Jesus, Francesca, I didn't know." He drags his hand down his face. "We were supposed to be in the front row with everyone else. I had no idea they'd moved us."

"You should have called me, Darian. If I'd known you weren't coming...you should have called."

"I shouldn't have *needed* to call," he says. "I should have been there."

"Why weren't you?"

"It's...complicated. I can't even begin to answer that question." He stands up, takes a step toward me, and stops. "I'm asking you to give me the benefit of the

95

doubt," he says. "I'm asking you to forgive me anyway."

I lean back against the fireplace with my arms crossed. "Why do you even care? After today, we'll never see each other again. Aren't you going back to Miami tomorrow?"

"Yes, but…I don't know." His gaze falls to his feet. "None of this makes sense to me. In less than a week, you've gotten under my skin, and I can't imagine not *knowing* you anymore."

I can't imagine that either.

"I'm in Austin a few times a year," he says, looking up. "I'd like to see you."

I laugh. "You want me to be your Texas booty call?"

"No, that's not…*shit.*"

"Darian, I'm kidding."

"Good because that's not what this is. I just…I like you. I like *knowing* you," he says. "But I can't get involved. Not romantically. I can't commit."

"I'm not looking for a commitment," I say, my voice low. "I think I might have mentioned that."

He nods. "You did. I just need to be clear. I don't want to let you down. *Again.*"

"We're both adults. You don't have to worry about me; I won't break." I push off the fireplace and walk toward him. "But that can't happen again."

"It won't," he says. "I swear."

"Then I forgive you."

Darian extends his hand, and I take it.

A shy smile spreads across his lips. "Friends?"

"Friends," I say, smiling back at him. My gaze slides past him to the front door. "With benefits. I need *that* to be clear."

A laugh tears from his throat. "You're such a surprise," he says. His grin fades, and he brings his free hand to my cheek. "You already know I'm attracted to you, but please don't think that's what I'm after. It's not. If you decide you'd rather keep this thing one hundred percent platonic, that's what we'll do."

I ignore the flutter in my stomach.

"With benefits," I say again.

Despite my stipulation, we spend the day stretched out on layers of blankets on my living room floor, fully clothed and talking. The exchange is light, mostly playful banter, but it takes a somber turn when Darian asks about my mom.

"I was eleven when she died," I say as casually as I can. "Car accident. But my dad was amazing."

"That must have been tough—a single dad raising a little girl all by himself." He leans back against the hearth, his knees bent, his spine bowed. "You said you guys were close?"

I swallow hard. "Yes, we were."

"That's good," Darian says, his eyes aimed at the floor.

He seems distracted, and even though he brought it up, I think talking about family is hard for him.

I glance down at the pieces of fringe I pulled from the pillow I'm holding. I guess talking about family is hard for me too. "So…"

"So…" Darian says, a smile touching his lips. He leans to the side, slides his hand in his pocket, and pulls out his phone. He pecks at it with his index finger and then turns it to face me. "Tell me about Party in a Box," he says, referring to my website loaded on the screen.

I'm grateful for the subject change, but my face heats from the attention. I always feel a little self-conscious talking about my company. My gaze shifts to my skirt bunched around my thighs. "It started as a class project in college and evolved into a one-size-fits-all party-planning business," I say, pulling the fabric taut. "I sell boxed party kits through online retailers."

Darian rubs his chin. "Can't you already buy prepackaged party supplies?"

"If you're throwing a birthday party for a five-year-old but not if you're planning a wedding for a hundred people in your backyard." I lift my head and my eyes are met with a mix of curiosity and amusement. "Not everyone can afford a pricey wedding with a personal planner. Think of it like high-end boxed wine. It fits a niche."

A grin pulls at his lips, and my blush returns.

"I sound like a commercial, don't I?"

"No," he says, shaking his head. "You're passionate; it's nice." He turns his attention back to my website. "So just weddings then?"

"I do a bit of everything—milestone birthdays, office Christmas parties, graduations. I used to do one-on-one consulting too, but not so much anymore."

I confess the name was Jane's idea.

It's from the *Saturday Night Live* skit "Dick in a Box." She fell off the couch in fits of laughter when it came to her. "That's it!" she screamed.

"I'm also a waitress," I blurt out. "Before you get all impressed by my mad business skills, I figured you should know that."

Darian straightens his legs. "I know nothing of your mad business skills," he says, "but I'm impressed you're a waitress."

My eyes narrow. "Why?"

"Francesca, you're twenty-one."

I hold up two fingers. "Almost twenty-two."

"Almost twenty-two." He grins. "You run your own company, which I assume doesn't turn a sustainable profit yet, so you hold a second job to compensate. Did I get that right?"

I shrug.

"That's some serious dedication." He darkens the display on his phone and sets it on the hearth behind him. "Not all businesses turn a profit right away. It took the label years."

"It turns a profit…usually," I say, stretching my toes toward Darian's. "Just not a comfortable one."

He laughs. "So you're saying you run a *successful* business and you work a second job…*just because*? That says a lot about your character."

My chest swells. "I've never thought of it like that. I'm just—I'm on my own, you know? Some months are great, but some really suck. I wait tables to give myself peace of mind. I guess I don't feel successful because I still have a day job."

"My guess is you're successful *because* of your day job and the fact that you're committed to keeping it. I don't mean to keep harping on your age, but, damn, Francesca, it's *impressive*." He smiles shyly. "And it's really fucking hot."

Blood rushes my cheeks. It's hot all right. I swear the temperature just climbed twenty degrees.

I pull my hair off the back of my neck and wrap it around my fist. "So what about you? What's it like to run your own label? Give me a typical day in your office."

"There are no typical days in the music industry," he says, "and because we're indie, everything falls on my shoulders."

"You don't have people?"

"I do. Great people actually. One of whom is in Austin right now picking up my slack." His toes press against mine. "Have I mentioned Riley?"

I think for a minute. "Yes, at the Stoli party. Your assistant?"

Darian nods. "I'm grooming him to take over the managing side for our bigger acts. That's the part of my job I hate the most—dealing with the arrogant assholes."

"They can't all be arrogant assholes," I say. *You're not.* "Come on, you never get star-struck?"

He rests his elbows on the hearth behind him and crosses his ankles. "Obviously not with anyone we've signed, but I did meet Jimmy Buffett several years ago in Key West," he says, pausing as if he's replaying the memory. "That was pretty fucking cool." His face lights in amusement, and then his eyes widen and flick to mine. "Oh shit, and Paul McCartney. How could I forget meeting a Beatle?"

"Jesus."

"Not quite, but close."

"I recently met Cross to Bear," I say. "That was exciting." I crawl across the six feet of blue flannel bedding we're lounging on and kiss Darian's cheek before settling in next to him.

"Cross to Bear, huh? How did you ever manage that?"

"I have people too."

He drapes his arm over my shoulder, pulling me closer. "I'm really glad I'm here."

Yeah, about that...

"Me too."

He smells incredible—a dizzying blend of earthy male

and my honeysuckle bath oil. It's almost enough to wreck my train of thought. *Almost.*

I remove myself from the distraction of his embrace and return to my previous location, opposite him. "So how exactly did you find me?"

His head pitches forward, his smile wide. "I saw your driver's license, remember? Francesca lives at One Francesca Lane." He shrugs. "Pretty hard to forget."

"We've had this place forever. Dad named the street." I lean back against my hands. "We lived in San Antonio, but we were here almost every weekend."

"Your mom too?"

"No. This wasn't her thing. She was always…busy."

"That's a shame," he says. "I love it."

I love it too. Rustic and cozy with two fireplaces and a creek that runs through three acres of backyard. But I've never made it my own—a fact made evident by the giant wild boar head glaring at us from above the mantel.

Darian looks around him, his eyes lingering on the antique gun case in the corner, the fishing poles hanging over the windows, the antlers…everywhere. "You are aware this is every guy's dream, right?"

"Guys are simple creatures," I say, pointing to the taxidermy above him.

His gaze follows the line of my finger.

"All it takes are a few dead animals and a creek stocked with bass."

He whips his head back around. "There's a creek?"

"With bass. I'd show you"—I glance at the make-believe watch on my wrist—"but you probably need to get back to the festival."

Please say you don't. Please say you don't.

"What festival?" he says, his lips curling into a grin. He's silent for a moment and then, "She lives in a cabin

101

in the woods."

"She does," I say, smiling.

"I'm surprised you don't get scared...all by yourself...so *isolated*."

His attempt to act menacing makes me laugh. "You know you're about as threatening as a kitten?"

"A kitten? A *kitten*?" He shifts to his knees and crawls toward me, prowling up my body. "Maybe a lion."

My arms fail me, and I fall back against the blankets. "Okay, a lion," I say, giggling as he hovers over me, his nose poking at my collar.

He makes an unsuccessful attempt at unbuttoning the front of my dress with his teeth and opts for his fingers instead. "A very dexterous lion."

CHAPTER 6

Yes, the River Knows

Drew: Still feeling like a jackass?

Darian: Yep.

Drew: You should try apologizing. It works in the movies.

Darian: I did.

Drew: And?

Darian: I'm at her house.

Drew: Did not see that coming.

Darian: Neither did I.

Frankie

"I'm aware we've mostly talked about me today," I say to Darian as we wander the woods behind my cabin.

The air has a bite to it, and despite the cloudless sky, it smells like rain.

"You think so?" He pulls me against him. "Your arms are cold. Is this normal for March? Do you want to go back and get a sweater or something?"

"It's not so bad," I say, enjoying the heat radiating from his body. We turn a corner and arrive at *the bench*, which is actually just the trunk of an old tree we lost several years back. I stop and gesture to it. "Mind if we talk about you for a minute?"

Darian braces beside me, his arm becoming stiff around my waist before he drops it to his side. "I prefer to talk about you."

I lace my fingers with his and guide him to sit. I'm quiet for a moment, my eyes aimed at two squirrels chasing each other up and down a giant oak. They disappear beneath the underbrush, and I turn my head toward Darian.

"I Googled you," I spit out and then wait for his reaction. He doesn't give me one, other than sitting stoically and tightening his grip on my hand. "I wasn't snooping...*exactly*. It's just...I knew you owned the record label, and I was curious."

His gaze veers to his feet, which are now stretched out in front of him, crossed at the ankles. He lets go of my hand to pick at the frayed denim on his knee.

"I'm sorry," I say, watching the threads fly from his fingers in the breeze. "I wish I hadn't done it."

A loose hold on my chin, he gently guides my head until our eyes meet. "Don't be sorry, Francesca. You have every right to know who you're getting into bed with, so to speak."

"Maybe I should have said something sooner," I say. "I just didn't know how to bring it up."

"It's okay." His voice is so quiet I can barely hear him over the rustling leaves.

The wind is bitter now that we're sitting still. I fold my arms across my chest and peer up at the sky. The sunset peeking through the branches looks like stained glass, but beneath the canopy of trees, it's already dark.

"Come here," Darian says, wrapping his arm around me.

I curl into him, tucking my head in the crook of his neck.

"It's not your fault my past is broadcast all over the internet. I wish I could keep my private life private. And I do now—for the most part. But back then..." His words die on his lips as he lowers them to my forehead. He kisses me softly just above my brow, but before he pulls away, I feel his smile against my skin. "I Googled you too," he says. "And I *was* snooping."

I perk up, pulling my knees to my chest. "Me? That must have been uneventful."

"On the contrary. Your social media is very enlightening."

"How do you know I have social media? I only use Twitter, and it's anonymous."

"I have my ways," he says. "And FYI, at FrankieDawnV is *not* anonymous."

I furrow my brows. "What could you have possibly learned on Twitter?"

"I learned that if given the opportunity, you would, without a doubt, attend the Stoli and Seventh party, which you did," he says through a smug grin. "I wanted to see you again, and there you were."

My feet drop to the ground with a thud as my head snaps sideways. "I was staying next door to you. You could have just knocked." A smile threatens to surface, but I refuse to give him the satisfaction.

"Yeah but where's the fun in that?"

"There's quite a bit of fun in that, if I remember correctly."

His confession staggers me. Not that he stalked me—which, clearly, he did—but because he went above and beyond to be with me.

"So, the badge…"

"Bait," he says simply.

"And Cross to Bear?"

"Not scheduled to appear. I flew them in early that morning and did some juggling with the other acts. It was worth it to see the look on your face. Much like the one you're wearing now."

I blush, knowing I must look like a fool with my mouth gaping open, yet I can't seem to close it. "I can't believe you did that." *For me.* "Wow."

"You were right," he says. "They never tour Texas, and a girl should get to see her favorite band."

I watch as Darian's expression goes from self-satisfied to sincere, as a smile replaces the smirk, as the pride slips from his eyes. He holds his hand to my jaw and brushes his thumb over my bottom lip. He seems taken aback, and it makes me wonder if my happiness affects him more than he expected. The thought causes me to shiver, and he notices.

"You're cold; let's go back," he says, pushing to his feet. "You can show me the creek another day."

Darian stops on the patio to build a fire in the rusted-out barbecue pit. He leans over the barrel, assessing the damage, his hand gripping the back of his neck. "When's the last time you used this thing?"

"It's been a while."

His gaze travels the line of my cabin—from the far corner of the patio to the far edge of the house—until it lands on a water hose coiled in the grass. I walk to the faucet, turn it on, and close the valve on the nozzle.

"You think we'll need this?" I ask, smiling nervously as I pull it toward him. I let it fall beside his feet.

He shrugs. "Better safe than sorry, right?" He closes the lid and then lifts it open again. It makes a terrible screech. "You want to check on the steaks and I'll try to get this thing going?" he asks, his smile tight.

"Two New York strips, coming up," I say, turning toward the kitchen. I slide open the door and step inside.

"It's about time."

Jane's voice comes at me from across the room, and I'm lucky I don't slam my fingers between the glass and the frame.

"Jesus Christ, Jane!"

She stands with her back to the sink, arms crossed and eyebrows arched. She opens her mouth to speak, then closes it. Opens it again. My chest tightens. Suddenly I'm fifteen and just got caught with a boy under the bleachers. I stop moving and wait.

"He's here?" she whispers loudly, her eyes doubling in size.

The corners of her mouth lift slightly, and I relax, a wide grin breaking on my face. I look over my shoulder to make sure I closed the door all the way.

"Jane, he just showed up here this morning. Like, out of nowhere. I was thinking about him, and, *poof*, there he was."

"Poof?"

"Poof!"

"Why?"

"I think he felt bad for standing me up last night."

"I thought you said it wasn't a date."

"You know what I mean." Obviously she doesn't, but she has the good grace not to say so. "What are you doing here?"

"Dropping off pizza and leaving," she says, jerking her head at the oven. "Your text kinda worried me, but if I called, I knew you would've told me not to come." She looks past me to the patio, her face brightening. "I guess you would've had a good reason."

My mind replays my day with Darian. We never made it past second base, but, God, I hope we do tonight. Heat crawls up my neck and settles in my cheeks. I know there's no hiding it, especially from Jane. I quickly turn away from her, but I'm too late.

"Oh shit," she says from behind me. "You've got it bad."

"I do not." I walk past her to the oven and crack open the door. The distinct scent of Gabriel's deep dish permeates the kitchen. "Salami and smoked provolone?"

"You do too. Look at you. You're candy-apple crimson right now."

I glance at my flustered reflection in the oven door as it closes. "Oh stop. I'm not candy-apple anything," I say as I turn around. "How's Jacob? Is he feeling better? You didn't have to come babysit me, you know."

"He's good. Really good actually. Mom took him bowling." Jane tilts her head to the side, her soft eyes studying me. "Frankie, it's okay if you like him."

"Well, I don't. I mean, I do, but not like that."

"If you say so." She grabs her keys off the counter and slides her purse on her arm. "I guess I should go," she says, moving toward the door. Her feet drag behind her in an arduous shuffle, and I struggle to hide my amusement. "Call me tomorrow?"

"I will. Thanks for the pizza."

"Anytime." She reaches for the knob and makes a show of turning it, as if it's the most difficult task she's ever carried out. "You kids have fun."

"We will," I say, biting back a grin. "Drive safe."

"Okay…well…bye."

The door closes behind her, and I count to ten. The door swings open.

"Really, Frankie?"

Laughter erupts from my throat. "I knew you weren't going anywhere. Open a bottle of wine while I grab the steaks."

"Steaks too? This is right up your alley, isn't it?" She pats her stomach. "I'm going to eat myself into a food coma."

"Oh, no you don't. You're my best friend and I love you. But the second dinner's over, you're out of here." I check the steaks to make sure they're thawed while Jane digs for a corkscrew. "Better take it easy on the wine too."

"Aye, aye, captain."

With the lights on in the kitchen, the golden glow of the fire is barely visible through the glass. I move toward the door until my reflection fades and Darian comes into view. With my arms crossed over my chest, I lean against the side of the refrigerator and watch him work. He seems comfortable here, at ease, and that warms me in a way that's unfamiliar.

"Are we hiding this bottle?" Jane asks, her voice cutting through my thoughts.

"Hiding?"

"Your three-dollar merlot."

"No," I say, shooting her a glare. "It's fine. Darian's not like—oh whatever. Just stick it under the sink."

I turn back to the door just as it slides open, a burst of cool air rushing in.

"The fire's about ready," Darian says as he steps inside. "But you're going to need a sweater." His nose and cheeks are red from the cold.

I hold my hands against his face. "You're freezing. Did you bring a jacket?"

"You can keep me warm," he says, a seductive smile teasing his lips.

I slide my arms around his neck and lift up on my toes. "I can do that."

He lowers his head until our noses brush together, and our lips—

"Oh gross. I should have left when I had the chance," Jane's voice calls behind us.

I fall flat on my heels, laughing against Darian's chest. "Oh yeah, Jane's here. Darian, meet Jane. Jane, Darian."

"So, Jane," Darian says, reaching for a slice of pizza, "what do you do?"

"Web design," Jane mutters over a mouthful of steak.

"She's a writer too," I say.

Darian leans in. "Really? What do you write?"

"Nothing and everything," she says. "Mostly nothing."

"Jane's amazing." I give her a hard glance. "She just lacks focus. She's—"

"*She's* on borrowed time," she says, her eyes fixed on Darian. "Enough about me. We're talking about you."

She rests her elbows on the table, hands drawn to her chin. "Tell me everything—ouch!" She winces as my toe digs into her ankle and then follows it with a smirk. "Starting with your favorite sandwich."

Darian grins. "My favorite sandwich? That's easy. My buddy Drew's famous BLT."

I look up from my plate. "Yum. I love BLTs."

"What's so great about his BLTs?" Jane asks.

"Brie," he says. "Best hangover cure ever."

"Are you prone to hangovers? Dammit, Frankie!" Jane says, rubbing the foot I just toed again. "That was a fair question." This time, she glares. "Fine. Movies or TV?"

"Books."

"Good answer," Jane and I say in unison.

Jane takes a bite of her pizza, allowing Darian a brief reprieve as she chews. Taking a slow sip of wine, I look over to him, and our eyes meet. We both smile. Darian returns to his steak, and I sink back in my chair.

A cool breeze blows across the patio, setting off my old rusted weathervane. It makes a loud, familiar creak only I seem to notice. The wind has died down from earlier, but it's still a bit nippy. I hug my sweater closed, happy we didn't sit inside. The Texas Hill Country is crisp and fresh this time of year, and with the cicadas and the stars and the lingering scent of smoke from the grill, it's worth it to weather the cold.

I stab a piece of steak into a piece of salami and swirl it in melted cheese as Darian watches with amusement over the rim of his glass.

"Pizza and steak should totally be a thing," I say, my eyes rolling back as I take a bite.

"Frankie has a weird obsession with foods that shouldn't go together. Exhibit A." Jane waves her hand over the table. "I'd say she was crazy, but she's usually right."

"Usually?" I say. "Try always."

Jane looks at me with mock irritation. "When chicken and waffles became popular, I thought this one was going to lose her shit."

"That was totally my idea! Burgers and waffles too, but that one hasn't caught on yet."

Darian grins and then tips back the last of his wine.

"So how do you like the merlot?" Jane asks him, sliding her feet a safe distance away from me.

"It's, um…fruity," he says, turning his attention toward her. He holds his empty glass to the light, pretending to study it. "I taste plum."

"This steak is cooked perfectly, don't you think, *Jane*?" I cut off another bite, then turn to Darian. "Jane and I tend to get sidetracked and overcook…well, pretty much any type of meat."

"Don't listen to her," Jane says, picking off a piece of provolone and popping it into her mouth. "Frankie can cook when she wants to. She just never does."

"I live alone," I say in my defense. "It's not worth the hassle."

"Darian lives alone," she says. "Don't you?"

Darian clears his throat and smiles. "I do. And I cook a little. Gives me something to do."

"What's your favorite thing to make?" Jane asks, then holds up her hand. "Sorry, new question. What are your intentions for my girl?"

My head snaps sideways. "Jane!"

Still wearing a smile, Darian sits back in his chair and folds his arms across his chest. His eyes slide from Jane to me and then back to Jane again. The air thickens between them. I hold my breath, wondering if I should save him, but the truth is, I want to hear this.

"I wish I could give you a definitive answer, but I don't have one. All I know is, I like *your girl* a lot." Leaning forward, he pushes his plate aside and trails his fingers along the base of his wine glass. "I'm not going to pretend you don't know my story. You'd be a terrible friend if you didn't."

I look from Darian to Jane. Her expression is unreadable, her features schooled but soft.

Darian reaches for my hand and squeezes it. "Francesca makes me smile, and I don't do a lot of that. I think sometimes I make her smile too."

Jane's poker face begins to slip, her eyes growing wide and curious. I know from experience, her mouth will follow.

I push back loudly in my chair. "We need more wine. Jane? Wine?"

Her gaze is glued to Darian. "None for me, thanks. I have to drive."

"Jane, I need *help* with the wine. Please."

"Oh yeah. Right."

My fingers prodding her back, I usher her inside, sliding the door closed behind us. "Jane, before you say—"

She kisses my cheek. "I'm gonna go. For real this time. Tell Darian it was nice meeting him." She grabs her purse and keys. "I love you, Frankie, and I'm here. Always, okay?"

"Okay?" I laugh, quirking a brow in confusion. "You're acting weird. You're good to drive, right?"

"Yes, Mom. Obviously you were too preoccupied to notice, but I only had water tonight." Her keys jingle from her fingers as she steps onto the porch. Closing them in her fist, she turns around. "I like him, Frankie, and I can tell you do too. Just be careful, okay?"

I wave to Jane as she settles into the driver's seat and wonder what the hell got into her. *Be careful? I'm always careful. Usually.*

I hear the sliding glass door open and close behind me. The breeze from the patio charges in ahead of Darian, chilling the back of my neck.

"Damn wind can't make up its mind," he says over the rumble of Jane's engine starting up in the driveway.

I close the door in front of me and turn around just as he passes with a tray of dirty dishes.

He sets them on the counter by the sink and glances out the window as Jane's car backs onto the street. "Everything okay?"

"Everything's fine," I say, sidling up beside him. I turn on the faucet and hold my hands beneath the stream while waiting for the water to warm. "I wasn't expecting her, although I guess I probably should have after coming home a day…" I feel Darian stiffen beside me, and I let my sentence fall away. "Anyway, she needed to get home, but she said to tell you it was nice meeting you."

I slowly lift my head, and our eyes catch in the window.

"After coming home a day early," Darian says somberly. He takes a step back and leans against the edge of the table. "Francesca…"

"Don't. You apologized, and I forgave you. I didn't mean to bring it up."

Once the water begins to warm, it gets hot quickly. Balmy steam rises from the sink and fogs up the glass, our reflections disappearing beneath a layer of condensation. Darian stands behind me, his head downturned, his breath warm on my neck.

"Leave this," he says, reaching around me to turn off the faucet.

His lips vibrate against my skin, and I can feel it in my toes. He slips his fingers inside the neckline of my sweater, sliding it off my shoulders and onto the floor. I kick it away as I turn around.

Fighting a smile, he unbuttons the bodice of my dress.

"What? No teeth this time?" I tease.

Amused eyes briefly cut to mine. "My mouth is better suited for other endeavors."

Heat spreads from my cheeks to my core as lavender linen balloons around me, hanging by a single spaghetti strap to my shoulder. Darian brushes it off with the tips of his fingers, and the dress plummets. I'm left in only my panties and sandals, and Darian's still fully clothed. I reach for the hem of his T-shirt, but he stops me, returning my hands to my sides. He shifts closer to me, pressing the small of my back against the edge of the sink, and I can feel his lungs expand and contract against me, his erection pushing into my stomach.

"Just you right now, okay?" A soft whisper, a request, before he slides his fingers inside my panties and between my legs.

"Just me. Okay. Just...*ahh*..." My words latch on to labored breaths, slipping away with each feathery stroke. I clench my legs together, thrust against his hand.

Fuck.

He's barely touching me, and it's making me crazy.

He pulls his hand away from me, curls his fingers into the band of my panties, and pushes them down my legs. They catch at my ankles, and I have to be told to step out of them, to relax, to breathe.

Darian lifts me onto the small strip of counter

bordering the sink and reaches for the shelf above the window, pulling down an unopened bottle of mandarin-infused olive oil. A million thoughts spin in my head, not the least of which is, *Shit. That's a really expensive bottle of olive oil.*

Darian's darkening eyes capture mine and hold them as he slowly twists off the cap. He slides off my sandal, cups my heel, and straightens my leg. He drizzles a thin line of oil from my foot to my hip and massages it into my skin. A low, throaty moan builds inside me at the feel of his fingers working their way up my leg.

The mandarin bouquet is erotic, and my only lingering thought is, *I wonder if I can buy this stuff by the case.*

I kick off my remaining shoe as Darian repeats the entire act on leg number two. He pours the oil and rubs it in. I squeeze my eyes shut as he lowers his lips to my ankle, and when his tongue flicks against it, I throw my head back.

He draws his tongue up my leg, and I suck in a breath, holding it tight in my chest. He gets *close*, so close my body goes rigid and my stomach knots in anticipation. But he doesn't do what I think he's going to do—what I *want* him to do—and when I feel his lips begin their descent back down leg number one, I blow out an involuntary sigh.

Darian's smile is so wide, his cheeks expand against my thighs. "You don't want me to cheat *this* leg, do you?"

His lips graze my skin and his words vibrate against me. I grip the counter with white knuckles.

"Francesca?"

"Don't worry about that leg. That leg's fine. Just—"

Oh holy fuck.

He dips his tongue inside me and takes one long, slow drag. "I need you to lean back," he says, his voice muffled. When I don't move, he chuckles, straightens, and brings his mouth to my ear. "Francesca, can you lean back?"

I move my hands behind me and lean against them. I'm suspended over the sink, the rough edge of the windowsill jutting into my spine. It's not the ideal position, but I manage, and as soon as I feel more oil pool beneath my belly button and trickle between my legs, I decide I can handle the discomfort.

Darian crouches down, pushing my knees apart, wedging himself between my thighs. His hot breath against the cool oil is maddening. He blows softly, and my desire fuses with overripe oranges, intoxicating the air around us.

"Goddamn, Francesca."

I can't remember ever wanting anything more than I want his mouth on me right now. I want to wind my fingers in his hair and pull him closer, hold his head between my legs and guide his tongue.

If I didn't need my arms to hold me up…

Instead, I arch my back, pushing my body forward. I'm met with a tender kiss and a smile against my inner thigh. Darian drapes my legs over his shoulders and takes hold of my hips. I expect him to tease me with his tongue or torture me with his fingers, but I get his mouth, hungry and impatient, devouring me in a way that has me convinced he read my mind.

I can't help but to writhe against him, and the movement causes me to slip toward the sink.

"Stay still," he says.

Mother of God, Darian Fox is fucking me with his face.

Lips, tongue, teeth, stubble. Even his nose is brushing against my clit.

Stay still? Is he serious? Okay. Try to focus. Focus on keeping your ass out of the sink. And maybe focus on not popping his head like a balloon between your thighs. Hey, is this how Suzanne Somers invented the Thigh Mas—

"Dariannnnnn…" His name bursts from my throat in a garbled cry.

Then I lose focus. On everything.

I feel weightless. Limbless.

Darian catches me just as my arms begin to give. I nestle against his chest, a giddy, drunken feeling coming over me as he carries me to the bathroom. He returns my sated smile with a grin of his own as he puts me down. I don't even care that I'm naked.

"Happy?" he says, squatting beside the tub. He pushes in the stopper and turns on the faucet.

The faded cotton of his T-shirt shifts with each movement, and I long to slide my hands beneath it, to feel my knuckles brush against the fabric while my fingers dance over his skin.

"Never better."

Darian's smile is triumphant as he straightens and turns around. He gestures to the tub. "I can't very well send you to bed covered in olive oil, now can I?"

"Oh, sure you can."

He lets out a sharp laugh, rubs the back of his neck with one hand, and offers me the other. "You're killing me right now," he says, steering me to the tub.

I get in, sliding forward to make room for him, my knees pulled to my chest. In my peripheral, I catch him watching me, his arms crossed as he stands—still fully dressed—in the doorway.

"I know it's small, but I'm sure we can make it work," I tell him.

His smile tightens. He glances at his watch and then shoves his hands in his pockets. "I'm guessing there's nothing open this late," he says, rocking back and forth on his heels. "We, uh…never quite made it to the store today."

"The store?"

"Condoms."

Oh.

The need lying low in my belly flutters back to life. "Darian, there are other things—I mean, we don't have to have condoms to…" A sheepish grin chases the words from my lips. "I'm such a moron."

Darian gives me a blank look.

"Jane gave me condoms. In Austin."

"We've had condoms all day?"

"Yep," I say, drawing the word into two syllables. I slide my hand along the curled lip of the tub. "So you might as well join me, you know, now that you don't have to hunt down a twenty-four-hour quickie mart."

Darian slides off his watch and sets it beside the sink. "It's not like I have anything better to do." He takes off his shoes, his socks, his T-shirt, and while his eyes are locked on mine, my eyes travel his body shamelessly. "And you are impossible to resist," he says, unbuttoning his jeans, unzipping them.

My gaze follows them down his legs and then back up, back to his…

Smiling-taco boxers?

My shoulders shake with laughter. "You, Mr. Fox, are impossible to resist."

He kicks out of his shorts and the laughter stops. Desire swells inside me. Hungry sighs rise in my throat, but I swallow them back.

"Are you making fun of my underwear, Francesca?"

119

Darian asks, sliding into the tub behind me, his legs on either side of mine.

"No way. I love happy food."

His muscled arms close around me, holding me tight against his chest. I turn my head, pressing my nose into his neck, and breathe in the masculine scent of his skin mixed with a lingering trace of orange. My body relaxes into him as the silky water rises around us.

"This is nice," I say. "I hate that you have to go home tomorrow."

Darian turns off the faucet with his foot and the room falls silent. He picks up my hand and brings it to his lips, kissing it softly. "I want you to come with me."

"What?" I sit up, drawing my body into a ball. "You want me to go to Miami?"

"Just for a week or two. I'll take you salsa dancing and feed you mojitos."

He pulls my loofah down from its hook and fills it with body wash. He dips it in the water before sliding it over my back, my shoulders. It feels like heaven, and the thought of Darian not being around to do this—to do anything with me—sends a sharp pain to the back of my throat.

But I can't go with him. I can't just take off work with no notice and go with him. *Can I?*

"I'll take some time off," he says. "We'll spend our days by the pool and our nights—"

"Darian, my job…"

His hand stills at my neck, and he gives the loofah a final squeeze before hanging it up. "Fuck, I'm sorry. I wasn't thinking," he says, drawing in a deep breath and blowing it out. "I'm just not ready to be away from you yet."

I'm not ready to be away from you either.

Darian lies back, and I ease onto him, resting my cheek against his chest. He combs his fingers through my hair, working out the tangles.

"She'd let me have it," I whisper. "Lucy, my boss. She'd give me the days off."

I can't believe I'm even considering this. Jane's words come back to me.

"Maybe you've changed."

"Are you serious? You'll go?"

"I didn't say that. Darian, have you even thought this through?" I ask, tracing my finger over the water beading on his skin. "You have commitments waiting for you. I'll just be in the way."

"I promise you won't, Francesca." He tucks his finger beneath my chin, drawing my gaze. "I'm having fun. Aren't you?"

"Yes, but..."

I moan as his hands find my shoulders.

"We like spending time together, hanging out...*among other things*," he says, digging his thumbs into my back, his fingers into my collarbone. "It's as simple as that. Come with me."

God, I want to. I really want to.

But there is nothing simple about Darian Fox. Or the way I feel about him.

Frankie: He wants me to go with him to Miami for a little while.

Jane: The plot thickens.

Frankie: What's that supposed to mean?

Jane: It means I'm worried about you.

Frankie: We're just friends.

Jane: You don't act like friends.

CHAPTER 7

People Are Strange

Drew: What time are you getting back? Think we should grill some steaks and break into your Macallan 18.

Darian: No can do. I'm still at her place.

Drew: Interesting…

Darian: Give it up, Drew. Just friends.

Drew: I've seen that movie. It doesn't end well.

Frankie

With the first rays of sun peeking through the window, I tiptoe back to bed and slip as quietly as I can under the covers. Darian stirs beside me and then stills. I'm unsure if I've woken him. His face is relaxed in a way that makes me question his age. He looks so young when he's sleeping.

One eye slowly opens, and Darian shields it with his hand. He smiles a half-smile and I'm treated to the dimple

I usually only see when he laughs. My heart does an unexpected flip.

"Did you just stealth brush your teeth?" he asks.

"Maybe."

He pulls me close to him, and I melt into the warmth of his body.

"That's cheating," he says, both eyes open and narrowed at me. He slides his fingers over my temple and into my hair, holding my head still as he kisses me. His lips part, and his tongue breaches my mouth.

I smile into the kiss. "Tastes like you cheated too."

"I found your Costco-size package of toothbrushes," he says, adjusting his pillow, "between the six-pack of hand soap and the biggest box of Q-tips I've ever seen."

"Some people shop once a week; I prefer once a decade."

He reaches for my hand. "I thought girls loved to shop."

"I never got that memo."

"No," he says, glancing around my meager bedroom, "I don't suppose you did." His gaze falls to our twined fingers, to his thumb gently brushing mine. A slow smile spreads over his face. "Have you thought any more about coming with me?"

"I know I want to," I say, "but…"

"But?"

I squeeze his hand and his thumb stills. "Can I ask you a question?"

Darian pulls his pillow tighter into his side and props himself up onto his elbow. His eyes are set on me, his attention focused.

"You were hesitant to even kiss me a few days ago. Now you're here and we've had an entire night of marathon sex."

"That's not a question," he says.

I shrug.

"Do you want to know why I was hesitant or why I'm here now?"

"Yes."

Darian lets go of my hand and rolls onto his back, his gaze trained on the ceiling fan. "Francesca, you're the first woman I've been with in five years."

The first in five years?

My heart swells with pride it has no business feeling.

The corners of Darian's lips lift and then lower, as if undecided whether to smile or frown. "That's a pretty long dry spell to end on an out-of-town fling—which, at the time, is what I thought it was."

His use of the word *fling* bothers me, and I don't know why.

It's just a word, Frankie, like benefits.

"Then why did you?" I ask, not sure I want the answer.

He turns on his side to face me. "Like I said last night, you're kind of hard to resist." His small smile fades as his expression turns serious. "But I was worried about leading you on. I didn't want to hurt you."

"Lead me on? It was my idea. How could you have hurt me?"

Silence falls between us as Darian traces his finger along the lines of my palm. "Because I've done it before," he says, his voice splintering at the edges. "After I lost my family...*my wife*..." His words trail off and the soft, youthful face I woke up to hardens. "I missed her so goddamn much, and I just..."

"Darian..."

I watch his Adam's apple chase a swallow down his throat. He brings my hand to his lips, kisses my wrist, and then holds it against his chest. For a moment, he just looks at me, his gaze heavy and his smile sad.

"I used women to fill a void, Francesca. I hurt some of them. But I'm not that guy anymore, and I need you to know that."

"I do know that," I whisper.

"How could you?"

"Because you're here."

Darian pushes up against the headboard, and I sit Indian-style beside him. His clouded features clear, and the sadness he held in his smile slips away.

"Yeah, I'm here. And believe me, I'm as surprised about that as you are." He rests his hand on my knee and looks over at me. "I got your note, and the thought of never seeing you again just…didn't sit right.

"For the first time in ten years, I'm not lonely," he says, "and I have a feeling you aren't either."

My shoulders sag with a sigh. "It's going to be so weird. Going back to our normal lives after…*this*."

"It'll be fine. We'll visit each other, talk on the phone, or"—he grins—"Snapchat, as you young kids do."

"Snapchat?"

"Yeah. Drew showed me. We can even swap faces."

"BLT Drew?"

"The one and only."

Darian draws his knees in, pulling the sheet tight around his legs. His face is brighter, happier. "It's perfect, isn't it? I think this is exactly what we *both* need. And I know I'm the bee's knees, but you'll have to keep your feelings in check. No falling for this," he says, motioning to himself.

I laugh. "You totally just said 'bee's knees.' I'd say you're safe."

"True. And you snore, so…"

I pick up my pillow and lob it at his head. "I do not snore."

His expression sobers. "Hey, about what I said before. I promise, things have changed. I don't want you to worry."

"I trust you," I say. And I do.

The scent of cinnamon is strong as I step out of the shower. It wraps around me with familiar arms, taking me back to Sundays with my father, right here, in this very cabin.

"Cinnamon rolls again, Dad?"

"Always, kiddo. It's Sunday. You love these; they're homemade."

"Dad, they're canned. They're not homemade."

"Hey, if I have to turn on an oven, they're homemade."

I catch myself smiling in the mirror as I towel-dry my hair. Dad was right. I did love those stupid canned cinnamon rolls. I wish I had told him that even though I'm sure he already knew.

My rumbling stomach urges me to dress quickly in jeans and an oversized sweatshirt straight out of *Flashdance*. I walk barefoot to the kitchen and find Darian leaning against the sink, a beach towel wrapped around his waist. He's holding a steaming mug of coffee, and I smile at the *#1 Mom* peeking through his fingers.

"This might not be something you want lying around for your overnight guests to find," he says, holding up the mug for me to see. "Jane's?" Darian crosses his ankles, and the bright yellow and blue hibiscus print he's donning slips lower on his stomach.

"Jane's," I say, nodding, but it comes out scratchy. I tear my gaze away from his bare torso, clear my throat, and try again. "It's Jane's."

Darian laughs.

"Where are your clothes?" I ask.

"I knew I was forgetting something," he says, setting his coffee on the counter beside him. "I washed them." He pulls the towel tighter around his waist and walks past me into the living room.

The metal clanking of doors opening and closing is followed by the heavy thud of wet denim and the soothing hum of the dryer. I pull out a chair at the kitchen table and sink into it. The lingering scent of cinnamon settles around me, and my empty stomach answers with a growl.

"Did you bake?"

Darian rounds the corner with a fistful of lint and tosses it in the waste bin. "I found some biscuits in your fridge. A lot of biscuits. I swear you have twenty of everything."

I shrug.

"Well, if the apocalypse comes, I'm moving in."

I think I'd be okay with that.

He takes a platter piled high with what looks like sugar-coated doughnut holes out of the oven and sets it in front of me on the table.

"That smells like heaven." I pinch off a piece and pop it into my mouth. Cinnamon and brown sugar explode on my tongue. "You *made* this. I mean, obviously you made this. It's just…*wow*."

Darian backs against the counter with his arms folded

across his chest, his eyes turning emerald beneath the overhead light. "It's my mother's monkey bread," he says with a soft smile. His gaze shifts to the platter. "I haven't made it in a while."

"Your mother would be proud."

He looks up at me then. "You know, I can make other things. Lunch things. Dinner things. If you come to Miami with me, I may just blow your mind."

"Blow my mind, huh?" I turn in my chair and poke my head inside the refrigerator. The chilled air prickles my cheeks as I scan the shelves.

Miami. Why is this so hard? Rome or Paris? Red or white? French fries or tater tots?

Stay or go?

I close the door and slump back in my chair. No Diet Coke. I might as well go to Miami. Either that or go to the store.

Are you seriously going to do this?

"I'll go," I say, "but…when is your flight?"

Guess so.

Darian shrugs. "It's open, so whenever you want it to be."

"Is tomorrow possible? I need to buy a ticket, which means I should probably do my banking. And I need to talk to Lucy. And do laundry. And what about your stuff?"

Darian's smile is infectious as he squats in front of me. "Don't worry about a ticket. Company perk. We can go by the diner today; I assume you want to do that in person? Clean clothes are a plus, and my assistant has my bags."

My heart beats erratically. *This is crazy.*

"Okay," I say, running my fingers along his unshaven jawline.

I bend to kiss him, and he kisses me back.

"Okay."

The familiar bells ring loudly above my head as I enter the diner. Lucy's perched against the counter, a pot of coffee nestled against her stomach. Her yellow fifties-style uniform is starched to perfection and her dyed auburn hair is pulled in a tight twist.

"Who's that?" she asks as the door closes behind me.

I glance over my shoulder at Darian's retreating form as he makes his way across the street to the resale shop. "Just a guy I met," I say, turning around. "Nothing serious."

Lucy moves behind the counter and sets the coffee pot in front of Earl, one of our regulars and the only lingering diner from the Sunday lunch rush. He grunts under his breath, and Lucy waves him off.

"Now, Earl, Frankie here just pulled up with a man. A very handsome man from what I could tell. Refill your own damn coffee." Lucy pats the counter in front of her. "Come sit," she says to me. "I'd suggest a booth, but if I sit down I'll go right to sleep."

Lucy doesn't look tired. She never does. Even in her late fifties she's the liveliest person I know. Still, the after-church crowd is a force to be reckoned with, and I'm pretty damn happy to have the day off.

"Diet Coke, dear?" she asks me as I set my keys on the counter.

"Yes, ma'am."

"Let me grab some clean cups from the kitchen," she says. "I'll be right back."

I've been coming to this diner since I was a little girl, and barring a few new faces, nothing much has changed. It always smells like syrup and stale coffee, even during dinner. The clock above the register is always five minutes fast. And for as long as I can remember, Lucy's been a fixture behind the counter. Rumor has it she went on a date once with my dad, but she's never mentioned it and I've never asked.

I take a seat three stools down from Earl. He gives me a nod before biting into his patty melt.

"How's Lois today?" I ask.

Earl shakes his head as he swallows his food. "She's takin' to diggin' up my garden, and if she doesn't cut it out she's gonna be buried in it."

Lois is Earl's chocolate Lab and the love of his life despite his threat.

"Oh, Earl," Lucy says, handing me my Diet Coke, "you don't even have a garden. You have weeds. Don't listen to him, Frankie. He's extra grumpy today." She props her elbows on the counter and twines her fingers, her gaze aimed at the wall of windows behind me. "Spill it, kid."

I pull my soda toward me and bend the tip of the straw against my lips. The accelerated tapping of Lucy's perfectly filed nails against the Formica syncs with my heart rate, and I stall by downing my entire drink in one exaggerated slurp.

"Come on," she says. "Cut it out. Who's the hottie?"

Her choice of words sends me into a coughing fit.

Earl slides the napkin dispenser my way, and I mumble a, "Thank you." I answer Lucy, "There's nothing to spill. We met in Austin. We're friends."

"Yeah, right," Lucy says, squinting at me. "Then why are you here on your day off?"

"Well…" I scoot back on my stool and slide the heels of my hands along the tapered edge of the counter. "I was wondering if maybe I could take a little more time off. He lives in Miami and—"

Earl scoffs. "Miami? What's gotten into you, Frankie? Miami's full of nothin' but white-collar pansy-asses. You need you a nice, hard-workin' country boy. You know Jim's boy's livin' here now. What's his name, Lucille?"

"Jim Junior? No, Earl. Jim Junior's 'livin' here now' because he just got out of jail." Lucy refills my cup and slides it in front of me. "Miami, huh?" Her eyes soften and a smile warms her face. "Frankie, sweetheart, I've known you since you were knee-high to a grasshopper, and except for that time old lady Higgins spiked the punch on bingo night, I don't think I've ever seen you have any fun. I know you didn't come here to ask my opinion, but I'm gonna give it to you anyway. Do you like him?"

"Lucy, it's not like that."

She rolls her eyes. "In general, as a person, do you like him?"

"Yes."

"Do you trust him?"

"Yes."

"Then go, sweetie." Lucy reaches across the counter and squeezes my hand. "You're too young to be cooped up here in this tiny town with the likes of me and Earl."

Earl blows out a theatrical huff. "Speak for yourself."

"It's only for a couple of weeks," I say.

"Oh, honey," Lucy says, grinning, "a lot can happen in a couple of weeks."

Darian and I sit on the tailgate of my truck, munching on Dairy Queen french fries as our legs swing beneath us. The sun beats down on our shoulders, warmer than it's been the last several days.

I roll up the sleeves of my sweatshirt and take a sip of my shake. "Find anything exciting on your shopping adventure?"

"I did," he says.

There's a playful edge to his voice, and I toss him a suspicious glance. His lips curl into a devious grin.

"I bought the original *Friday the 13th*. It's supposed to storm later, and, well, cabin in the woods and all."

I peer up at the near cloudless sky. "What makes you think it's supposed to storm?"

"Rose at the resale shop."

I laugh. "Rose is a little on the crazy side."

"I gathered that when she tried to sell me a pair of heels," he says, straightening his leg and flexing his foot. "They weren't even my size. She seemed pretty adamant about her weather prediction though." He feeds me the last french fry and stuffs the empty box inside the to-go bag.

"Thanks for this," I say.

"Fast food?"

"No, giving me this day. You know, before I throw caution to the wind and travel to another state with a total stranger."

And before I have a nervous breakdown midair, and we have to have that *conversation.*

Darian picks up my hand and kisses it. "Come on. Let's get out of here." He glances at his watch. "If Rose is right, we have about fifteen minutes to get home."

Rose *is* right. The weather does a complete one-eighty the second we pull in my driveway. What began as a single raindrop bouncing off the windshield is now a torrential downpour. The storm is loud and the metal roof of my cabin only amplifies the sound.

Darian drops his bag on the kitchen table and moves to the sliding glass door with the DVD tucked under his arm. "It's really coming down out there."

"I love it," I say, glancing past him to the patio. I don't have gutters, so when it rains this hard, it slides off the roof in a solid sheet. I wave my hand in front of it. "When I was a little girl, I used to pretend that was a portal to another dimension, and I'd run through it, back and forth, until I was completely drenched."

Darian shakes his head. "Your parents let you play in a rainstorm?"

"Just my dad," I say, my throat growing thick with the memory, "and he didn't care as long as there wasn't lightning. Sometimes he'd play with me." I pull a container of Hershey's Cocoa out of the cabinet and set a pot on the stove. "Hot chocolate?"

Darian eyes the Hershey's and his face brightens. "From scratch? My mom made it that way."

I swallow hard. "Mine too."

I whip up the hot chocolate, and we take our mugs into the living room. I set mine on the coffee table while Darian holds his tightly in both hands, flinching with every clap of thunder.

"Maybe you should set that down before you burn yourself," I say, freeing the DVD still wedged beneath his arm. I peel off the cellophane and pull out the disc.

Darian places his mug beside mine and sits on the edge of the couch. "How does this not scare the hell out of you? It sounds like we're inside a drum."

"I'm used to it, I guess. It's comforting to me." I wave the movie in front of him. "And isn't *scary* the point?"

Darian glances at the ceiling. "Will we even be able to hear it?"

"Oh, you actually want to *watch* it?" I slide the DVD into the player and crank up the volume.

The familiar digital sound effect roars above the storm and Darian's eyes light up.

"Surround," I say, chucking off my Converse and plopping beside him on the couch, "and killer acoustics."

We sit back, and Darian hands me my hot chocolate. I settle into the hollow of his body with the mug cupped against my chest and bask in the warmth of his arms.

It's easy and lazy and perfect.

But three gory deaths later, I've changed my mind. A horror movie at top volume in the middle of a raging storm isn't any of those things. I'm a ball of nerves with my hand in front of my face, watching through an opening between my fingers. Thunder crashes overhead and I let out a surprised yelp. Lightning strikes fast and close, killing the power. I jump, showering Darian with a full mug of untouched chocolate.

He lunges forward. "Oh, man, that's cold."

"Shit. I'm so sorry." I set my empty cup on the coffee table and turn toward him, blindly feeling for his clothes. I grab fistfuls of the saturated cotton clinging to his stomach and hold it away from him. Chocolate drips through my fingers and onto his already soaked jeans, making an even bigger mess than the one we started with.

"Let me help you," Darian says, amusement coloring his voice. He pulls his shirt over his head and hands it to me. "You know, if you wanted me naked, all you had to do was ask."

"I was going for subtle," I say, my gaze snapping to the sound of his shoes hitting the floor.

Lightning flashes and the room floods with light. I catch a glimpse of his smiling-taco boxers and it makes me laugh.

"Admit it, you think they're sexy."

He pushes his jeans down his legs, and I bend to pick them up.

"Fine. I think they're sexy," I say, standing. I ball his clothes against my chest. "But you might as well take them off so I can wash them too."

As I turn toward the utility closet, Darian grabs my hand.

"I think laundry can wait," he says, curling his fingers around mine. His tone is suggestive and makes my cells tingle. "At least for a little while."

He pulls me toward him and guides me onto his lap, my back to his chest. He slips his fingers just inside the wide neck of my sweatshirt, and I let out a weak moan when he starts kneading my shoulders.

"God, that feels incredible," I say, my body turning to jelly beneath his touch. My arms go limp, and his clothes fall to the floor.

"There's no power anyway." He rakes his fingers down my back and then edges them under the hem of my sweatshirt.

"Power?"

"For laundry."

"Oh right. Laundry."

I lean against his chest as his hands snake around my waist to the front of my jeans. Pinching the denim between his fingers, he unfastens the button.

"Hmm, I wonder what we should do then," I say.

"I bet I can think of something." He slowly slides my zipper down, and I stop breathing until he speaks again, "Charades maybe?"

"Won't work. Too dark."

"Good point." His fingers dip into my panties, and I push against them. "We could build a fire…roast marshmallows…" He teases me with soft, careful strokes.

"No marshmallows," I say, almost breathlessly. "Wet firewood."

"Let me think. What about…" His voice is reduced to white noise as I close my eyes, my body tuned to his. "*Shit*," is the next word I hear him say and only because his hand stills.

I jerk up. "What? What's wrong?"

Laughter rolls off his tongue like an afterthought, and he drops his forehead to the back of my neck. "It's dark as hell, and I have no clue what I did with the condoms."

My face splits into a wide grin. His concern is adorable, like he must have me right now, storm be damned.

I turn my head to speak over my shoulder. "Hey, that reminds me. If it's been so long since you've had sex, why did you just happen to have condoms in Austin?"

I feel his smile form against my skin. "I was drunkenly attacked, if you remember. I bought some in case you tried it again."

"Fair enough," I say, standing up and turning around.

"You think you can find them?" he asks.

"Yeah…" I peel my sweatshirt over my head and unhook my bra.

Lightning flashes outside the window, just long enough to illuminate my naked chest as the straps fall from my arms. Darian's eyes narrow and one corner of his mouth quirks up.

"They're in my medicine cabinet," I say, "but…" I push my jeans down my legs and step out of them.

"But?"

"But…we don't *need* them."

Another flash of light as I slip out of my panties. Darian's gaze sweeps over me until darkness steals his view. I step forward and straddle him.

"We're covered. *I'm* covered…just—"

"Just what?" His voice is a sultry whisper that spreads through my veins like a shot of courage.

I dip my hand inside his boxers and take him in my fist. I stroke him up and down and around, tightening my grip with each rotation.

His breath comes out in short gasps, and his fingers dig into my hips as he rocks into my hand. "Just what, Francesca?"

"Just fuck me."

A growl stirs deep in his chest as he throws me down on the sofa. His body swallows me, its sudden weight driving my back into the cushion. Without warning or preamble, he pushes into me, and I take a gasping breath. He pulls out, and my breath leaves with him. His thrusts aren't gentle or careful; they're aggressive and hungry.

"Look what you fucking do to me," he says, but no sooner do the words leave his lips than the power returns, sucking them out of the air.

Darian's expression softens. He lifts onto his elbows, holding his face just above mine. His fingers dig into my arms, and he watches me with curious eyes as his rhythm slows to the natural beat of the storm.

Whatever's changed—whatever's happening now—it's unexpectedly intimate. Maybe it's the feel of him naked inside me or, more likely, the *idea* of him naked inside me. Maybe it's his slow, measured movements, his fixed gaze as he slides in and out. His breath, warm against my lips, or my name, a whisper on his. Whatever it is, I want more of it.

I stare into his unblinking eyes and dissolve into an orgasm that's unlike anything I've ever experienced. It's more emotional than physical. It's foreign and amazing and fucking terrifying.

And as I lie there trying to make sense of it, I *feel* him come.

"Darian."

At the mention of his name, his gaze cuts away, and he pulls out of me. He rolls onto his side and I press against him, a grin creeping over my face, a giggle rising in my throat.

"Mmm, that was different. Really different. *Good* different." I trail my fingers down his chest, but his hands stay at his sides, his stiff body unyielding. "Darian?"

He clears his throat and sits up, and I have to pull in my knees to accommodate him. He rubs his eyes with the heels of his hands and then looks at me without expression.

I prop myself up on an elbow, my other arm draped over my chest. "Is something wrong?"

"No," he says quietly. "Nothing's wrong. I'm just beat." He bends forward, reaching for his boxers. He picks them up and slides into them. "I think I'm going to call it a night."

"You're going to bed? It's...*early*. You sure you're okay?"

He leans over me and kisses the corner of my mouth. "I promise, I'm fine. Just tired. You want the TV back on?" he asks, standing. He reaches for the remote, but I wave him off. "Let me get you a towel then."

My voice quivers as it leaves my lips. "It's, um...it's okay. I think I'll just take a shower."

I don't though. As soon as Darian goes to bed, I clean myself up at the bathroom sink, pull on my underwear and sweatshirt, and curl into a ball on the sofa. The same hollow feeling I felt in Austin gnaws at me.

What the hell just happened?

I play the last hour over and over in my mind. I know it wasn't me. I know it. But that doesn't make me feel any less rejected.

You're the first woman he's been with in five years, Frankie.

This sucks. Feeling this way just *sucks*. I'm embarrassed for me. I'm scared for me. But I ache for him.

The morning sun stabs me like a hot poker, and it takes me a few minutes to orient myself. I'm in my bed, under my covers, Darian's heart thrumming beneath my ear. He strokes my hair with long, leisurely drags of his fingers. The sting of last night fades, and if I wasn't still in yesterday's sweatshirt, I'd wonder if I'd dreamed it.

"I didn't mean to run off on you last night," he whispers.

"Why did you?"

"I don't know. I just…" His hand stills in my hair. "I had some sort of déjà vu. I guess it shook me."

I tilt my head to look at him, and he kisses me. It's soft and quick. Just a peck on my lips.

He carefully disentangles himself and sits on the edge of the bed, his hand resting on my hip, his gaze aimed at my feet. "We've got time if you want to sleep in."

"Darian, are you sure about this?"

"Yes," he says, his eyes flicking to mine. "Please, Francesca. I want you to come. I'm sorry if I scared you. This is all new to me."

"It's new to me too."

"I know."

"Stay with me next time."

He squeezes my hand. "I will."

CHAPTER 8

Land Ho!

Darian: We're headed back.

  Drew: We?

Darian: Yes, we.

  Drew: This girl have a name?

Darian: Francesca.

  Drew: I like that. Racquetball this week?

Darian: Maybe. I'll call you.

Frankie

Darian hires a car service to take us to the Austin-Bergstrom International Airport. The perplexity of last night along with my healthy fear of flying have my nerves on overdrive. I'm anxious about flying. I'm anxious about Darian. I'm anxious about flying with Darian. I shift uncomfortably in my seat as I try to relax. I bounce my foot and pop my knuckles.

Chill out, Frankie.

I hate it when people pop their knuckles, yet I can't seem to stop. I glare at my hands and will them to stop. I could use a manicure.

I wonder if the airport has a salon, I think absently as I pick at a hangnail.

I glance up to find Darian's eyes on me, his brows knitted.

"The weather's been great, hasn't it?" I ask.

Hey, Frankie, we had a ridiculously strong and potentially damaging storm last night. Idiot.

He chuckles, clearly amused with me. He turns sideways a little and props his ankle on his knee. His laughter settles into a smile. "Yeah, Francesca, awesome weather."

"How's the weather in Miami this time of year?"

"Much more pleasant than it is in August." He reaches for my hand. "Are you okay?"

The car veers to the right as we exit the toll road. I look up just in time to see the airport sign looming in front of us like an omen.

"I'm okay." *I'm so not okay.* "I'm just worried about what to tell Jane," I lie. Nope. That's not a lie. Now, I'm anxious about that too.

Darian cocks his head. "You haven't told her yet?"

I shrug. "It's safer this way. We'll be airborne before she can kill me."

"I don't know," he says, snorting a laugh. "I wouldn't put anything past that one."

He turns his attention to the driver, and I turn mine to my phone, my fingers flying over the screen in a series of texts.

Frankie: I'm on my way to the airport.

Jane: What?

Frankie: I told you I was probably going.

Jane: No, you told me he invited you.

Frankie: Same thing.

"Well?" Darian says. "What's the verdict?"

"Too soon to tell."

We ease into the turn lane. The rhythmic click of the blinker sounds through the car. It's unusually loud, but no one else seems to notice.

Jane: Do you even have Xanax?

Frankie: All major airlines have booze. I'll manage.

We turn left when the light changes. The blinker stills and peaceful silence returns to the car. I stare blankly out the window as we coast down a long stretch of road. This airport is smaller than I expected, especially since the word *International* is in its name. So far I've seen nothing but a row of planes behind a chain-link fence. No parking garages, no buildings.

Jane: It just seems fast. Couldn't you have planned a trip? For like…later?

And give myself time to change my mind?

The muffled rumble of takeoff quickly grows into a crescendo of roaring jets the closer we get. I keep my head down, my eyes on my phone. The little dots dancing on the screen tell me Jane's typing, but the text never comes through. She's waiting for me. As I begin to reply, the car slows and then stops. The driver cuts the engine, and my fingers still.

I lift my head. "Where are we?"

"Tarmac," Darian says.

No wonder it looks different.

I turn to look out my window and I see a small jet, dark blue and silver with burgundy trim. The paint looks

143

new, and I wonder if the plane is new or if it just got a fresh coat. *Is that even a thing? To paint old planes so they don't look so terrifying?*

My phone vibrates in my hand and I drag my gaze back to the screen.

> Jane: Ignoring me now?

Darian kisses my cheek. "I'll be right back."

He gets out of the car, and I watch as he walks across the pavement to a man standing beside the plane. They shake hands. Darian speaks to him, his arms crossed, his thumb propped at his chin. The man replies and Darian's head falls back in laughter. He turns to look at me, nods, and then turns back to the man. They shake hands again.

"I've only flown commercial," the driver says, pulling my attention to his face in the rearview mirror. His eyes are bright and carry a subtle optimism I wish I shared right now. "I can't even imagine how nice a private jet must be. What about you, young lady? This your first time?"

Oh holy fuck, I'm flying on that thing.

The air escapes the car in a big whoosh, and it's replaced by a sort of loud silence, thick and heavy and suffocating. I nod my response, but my head feels like it's stuck in a vise and I'm not sure it even moves.

> Frankie: WTF!
>
> Jane: Don't get pissy. I'm just worried about you.
>
> Frankie: Not you. Darian! He has a private jet!
>
> Jane: Oh shit.

I glance back at the driver. He says something, but the words don't register. Smiling tightly, I turn back to the plane. My stomach churns.

Frankie: It's so small.

Darian opens my door and leans in. "You ready?"

I swallow a sharp gulp of air. "You have a plane?"

"Don't you?" His lips quirk up in a playful smirk. "It's chartered. I'm trying to impress you. Is it working?"

"I…"

"Look," he says, his smile fading, "I don't want you to think I'm some pretentious plane snob, too good to fly commercial, but I do go to great lengths to avoid it." He glances over his shoulder at the small jet and then back to me. "It's not even the planes. It's the airports. Specifically the one we're flying into. That's the last place I— anyway…" His voice softens and his eyes hold mine in their olive-green depths. "It's better for me if I don't have to go inside."

I feel foolish for freaking out. It's just a plane.

A private plane.

I don't know the statistics, but don't most crashes involve private jets?

Good Lord, Frankie. Just stop.

I step out of the car and wrap my arms around his waist.

Giving me a tight squeeze, he lowers his mouth to my ear. "This phobia charges by the hour, so we should probably get going."

I relax slightly as we board the plane. With the absence of screaming kids and irritable passengers, it's hard not to. The interior is decked out with cream-colored leather chairs and glossy wood-grain tables. The walls are trimmed in the same wood-grain with leather accents.

Darian rests his hand on my back and guides me to our seats. A bottle of champagne awaits us, and I grit my teeth when I see it. The champagne, the private jet, the car service…it all feels so fancy, and I'm dressed in yoga pants and a hoodie.

I elbow Darian's arm as we sit. "I think I missed the dress-code memo."

He laughs and thumbs the V-neck of his white undershirt. "Technically this is considered underwear, but it was all Rose had in my size."

"She tends to cater to old ladies."

Darian eases the cork out of the champagne with a subtle pop. He pours two glasses and hands me one.

The bubbles go straight to my head as I take a sip, and I savor the sharp tang that's left behind on my tongue. "This is perfect. Oh, we should toast." I raise my glass. "To living a little."

Darian's enthusiastic grin exposes his dimple as our glasses clink together. "I think that's a good plan for both of us."

The pilot and copilot enter the cabin, and there goes my smile. Dressed predictably in crisp white shirts beneath navy-blue blazers, they're an unfortunate reminder that we're about to be airborne. I focus on my champagne and let their voices slide over my head. I take a large swallow, which results in an empty glass. I place the stem between my knees and let it rest there. My hands are damp from the condensation, so I wipe them on my cotton pants before clutching the armrests. We've yet to move, but I can already feel my stomach crawling up my throat. The pilots turn toward the cockpit, and I turn toward my window, tightening my grip on the smooth leather.

"We're a pair, aren't we?" Darian says as he pries the fingers of my left hand free. "I hate airports, and you hate flying."

"Is it that obvious?" I close the shade, but I continue to stare in its direction.

Darian takes the empty glass from my lap, refills it, and nudges my hand.

"Thanks," I say, accepting the champagne with a timid smile. "But I'm okay. Really." The plane begins its taxi to the runway, and I squeeze my eyes closed without ever taking a sip. "Or at least I will be in a few minutes."

Darian trades my glass for his hand, and I practically crush it when the plane picks up speed. I hold my breath until the nose lifts off the ground, and once we're airborne, I only loosen my grip enough for Darian to stretch his fingers.

"The odds of dying in a plane crash are, like, one in eleven million." The words roll off his tongue in a whisper so soft, I question who they're for.

I look up at him and expect to meet his gaze, but his eyes are closed and he's biting his lip. I rest my cheek against his arm, and he exhales a long, shaky sigh.

"It's not a mantra or anything, if you're wondering," he says gently, "just a fact. One I tell myself all the time." He faces me then, his smile cautious. "I thought maybe it would do you well to hear it, but…"

"It's okay, Darian. I'm okay, I swear."

"I guess facts don't hold much weight coming from their exceptions." He brings my hand to his lips and kisses it. "I just want you to know it can't happen. It *won't* happen again."

They're reassurances. Ones he makes to himself, only now, he's sharing them with me.

"I know."

The plane jerks as the wheels draw in and I gasp, a shrill, uneven sound that makes us both laugh.

"And when facts aren't enough," Darian says, handing me my champagne, "there's alcohol."

We land in Miami just before five o'clock. I step off the plane and the humidity hits me like it's swinging a bat.

A Mercedes SUV sits on the tarmac, its shiny black surface capturing the low-hanging sun and deflecting it in beams of blinding light.

I cast a squinted glance at Darian. "Still trying to impress me?"

"Is it working?" A smile slides over his face. "It's a service, like the one I had in Austin." He throws my duffel and laptop bag over his shoulder and grabs my hand, gently squeezing it before we set off toward the car.

The driver rounds the back of the SUV, popping open the hatch on his way to us. He extends his hand to Darian, but his gaze is aimed at me.

"You must be the lovely Ms. Valentine," he says in a botched Irish accent. "Name's CJ, milady, and today I'll be playing the role of the handsome driver."

A giggle bursts out of me and any leftover tension I carried off the plane melts away. "Nice to meet you, CJ."

He opens the back passenger door and waves me inside. "In you go," he says, grinning. "Unless you want to run away with me. In which case, hop in the front."

Darian clears his throat with a chuckle.

"Yeah, yeah. Welcome home, Fox," CJ says, accent-free. He glances at my bags still slung over Darian's shoulder. "You mind?"

With a good-humored groan, Darian hauls them to the back of the SUV and stows them inside. "You want me to drive too?"

Leaving the boys to banter, I settle into my seat and power up my phone. The air is thick with the scent of leather—masculine and earthy—and if I give it half a chance, it will easily lull me to sleep. Darian climbs in beside me and slips me a curious glance as my phone buzzes with Jane's texts.

Jane: How small?

Jane: Frankie?

Jane: Text me the second you land!

Frankie: We're here.

Jane: And?

Frankie: Wasn't too bad.

Jane: Tequila?

Frankie: Champagne.

I breathe a long-awaited sigh as the car rolls toward the exit. All things considered, the flight was uneventful. Once the champagne kicked in, I relaxed, and shortly after that, I slept.

"Everything okay?" Darian asks.

"Better than okay."

He tucks a loose strand of hair behind my ear and draws his palm down the side of my face to rest beneath my jaw. "Happy to have your feet back on the ground?"

I smile and give his hand a squeeze against my cheek.

I don't think my feet have been on the ground since the day we met.

It's a quiet ride to Darian's place, which is in an upscale Miami neighborhood called Coral Gables. To someone like me, Miami is the epitome of upscale, so this

Coral Gables place must be lined in gold. Where I'm from, *upscale* just means you don't have a recliner on your front porch.

I turn to ask him about it, but the content look on his face drives the thought away. His head is tilted back against the headrest and his eyes are closed, but the slight curve of his mouth tells me he isn't asleep.

"Why are you smiling?" I ask as I curl into his side.

He doesn't answer, nor does he open his eyes. But his smile stretches wide across his face, and for the first time today, I feel at peace with my decision to come.

Despite the jetlag trying to pull me under, I stay awake for the drive. Everything is shiny and new, and I scan the unfamiliar landscape with a child's eyes, full of curiosity and awe.

"Traffic is at its worst this time of day," Darian tells me.

But I don't mind. It just gives me more time to digest it all.

Urban becomes rural, and buildings become homes as we close in on Darian's neighborhood. Excitement builds inside me at every turn, and by the time we pull up to his gate, I'm ready to hop the fence and run inside.

"We're here," Darian says in a singsong voice.

I can tell he's happy to be home.

CJ punches a code in the keypad and the ornate wrought iron gate opens before us. I sit taller in my seat, craning my neck in every direction to look out the windows. The driveway to Darian's house is laid in cobblestone and bordered on both sides with palm trees. It culminates in a big, circular forecourt surrounded by lush greenery.

CJ parks the car, and I tell him goodbye as I hop out, my attention already lost to the structure in front of me.

"Wow, Darian," I mumble under my breath.

The house is plantation-style but modern, painted stark white with black shutters, and has a large, columned front porch. It's lovely and not at all what I expected.

"You want these upstairs?" CJ asks.

"No, man. I got it."

My eyes roam the exterior of the house while Darian finishes up. He returns with my bags hoisted over his shoulder and a set of keys in his hand.

"I kind of figured it would have a keypad or something," I say as we scale the steps.

"Nah, I'm old school."

The heavy wood door looks ancient and even sounds ancient by the loud creak it makes when Darian pulls it open. I walk in ahead of him and stop to wait in the foyer. It's modest with a round cherry wood table in the corner. A large delft vase sits on top, and I wonder if it's ever seen fresh flowers.

"This way, milady," Darian says in an even worse brogue than CJ.

With a dramatic bow, he takes my arm in his and guides me through the house with our elbows linked together. We pass a glass-walled office, a formal dining room, and a freestanding staircase with a set of double doors tucked beneath.

"Keep going," Darian says. "The kitchen's straight ahead. I'll just drop off your bags and then I'll be right there."

The walls are painted a creamy white, similar in color to the polished limestone floor. Black beams crisscross the ceiling and match the exterior shutters. The glass light fixtures add bursts of color and look like they're handblown. The house is stunning, but it doesn't look lived in.

I may not have been the one to decorate my cabin, but my entire life is still present in every nook and cranny. Darian's house is…empty. So far, I haven't seen anything personal—no photographs, no mementos, no books, nothing.

"They came with the house," Darian says of the massive oil paintings I'm staring at in his kitchen. "Haven't gotten around to replacing them." There are two that flank a mahogany range hood, both of undeveloped coastline.

"Why would you?"

"I don't know," he says as he sidles up beside me at the island. "They're not really my style."

"What's your style?"

He leans forward against the granite, his eyes fixed on the oils. A deep laugh rumbles in his chest, and he wears a smile when he turns to look at me.

"That's a good question," he says. "I haven't thought much about it. I just moved in and unpacked my toothbrush; that's as far as I've gotten."

"So you haven't been here long?"

"Almost ten years." Darian pulls out a barstool. "Make yourself at home. I'll open a bottle of wine."

I'm too anxious to sit, so I wander along the trio of French doors on the back wall of the kitchen and peer into the backyard. It's completely private, enclosed in the same dense jungle of vegetation that borders the forecourt. The doors open to a covered patio, and just beyond that is an impressive rectangular pool.

"This might be a little sweet. It's homemade," Darian says as he slides a glass of white wine across the island. He watches me as I look around, as if he expects me to say something.

I'm kind of speechless. "It's just—"

"Not what you expected?" he asks.

I take a seat on the barstool he pulls out for me and rest my back against the wooden slats. "No, not at all. It's gorgeous, but it's not pretentious. Not that I thought it would be. I actually envisioned you in a high-rise. It's smaller than—okay, now I'm babbling." I pick up my glass and take a long, slow sip. "The wine's good. It's homemade?"

Darian laughs, his eyes glinting beneath the pendant light that hangs above him. "Yes, Gloria made it. It's her new thing—making wine. You'll meet her tomorrow. She's my, um…how does one explain Gloria?" He raps his fingers against the granite, his lips pursed. "She's like an overbearing mother who stops in unannounced and does things without being asked."

"And she forces her wine upon you," I say.

"And she forces her wine upon me."

"She sounds terrible."

He smiles. "She's the worst." His cheeks redden the tiniest bit, and I can tell he's very fond of her. "Speaking of," he says as he opens the door to the fridge, "she texted me earlier that she left some marinated, uh…something and asparagus in here…somewhere."

"Mmm, I love marinated something. Do you grill that?"

"Hold on, smart-ass. Give me a minute." He rummages through a stack of plastic containers, takes one out, peels off the lid, and sets it on the counter. "Marinated snapper, and yes, I can grill it…I mean, if you like seafood. You like seafood, don't you? But if you don't, that's fine; we can order in. Or go out if you're up to it."

"Snapper sounds great, but I'd like to freshen up and check my e-mail first." I hop off the barstool and head toward the door. "Is my stuff in your…"

"Right down the hall," Darian says. He puts the container back in the refrigerator and closes it with his foot. "Let me show you."

I follow him to the set of double doors we passed earlier.

An odd place for a master, I muse, noting its proximity to the dining room.

"Here we are," he says, standing against the door to hold it open. He jerks his chin at my bags sitting on the bed, atop a pink floral comforter folded over the foot.

With my back to Darian, my eyes sweep over the details—the perfectly fluffed pillows, the uncluttered nightstands, the empty closet—and then burn with realization. The room is beautiful. It smells like lavender and fresh linen. It's decorated like a five-star suite—formal but comfortable. And not his.

He put me in my own room?

"There's a private bathroom with a Jacuzzi I thought you might like," he says, still leaning against the door like he's afraid to let it go. "I'll get the grill fired up. Take your time, and if you think of anything you need, just let me know."

I need to be with you. In your room. In your bed.

The heavy door crashes against the frame when it closes and makes me jump.

Welcome to your dungeon, Frankie.

Under different circumstances, I could really dig this. Every piece of furniture is oversized and nothing looks cramped. I doubt I could fit this stuff in my entire cabin, much less my bedroom. There are doors that lead into the backyard, which I already know accommodates a pool fit for a resort. And Darian did say Jacuzzi…

There are worse dungeons.

I don't want to overthink this, but my mind is reeling and there's no stopping it now. He kind of freaked out last night. Maybe this is his way of putting on the brakes.

Maybe it isn't personal.

I drag my fingers along the smooth beveled edge of the dresser, catching sight of my appearance in the mirror as I pass. My hair looks like I slept on it all day, which I suppose I did, though my puffy, blood-shot eyes and sallow skin would beg to differ.

Maybe it is personal.

I pull my toiletry bag out of my duffel and take it into the bathroom. Except for the almighty tub with jets, it's not *that* fancy. The lighting is better, and that's all I really care about right now. My hair still screams light socket, but my face doesn't look nearly as wasted as it did under the unforgiving lights of the bedroom.

After a five-minute shower and a change of clothes, I exit through the patio doors in my room and walk barefoot across the cool stretch of flagstone to the barbecue area at the opposite end of the house. Darian's head whips around as I drag one of the heavy black iron chairs away from the table. The man is a paradox. The smile he gives me suggests nothing of the last thirty minutes, and for a brief moment, I almost forget I'm upset.

Are you upset? It's just a room.

"I poured you another glass of wine," he says with his spatula pointed toward me.

I open my mouth to speak and then close it. *You're such a wuss, Frankie.* "Thanks," I mutter instead as I sink into the cushion.

"Fire's almost ready. It won't take long after that."

The far corner of the patio houses an outdoor kitchen complete with a built-in gas grill, and directly in front of it sits a black charcoal pit with smoke rising from the coals. It's just a basic barrel with a grate, like something you'd find in front of a grocery store. Like the one I have, only safer.

"Fire's good," Darian says, striding toward the kitchen door. "Let me just grab the—hey, are you okay? You don't look well."

My eyes flick to his as he pulls a chair next to mine and sits beside me. His smoky fingers run the length of my hairline, tucking the frizzy pieces behind my ear that have taken to blowing in my face.

Here's your chance, Frankie. Say something.

"Why don't you use the gas grill?"

Seriously?

He sits back in his chair with his fingers steepled beneath his chin. "Never been a fan of gas, I suppose." His head slants to the side, like he's studying me. "I'm not used to having company. If you want anything at all, please...is it the wine? This batch is sweeter than normal. I can get—"

"The wine's perfect. I'm just..."

Tell him what's bothering you. Drink a glass of wine. Eat dinner. Have lots and lots of sex.

I stare at the rivulets of condensation as they trail down the side of my glass. Darian moves it out of his way and reaches across the table to take my hand. I only let him hold it for a second before I pull it back and tuck it in my lap.

"I'm just worn out," I say.

Darian leans forward with his elbows propped on his knees. "It's okay if you don't feel like eating. Or do you want something else?"

"No. Thank you. I'm not very hungry. I feel terrible though. Gloria went to all that trouble, and you—"

"Haven't done a thing. It's okay, Francesca. Really." He rests his hand on my knee. "It'll keep. We can have it tomorrow, and on my way home, I'll stop and pick up a few things to go with it…like chocolate."

"Fish and chocolate. Now that's a combination I haven't considered," I say with a hesitant smile. "On your way home?"

"I need to drop by my office in the morning, but I shouldn't be long. And Gloria will be here."

Darian stands when I do and reaches for my arm. I think he might try to kiss me, but he doesn't.

"Take your time," I say as I wrangle my chair under the table. "I still haven't checked my e-mail, and I'm sure there are a few things that need my attention."

With a single nod, he pulls open the kitchen door and extends his hand. "Then come with me, milady."

I try to smile, but his enthusiasm has a sharp edge that's beginning to cut. I think the only thing worse than having my own bed is that he wants to tuck me into it.

"It's okay. I've got it," I say as I turn toward the patio outside my room. I make it a whole two steps before my eyes begin to burn.

You're just tired. Get some sleep.

"Francesca?"

I stop. Clear my throat. "Yes?"

"Nothing. Goodnight."

"Goodnight."

I open my eyes in an unfamiliar bed in an unfamiliar room, and to my surprise, relief is the first thing I feel. Relief that Darian's at work and I don't have to face him just yet…and relief that he won't catch me in his Doors tee that I slept in last night. I trade his shirt for one I actually own, but I stay in my fuzzy monkey-print guys-suck pajama pants, which, thankfully, I had the forethought to pack.

The second I open my door, the irresistible pull of bacon wraps around me and lures me toward the kitchen. I poke my head around the corner and watch Gloria conduct breakfast like it's a symphony. A short, slightly plump little thing with a head of graying curls, she scurries from the stove to the sink to the pantry to the fridge and then back to the stove where her gaze finds me.

"Ms. Valentine, good morning," she says, wiping her hands on her apron.

She rushes toward me, and I brace myself for a smothering hug, but she pinches my cheeks instead.

"I am Gloria, Darian's, uh…Darian's Gloria."

"It's nice to meet you, Gloria. Please, call me Frankie."

"Yes, Ms. Frankie."

She smiles brightly, and her unflinching gaze follows me to the other side of the island where it lingers on me for long seconds before it falls away. Heat rises in my cheeks from the attention.

"Darian says you'd be hungry this morning, so I fry up bacon and eggs to go with tostadas. You sit." She points to a barstool, and I do as I'm told. "You sleep good, Ms. Frankie?" she asks, turning back to the stove.

She bends to check the flame and then glides across the limestone to the far right cabinet for a glass. I'm so amused by the way she darts around the kitchen, I fail to answer her, which is evident when she turns to face me, hand planted firmly on her hip.

"Yes?" she says. "You sleep good?"

"Yes. Yes, thank you."

Now bent over with her head in the freezer, I struggle to hear her muffled voice above the clanking of ice.

She shoots up and stares at me again expectantly. "Yes? Texas?"

"Texas, yes," I say, fingers crossed I heard her right. "Outside of Austin."

She grabs the milk from the fridge, takes a mug from the stand on the counter, and then turns on the Keurig. It gurgles and hisses as the rich scent of fresh coffee wafts toward me.

"You don't have much of an accent, Ms. Frankie," she says. "Unlike me."

She breaks into a fit of giggles, and it's impossible not to join her.

"Not really. It only comes out when"—*I drink tequila*—"I'm tired."

She sets a cup of heavily creamed coffee in front of me. "Café con leche. Strong coffee and milk. Darian says you like Coke Light"—she pours a miniature glass bottle of soda over ice and places it beside the mug—"but café con leche is traditional so you have that too."

"Thank you." I'm not much of a coffee drinker, but no way in hell am I arguing with her. "So how do you know Darian?"

"Oh, that boy. I changed his diapers." She waves her hand in the air as if to downplay their relationship, but there's an unmistakable gleam in her eyes and a hint of pride in her smile.

It's clear she's just as fond of him as he is of her, and for some reason, that thought comforts me.

"I used to work for his mama," she says as she flutters about the kitchen. "But then, you know..." Her head tilts from side to side and her eyes widen. "Wait, you *do* know, yes?"

I nod over the rim of my mug. "About the accident? Yes, he told me."

"Well, the dummy decided he had no use for me after that, but I knew better. Can you believe he tried to fire me?" She pushes a basket of grilled buttered bread toward me. "Tostadas," she says, gesturing toward the coffee I'm holding. "You dip."

I nearly choke. "He what?"

"Men are loco, Ms. Frankie," she says. She transfers bacon and scrambled eggs to a plate, slides it to me across the island, and then leans back against the counter with her arms crossed. "Half the time, they don't know what they want, and when they do, they don't know how to ask for it. He needs me; I stay. Simple. Plus, I'm a lonely old lady. I make him play cubilete with me."

I pick up my fork. "What's cubilete?"

"Oh, Ms. Frankie," Gloria says, flashing the biggest grin I think I've ever seen. "You eat up and I show you."

Gloria is a wonderful distraction. She regales me all morning with stories Darian would probably wish she'd kept to herself. I laugh so hard and for so long my stomach muscles ache. She seems thrilled that I'm here, like I'm the only living proof she has that Darian exists outside these walls. We munch on tostadas, drink mug after mug of café con leche, and play countless rounds of the Cuban dice game. At a quarter 'til noon, my phone vibrates with a text from Darian, and Gloria stands.

"You take that, Ms. Frankie," she says, patting my shoulder. "I need to get to this mess anyway."

My brows furrow. "Absolutely not," I say. "You made me an amazing breakfast, and I'm cleaning up." I hop off the barstool and make for the sink while Gloria stares after me. "Besides, it will give me something to do while I wait for Darian." I glance at my phone, to the text that tells me he's going to be late. "And it looks like I'll be waiting a while."

It's strange being alone in someone else's home. You get this sense of who they are, and it's usually vastly different from the person they claim to be. But as I wander through Darian's house, I get nothing, except what I already know—that he's incredibly private. Other than his mail stacked on the kitchen counter, there isn't a single thing that suggests he lives here.

The home's plantation-style is in the details; the layout itself is much more modern. Each room leads to another, so if you keep walking in the same direction, you'll end up right where you started. It's one big square, and in the very center is a courtyard, which is where I spend most of my day.

Despite the constant humidity, it's surprisingly cool, and the four walls that enclose it don't do a thing to stop the breeze blowing in from the gulf. It's furnished with black wicker couches with cream-colored cushions and a teak dining set. Giant turquoise planters of yellow lantana adorn each corner, and a stone fire pit sits in the center. It's hands down my favorite part of the house.

I bring my laptop outside and work from the dining table beneath the generous shade of an umbrella. Party-planning is a get-what-you-give kind of business, and maybe, if I gave a little more, I'd feel better about eventually quitting my day job. It's easy to sell prepackaged boxes. It's also incredibly boring. My heart is in consulting, but ever since my father died, I've lost interest. There's nothing worse than helping other people celebrate while you're grieving. But the truth is, some part of me will always grieve him, and I can't keep pushing everything else aside because of it.

The table rattles beneath my vibrating phone as "Pony" by Ginuwine blows up the quiet courtyard. With my thumb hovering over the Answer button, I stare at Jane's smiling face until the call goes to voice mail. It's safer to text her. That girl is like walking truth serum, and the second she hears my voice, she'll know something's off.

Frankie: Hey!

> Jane: Too busy to talk to your BFF?

Frankie: Sorry, bad signal.

> Jane: So? How's Darian? How's the house?

Frankie: Darian's good and the house is amazing.

> Jane: Is it weird being surrounded by his family?

Frankie: I'm not. I haven't seen a single picture.

> Jane: Nothing? Not even Anabel?

Frankie: Nothing.

> Jane: I was worried her pictures might trigger your nightmares.

Frankie: How's Jacob?

> Jane: He keeps asking if you've met Mickey Mouse.

Frankie: LOL. Tell him he'll be the first to know.

When the sun dips below the walls of the courtyard, I close my laptop and head inside, but as I reach the double doors to my room, my eyes lift to the staircase that frames them. I set my laptop on the floor at my feet and circle around the banister.

I'm not snooping; I'm exploring, I tell myself as my feet navigate the steps.

The staircase culminates in a rectangular landing flanked by two more sets of doors. The one on the right is ajar. I poke my head inside and find a small library with floor-to-ceiling shelves lined with more books than I could ever imagine a personal library to hold. Unable to resist the pull, I step over the threshold and drag my gaze over the hundreds of titles.

I take it back. *This* is my favorite part of the house.

Darian has a little of everything—from English lit to true crime—but science fiction is the clear front-runner.

Finally. Something personal…and something he would've shared with my dad. The thought warms me, but at the same time, a wave of unease crawls over my skin because I know I shouldn't be up here.

As I slip out of the library, I come face to face with the only other room making up the second floor, and it's hidden behind a set of closed doors. My heart aches to learn the secrets that lie within, but…

"Now is not the time," I whisper to myself as I head downstairs.

A faint rap on my door pulls me from my book. I look up as Darian pokes his head inside. Apart from the dim light that spills from my Kindle app, the room is dark. I push myself up against the headboard and fumble for the lamp on the nightstand.

"You can come in," I say when I realize he's still standing there, waiting.

He's dressed in ripped jeans and a Ramones T-shirt. His hair is damp, and as he sits beside me on the edge of the mattress, I notice he smells faintly of soap.

"How long have you been home?" I ask, drawing my knees in to give him more room. "I didn't hear you come in."

He lies sideways across the bed, his body held up by his forearm. "Maybe an hour? I thought you were asleep and I wanted to clean up and get dinner going before I woke you."

"I was just reading," I say. I hold up my phone as evidence. "How was work?"

He shrugs, and his gaze dips to my ankles, to the hem of the pajama pants I never bothered to change out of. A small smile plays on his lips as his fingers graze the fuzzy fabric. "I like these," he says, looking up at me. "Work was work. I'd rather have been here."

I wrap my arms around my legs, hold them tight against my chest, and rest my chin on my knees. My hair falls forward, forming a curtain over my face. Darian sweeps it back behind my ear, and his fingers linger there.

"Are you okay?" he asks, his voice gentle.

I sit up a little. "Just hungry. Gloria made me a feast for breakfast, but I got distracted and haven't eaten since."

"I'm sorry," he says. "I should have sent something over."

"Oh no, it's fine." I lean back against the headboard and narrow my eyes at him. The corner of my mouth lifts in a half-smile. "I mean, as long as you remembered to bring home chocolate."

Darian laughs. "I got ice cream. Will Rocky Road work?"

"Rocky Road is my favorite."

I send Darian ahead, and I stay behind for a shower and a change of clothes—a pair of black leggings and a gray chevron tunic. Then I set off to find him. I go through the house this time, to the kitchen where all three French doors are open to the backyard. Classic rock filters in from the patio and I follow it outside. Darian's at the grill with his back to me. He doesn't hear me come out, which is good since the look on my face is probably not the one he's expecting.

The same table we sat at last night is *set*. Dressed in a white tablecloth and topped with tea lights and a small vase of assorted roses from his garden, it's romantic. Really romantic.

And I'm not sure how I'm supposed to feel about it.

Darian doesn't want to share his bed with me, but he does this? I know we're technically just friends, and I suppose, as such, a friend would have her own room. Except we're *fucking* friends, and logistically speaking, not sharing a room is just stupid. But this? Friends don't have candlelit dinners with wine and roses. They eat Chinese takeout on the floor in front of the TV.

Jane's text flashes in my mind. *You don't act like friends.*

"Perfect timing," Darian says, walking toward me with a platter of grilled fish and asparagus. He sets it on the table beside a bowl of pasta salad. "This stuff is craveable. Drew turned me on to it."

"The pasta?"

"Yeah. Wait 'til you try it." He pulls out my chair as if he's done it a thousand times. "There's some secret ingredient we can't place. Maybe you'll have better luck."

I feel a twinge in my chest. Darian sits next to me, and the ache spreads to the pit of my stomach.

He always sits next to you. What's the big deal?

Darian's hand slides over mine and the sudden contact gives me a jolt. My eyes dart to his. He looks as confused as I feel.

"Sorry, I'm—"

"Hey, I think we—"

"A little out of it," I finish. I reach across the table for a serving spoon.

Darian sits back in his chair and silently watches me as I transfer pasta salad to my plate. I scan the table for a pair of tongs but come up empty. I'm about to stand when I feel his fingers wrap around my wrist.

"I was just going to get some tongs or something for the asparagus," I say, keeping my eyes trained on the table. "And I guess a spatula for the fish would be good."

"Can it wait a second?" Darian turns in his chair until his knees brush the side of my thigh. "Will you please tell me what's wrong? I can tell something's bothering you. I just don't know what it is."

I lift my eyes, slowly meeting his gaze. "You gave me my own room."

"Was I not supposed to do that?"

"No, it's...I thought maybe you did it because of what happened the other night. Like you were just setting boundaries or something, and I totally get that. But then tonight, I come out here and see this romantic"—I wave my hand over the table—"spread, and I realize...that can't be it." My throat tightens. "You don't want to share your room with me, but you do...*this*? Candles? Flowers? I'm not saying I don't appreciate it; I'm just saying it's confusing."

Darian sinks back in his chair. "I didn't think of it like that. I left you here all day by yourself. I felt bad. I wanted to do something nice for you."

"And I love it; I do. But you're drawing a line with one thing and crossing it with another. I don't know what to think."

He leans toward me and reaches for my hand. "I gave you your own room because I wanted you to be comfortable. I didn't want you to feel pressured and I didn't want to be presumptuous." His thumb grazes my knuckles and he lets out a deep sigh. "You didn't say anything so I figured I'd made the right decision."

"I know," I say. "I should have just asked."

"And I should have talked to you about it instead of assuming." He lifts his hand to my jaw, his long fingers tangling in my hair. "This is new territory for both of us, and I think we can agree sex blurs the lines a little bit. The last thing I want to do is confuse you. I'm trying like hell to do the right thing, but I don't always know what that is."

I scrunch my face. "I guess that makes two of us."

"I admit our friendship is a little…unconventional."

Laughter bubbles out of me. "That's one way of putting it," I say as my eyes roam the table. "Yes, sex blurs the lines, but so does holding hands and kissing…and *this*." I point to the vase of roses and then pluck one out, bringing it to my nose. "It feels like we're dating."

Darian stiffens beside me, and my gaze drops to his fingers wrapped tightly around the armrests.

"We're not dating," he says, his tone brisk.

"I don't mean it like we're serious or anything."

"Because, Francesca, I…*can't*."

I put the rose back in the vase. "I know."

167

We both fall silent as the angry thrashing of drums in Led Zeppelin's "Babe I'm Gonna Leave You" fills the backyard.

Darian pulls a remote out of his pocket and aims it at the house. The music fades. "What do you say we try this again?" he says, looking over at me. His lips curve into a half smile. "Open the wine? Have some cold snapper?"

An uneasy feeling flits in my stomach, then flutters away as I smile back at him. "I'd like that."

"Good." He reaches across the table for the chardonnay and sets it between us. "So will you stay with me tonight? I *want* you to stay with me. Please."

"I'd like that too."

I'd like that a lot.

CHAPTER 9

Hyacinth House

Drew: I hear you're playing hooky.

> Darian: Taking Francesca to SoBe.
> Doing a show with CTB, so technically
> working.

Drew: Make sure you take her to Rustica. Do they even have pizza in Texas?

> Darian: Ha ha. I promised to take her
> salsa dancing. We'll grab dinner there.

Drew: Grab dinner? At a SoBe hotspot?

> Darian: Fuck off.

Drew: Just sayin'. You've never taken me salsa dancing.

Frankie

Mmm, last night was just…*mmm.*

I stretch my naked limbs in Darian's bed, hyperaware he's not in it, and make sheet angels in the cool cotton. A stupid grin unfurls on my face, and I'm a little relieved he isn't here to see it. *Did he say he had to work today?* I don't remember a thing after "stay with me tonight."

I push myself up against the headboard and clear the sleep from my eyes as Darian's room comes into focus. The walls are painted the same creamy white as downstairs and the bed and windows are dressed in a mix of grays. It's just as lovely as the rest of his house, but as I suspected, it's just as bare. The only personal items I can see from this vantage point are his glasses on the nightstand and his watch on the dresser.

I shake off the covers and sit on the edge of the bed. Darian's Ramones T-shirt is still draped over the lampshade where it landed last night.

Convenient, I think as I pull it over my head. My clothes are still outside.

I find Darian in the kitchen, hunched over a cup of coffee. His gaze briefly meets mine before it slides down my body, over his shirt, and along my bare legs. One corner of his mouth lifts, and by the time I get to him, he's sporting a full-fledged grin. He takes my face in his hands, bends as if he's going to kiss me, and pushes his fingers into my hair.

"Hey," he says.

"Hey," I say back.

"Nice shirt. Good thing Gloria isn't here." He brushes his nose against mine. "You'd have given her a fright."

"Maybe you should consider that the next time you want to disrobe me in the backyard."

"Next time…I like the sound of that."

He kisses me, and I taste the rich flavor of sweetened coffee on his tongue as it sweeps inside my mouth. His teeth pull at my bottom lip, sending heat curling down my spine. I wind my arms around his neck and melt against him. Then the kissing stops, and I hear the faint buzzing of a cell phone set to vibrate.

"What now?" His tone is gruff. He steps back, pulls his phone from his pocket, and narrows his eyes at the screen. "Sorry about that," he says, running a hand through his hair. He tosses his phone on the island with enough force to send it skating to the other side. "Where were we?"

"I think we were about to have sex in your kitchen," I say, sidestepping him for the refrigerator. "Everything okay?"

"Yeah, it's nothing." He waves off the question with a flick of his wrist.

I pull out a Diet Coke and rifle through his utensil drawer for an opener.

"Next one over," he says. "And we can still have sex in my kitchen."

"You keep your bottle opener with the oven mitts? Because that makes sense." I pop off the cap and take a long pull. I love that he got me glass bottles. I don't think I've ever had Diet Coke in a glass bottle before yesterday. "You got up early this morning."

"Someone was snoring," he says, arching his brows. "Couldn't sleep."

I give him a pointed look. "Whatever."

He jerks his chin in the direction of his office. "I had a few e-mails to get out."

"You don't need to go in today?"

"Not today," he says. His smile is suspicious.

I cross my arms. "What are you up to?"

He disappears into the family room and returns with a sizeable box wrapped in silver paper. He sets it on the counter beside me. "I did a little shopping while I was downtown yesterday."

"What is it?" I ask, my voice hesitant.

"It's a surprise. Sort of. Well, those are clothes," he says, nodding toward the package, "but where you're going in them is a surprise."

"Clothes?"

"Yes. And because of our talk last night, I have a feeling you're going to fight me on them, but please don't. Just let me do this for you today." His eyes are intent on mine until I nod, and then he takes his mug to the sink and pours out the last dregs of his coffee. "I have a few more things to do this morning, so go get dressed and meet me back here in"—he peers up at the clock—"forty-five minutes?"

"I'll be ready."

Darian grabs his phone off the island, slides it in his back pocket, and turns toward the door. "Don't overthink it, Francesca."

I open my mouth to argue, but he's already gone.

"Okay, Darian. What am I not supposed to overthink?" I whisper before tossing back more of my Diet Coke.

Excitement and apprehension knot my stomach as I pick up the box. It isn't as heavy as it looks, and I don't know if that's good or bad. I carry it upstairs and sit beside it on Darian's bed, staring at it hard enough to melt the paper. I'm not used to gifts, and Darian's already given me more than any man has ever come close to.

Stop overthinking it, Frankie.

I tear off the wrapping and lift the lid. Buried beneath layers of tissue paper are two smaller boxes. In the first, I find a pale pink bikini and a matching pink halter dress. Relief softens the hard edge of my anxiety. It's just a swimsuit. A gorgeous swimsuit, a *tiny* swimsuit, but just a swimsuit.

I dig out the second box. It's a shoebox, red, with *Valentino* printed on the top.

Holy shit. This is not just a pair of shoes.

My hand flies to my chest as a piercing laugh bursts out of me. I take off the lid, and my heart hammers in my ears as I pull the drawstring on the little red bag inside. Using only the tips of my fingers, I carefully take the first shoe out, as if actually touching it will damage it somehow. It's a black sandal studded with little silver pyramids. It's absolutely stunning. And way too much.

I glance at the clock on Darian's nightstand. I'm down to twenty minutes, and I haven't even started getting ready yet. I take an impressive five minutes to shower and shave my legs. I choose sunscreen over makeup and scrunch my damp hair into beachy waves. At three minutes and counting, I get dressed. Everything fits, even the shoes, which I promptly take off.

My ears perk up as I open the door. Darian's voice, hushed but clipped, echoes from downstairs, and he's not alone. He's arguing with a woman I hope I don't have the pleasure of meeting; she's loud, and she doesn't sound very friendly.

By the time I reach the bottom step, the exchange has become heated. Darian's tone is on par with the woman's, and without the buffer of carpeting, the effect is jarring.

I crane my neck to peek over the banister. Animated shadows battle it out on the limestone floor in front of the kitchen and grow larger as the voices near. I jerk back against the wall with the sandals dangling from my fingers, hoping to remain unseen.

"Yes, I agreed to handle things when I thought you were still in Austin, tying up loose ends," the woman says. "Then I find out you left days ago and you've been shacking up with some bottle-blonde adolescent. You have commitments, Darian, and you need to honor them."

Bottle blonde?

"Adolescent?"

"She's a kid. I saw your picture on the S&S website." Her voice advances and then retreats as her shoes click back and forth across the tiles.

"That's right, Amanda," Darian says, his voice steady. "I am committed today. Just not to you. I'm sorry you're having so much trouble with this, but I think you're forgetting who cuts your check."

Steady but pissed.

"That's fine. You two have fun playing Sharks and Minnows and I'll handle the showcase."

"Thank you for being so amenable. The *kid's* name is Francesca, and I think Marco Polo is more her style. But I'll keep Sharks and Minnows in mind."

Nice.

"Fuck you, Darian." The *click, click, click* of her shoes grows louder with each step in my direction.

It's too late to bolt. I hug the sandals against me and the heels dig into my stomach.

"You must be Francesca," she says when she spots me. Her lips are drawn in a smirk. "I'm Amanda."

She extends her hand, and I have half a mind to leave it hanging...but I don't.

"Please, call me Frankie."

Frankie? That was stupid. Way to go, kid.

Darian sighs, defeated. "Francesca, this is Amanda Harris, my COO. Amanda, Francesca Valentine."

"Francesca Valentine, your..."

"My date," he says.

"For Marco Polo," I add.

Shut. The. Fuck. Up. Frankie.

Her keys rattle in her hand. "Lovely to meet you, *Frankie*," she says, over-articulating my name. She turns toward Darian. "See me out?"

Their back and forth banter tells me there's more to their relationship than boss-employee, and I'd be lying if I said that didn't bother me. Plus, she happens to be a knockout. Ms. Miami Beach in business wear and heels, Darian's COO is tall and tanned with long, dark hair that almost reaches her tailbone. Darian's too smart to be cliché, so I know she must have a brain in that perfectly symmetrical head of hers, and somehow that makes it worse.

I sit on the bottom step with my elbows propped on my knees and the sandals hanging between them. I hear the door close, then more arguing, and then the door opens.

Darian marches toward me with purpose, his grin wide. "Oh, Francesca," he says, pulling me to my feet. "I'm going to kiss you now."

He does, and it makes this morning's kiss pale in comparison.

"What was that for?" I ask, my grin matching his.

"For being you." His gaze falls to the shoes in my hand and he takes them from me. "You ready to go?"

"Darian, about those…"

He stops me with the touch of his thumb to my lips and then kneels on the floor in front of me. "The label's co-sponsoring a spring break party at the Clevelander in SoBe…South Beach. Lift."

Holding his shoulders for balance, I pick up my left foot, and he slides on a sandal.

"Several of our top bands will be performing. Lift," he says again.

I pick up my right.

When he's finished buckling the straps, he stands. "Including Cross to Bear."

I grab his hands. "Seriously? Why didn't you tell me? I had no idea it was spring break."

"The spring break show is Amanda's thing. I usually back her up, but it'd completely slipped my mind until I went in yesterday. I've been a little preoccupied," he says, his lips curving into a smile. "That's one of the reasons she's so pissed."

"One of the reasons?"

"With Amanda, it's complicated. She's been with me—with the label rather—since the beginning. We don't really have the typical boss-subordinate relationship, if you didn't notice. Oh, I almost forgot. I made pancakes. You eat while I finish up, and then we can go."

The grin splitting my face gives him pause.

His brows draw together. "What?"

"It's just been a really good day."

"How so? It's barely ten and you've already been boorishly affronted by my COO."

"Well, despite her, you dressed me like a supermodel, you're taking me to see my favorite band, *and* you made me pancakes."

Darian smiles. "You look beautiful, by the way."

"I feel beautiful. I'd like to say it wasn't necessary, but if this is what people wear in South Beach, you were right in assuming I didn't pack anything even close."

"It's not that," he says. "I just wanted to treat you. I like making you happy." Leaning forward, he brushes his lips against my grin. "And call Jane to let her know about the show. It'll be live on WMN."

"Is that that new one? World Music Network?"

"That's the one. Now go eat before it gets cold."

I wait for Darian on the front porch with my purse hanging on my shoulder and a pair of wide-framed sunglasses perched on my head. I hear the metallic clank of a garage door opening, followed by the smooth purr of an engine. Darian's car edges past the side of the house, and my eyes double in size. An electric-blue convertible, the color brilliant beneath the Miami sun, turns the corner and then rolls to a stop in front of me.

"Wow," I say as Darian opens the door and steps out. "What's that?"

His smile is wide. "*She* is a Maserati GranTurismo."

"*She?*" A grin breaks over my face as I cross the pavement to the passenger side. "Does *she* have a name?"

"Not yet," he says. "Maybe you can come up with something."

He holds the door open for me and I climb in, dropping my purse on the floorboard by my feet. I slide my sunglasses over my eyes and tilt my head back against the headrest.

"I haven't been in a convertible in ages," I say.

After Darian buckles himself in, he leans over me and pops open the glove compartment. He takes out a pair of shades and puts them on before pulling out a scarf. "For your hair," he says, setting the scarf in my lap.

"Really?" I shoot him an amused look. "You can't be serious."

"What?"

"You keep a scarf on hand for all the girls you drive around in your come-fuck-me car?"

A laugh bursts from his throat. "Come-fuck-me car?" His hand smooths over the dashboard with reverence. "I think Francesca just named you," he says to *her* before turning to me. "Are you jealous?"

"No!" I say a little too loudly. "I'm just making fun of your communal scarf."

Darian bends over the wheel, his head buried in his arms, his shoulders shaking with laughter.

"Why is this so funny?" I ask, leaning against the door with my arms crossed.

He rolls his head to the side and lays his shaded eyes on me. "This overreacting thing you do? It's fucking adorable." He sits up. "Francesca, look at it. It matches your dress. I bought it for you."

"Then why was it in the glove compartment?"

"Because I bought it *after* I had your box wrapped. I threw it in there so I wouldn't forget to give it to you." He holds up his hands. "Simple as that. I swear. And by the way, you are the only girl I've ever driven in my come-fuck-me car. You also happen to be the only girl who's ever been to my house—aside from Gloria, obviously, and Amanda. And until today, she's never made it past my front office."

I sit tall in my seat and pull on my seatbelt. "Really?"

"Really." His fingers brush my cheek. "Francesca, I wasn't lying. It's been five years."

What the hell, Frankie?

"Ugh. I know. I've never doubted you either." I turn my face toward the window. "Thank you."

He smiles. "For what? Not being an asshole?"

"That too."

"You're welcome."

I wrap my hair in the scarf and tie it tight at the back of my neck. Darian shifts into drive and we coast slowly down the long driveway, coming to a stop at the gate.

"You really thought I had a communal scarf?" he asks, incredulous.

I shrug. "I don't know what's wrong with me."

As the gate slides open, Darian picks up my hand and caresses my knuckles. My stomach flutters.

I *am* overreacting. More than normal. My age, his guest room...a scarf? I sure hope it's fucking adorable because I'm turning into a crazy person.

I glance at Darian through the dark lenses of my sunglasses. He squeezes my hand, then brings it to his lips and kisses it.

"How about some music?" he says, turning on the radio.

Culture Club's "Do You Really Want to Hurt Me" fills the open air of the car, and I bite back a laugh.

This man is going to crush you into a million little pieces, Frankie, my subconscious warns.

I lean forward and change the station. *Not today.*

My head perks up when Darian pulls into the valet area at The Ritz-Carlton. "I thought we were going to the Clevelander." I slide my sunglasses down my nose and turn sideways in my seat.

"We are," he says, giving me a sly smile as he puts the car in park.

A valet attendant opens his door. "Checking in, sir?"

Checking in?

"Yes. Darian Fox," he says, glancing at his watch as he gets out of the car. "Please see to our luggage, and we need a lift to the Clevelander."

"Yes, sir, Mr. Fox."

A second attendant opens my door and I step onto the sidewalk, a huge grin spreading on my face as Darian makes his way around the car. "We're staying? Here?"

"We're staying here."

I push up on my toes and throw my arms around his neck. He bends, meeting me halfway, and laughs softly against my lips.

"It's okay, baby," he says. He pulls off his sunglasses and hangs them on the neck of his T-shirt. "We don't have to stay if you don't want to."

Baby?

My feet fall flat and we break apart.

Did he just say baby?

His eyes narrow. "I was joking, but if you don't want to stay…"

Oh thank God, he was joking.

I wait for relief to flood me, but it never comes.

"No, um…" The words dissolve in my throat as a white stretch limo pulls in behind the Maserati. My eyes snap to Darian's. "Is that for us?"

"I guess so. Shame we're only going down the street."

The driver, a tall, dark-haired woman in a chauffeur cap and aviator shades, steps out of the car. "Mr. Fox?"

Darian nods. "We're headed to the Clevelander."

"Yes, sir."

We settle into the car, and a smile pulls at my lips as I extend my legs in the open space in front of me. I can't believe I'm taking a limo to a spring break party in South Beach. To see my favorite band. Who happens to be signed to my *unconventional friend's* record label. A couple of weeks ago, true excitement came in the form of a Netflix marathon and a package of Oreos. *This is a little surreal.*

Even at this early hour, the city is one big ball of energy, but inside the car, it's peaceful and silent. Darian scrolls through his messages while I stare out my window at the row of hotels lining the street. After a few blocks, he slides his phone in the pocket of his shorts and picks up my hand.

"You're quiet all of a sudden," he says.

I angle my body toward him and lace our fingers together. "Just sightseeing."

"Not a lot to see on Collins," he says. "I need to take you down Ocean."

"I'd love that." My head rests against his arm as I look out the window on his side. "Everything is so white. This is nothing like Texas." The architecture is stunning, and I can only imagine what it looks like at night, all lit up.

Another block passes as we sit in silence. We stop at a light, and Darian brushes my hair back from my face.

"Should I have asked you?" he says, drawing my gaze. "About staying? I wanted to surprise you, but maybe I should have asked."

"No, I'm happy we're staying." I turn, tucking my feet beneath me, and rest my knees on his thigh. "Wait," I say, pushing my sunglasses on top of my head, "you did bring my bag, right?"

Darian laughs. "Sorry, babe. After this party, you'll be in clothes-free territory. All you'll need is a toothbrush, and I'm sure the hotel will have one."

I smack his arm. "Very funny."

"I didn't bring your duffel, but I grabbed your makeup and toiletry bags. I promise you'll want for nothing else."

The car slows and moves into the turn lane.

Darian bends to look out the window. "It's going to

be a madhouse," he says. "You ready?"

I nod, a nervous excitement building in my stomach as we pull up to the Clevelander. The driver opens my door and I slide out, followed closely by Darian, into a dense crowd of people. I slip my hand in his as we navigate through them.

"Where are we going?" I ask, unable to see more than a few feet in front of me.

"Roof deck." He laughs. "If we can get to it."

I peer down at the gorgeous pink silk dress I'm wearing and stand a little taller beside him. Even in swimwear, South Beach women are impeccably dressed, and thanks to Darian, I don't feel as out of place as I thought I would. South Beach guys, on the other hand, are much more casual. Darian's sporting gray hybrid shorts and a Led Zeppelin T-shirt. I tug at the hem.

"You own a record label," I say. "Has it ever occurred to you to advertise the bands you're trying to sell?"

He scoffs. "You sound like Amanda. I told her I'll do it when she does."

"Wow. What are you, five?" I'm gifted a boyish grin, and I have my answer. "Will we see her today?"

"Not if I can help it," he says. "Today's about us. I'm not Darian Fox, CEO. I'm Francesca's Marco Polo playdate."

I swallow hard. First, *baby*, and now, *us*.

They're only words, Frankie. Get a grip.

"I bet that's why she's pissed," I say. "She has to work and we're having fun."

"Blondes do have more fun." He puts his arm around my waist and pulls me against him.

"*Bottle* blondes."

"Oh, Francesca, I think I've seen enough of you to know you are definitely *not* a bottle blonde."

The ocean-scented air is thick with humidity when we get outside, and the wall of people block both the breeze and the view. Skipping makeup was one of my better ideas, but I wish I had worn my hair up. The scarf was fine for the car, but it isn't suited for South Beach.

Darian lowers my glasses over my eyes and presses a kiss to the top of my head. "It's miserable down here," he says, "but we're going up."

We come to a set of stairs. Darian releases my waist for my hand and climbs ahead of me to the roof deck. A hostess greets us when we reach the top.

"Mr. Fox, so nice to see you again," she says. "Right this way."

We're escorted to a reserved table, close to the edge with an unobstructed view of the ocean. Even with the chaos of spring break, it's breathtaking. I follow Darian's gaze to the stage below.

Another unobstructed view, I think, smiling. I give him a questioning look.

"What?" he asks.

"You're playing the VIP card," I say as I push myself onto the bar-height chair. "I thought you weren't Darian Fox, CEO, today."

He leans over the railing and shakes his head. "I'm also not twenty-one with finals next month."

I cross my arms at that, eyebrows raised.

"Nineteen. I'm not nineteen." He laughs. "It's hot as hell down there and there's a high possibility of being vomited on."

"Valid reasons." I wrinkle my nose. "Graphic but valid."

A server appears at our table with a beverage cart, and Darian takes his seat.

"I also appreciate bottle service." He picks up a sprig

of mint from the cart and rolls it between his fingers. The fresh scent permeates the salty, sticky air. "I believe I promised you mojitos, Ms. Valentine."

Two bands and two mojitos in, I'm kicked back with my feet resting on Darian's lap. There's just enough of a breeze to make it bearable and I'm beyond grateful he played his VIP card.

"You're smiling," Darian says.

"I am? I guess I'm happy." I pull off my sunglasses and set them on the table. "I liked that last band. Who were they?"

"Ela-ment," he says.

"Element?"

"Kind of. It's *Ela* and *ment*. *Ela-ment*. It's a play on the lead singer's name." He rolls his eyes and I laugh. "It was a battle I chose not to fight."

"That's the one," I say, pointing to his chest. "That's the T-shirt you should start with."

He juts his chin toward the railing. "I think you'd have a better chance of getting me to wear *this* band."

The familiar intro of Cross to Bear's opening number rises from the stage below and the same giddy expression I wore in Austin returns.

Darian laughs. "Come on," he says, holding his hand out to me.

I jump down from my chair, and he cages me against the railing.

"I can get you to the stage if you're interested," he says.

"You'd risk sorority-girl vomit for me?"

His smile is sincere. "Without question."

The seriousness of his tone gives me a shiver. I smooth my hands over my arms and settle against his chest.

184

"That's okay," I say with a grin. "I'm good here."

We stay just like that for the entire set. CTB finishes with an acoustic version of The Doors' "Love Her Madly."

Darian lowers his lips to my ear. "Aside from their encore genius, what is it about this band you find so appealing?"

I tilt my head back and peer up at him. "Shame on you, Mr. Fox. You represent them, and you don't know?"

"I know all I need to know; they're a lucrative asset."

I give him a glare and his face breaks into a smile.

"I'm kidding," he says. "The truth is, the label's been doing some restructuring and CTB is Amanda's find. I gave her free rein." He slides his arms around my waist. "But I asked why *you* liked them."

I turn back to the stage. "It's their lyrics. Their music feels light on the surface, but their lyrics are anything but."

"Amanda says they're unapologetic."

"She's right. Their melodies give nothing away and they don't explain themselves. They sing to their fans, even now with their newfound fame."

"Finally, someone who gets it." Amanda's voice is unmistakable as it creeps up behind us like a lioness stalking her prey.

I knew avoiding her would be impossible. Darian and I slowly turn around. Our matching grins are forced.

"I've been trying to explain their appeal to Darian here for some time now," she says.

"Amanda." Darian's tone borders on curt, but his smile remains. "Everything running smoothly?"

I take my seat at the table to watch the back and forth, but my eyes stay fixed on Amanda, on her perfect hair and her perfectly made-up face. Aside from the occasional gust of wind, it's hot—really hot—and her makeup isn't even running.

She called me a kid so I have to assume she's closer to Darian's age than mine, but she doesn't look a day over twenty-five. Her golden-brown skin is flawless and not a single strand of her long, silky espresso-colored hair is out of place. She's still dressed in the same business attire she had on earlier—a fitted black skirt that hits just above the knee and a sleeveless ivory blouse. Her long legs are toned and end in the same pair of four-inch heels that clicked around Darian's house. I shake my head. *Who wears four-inch heels to the beach?*

She's stunning, and I can't help feeling just a little bit jealous. Despite Darian's obvious irritation with her, they have a history. Bickering aside, I get the sense he cares about her.

"Of course everything's running smoothly," Amanda says. "*I'm* here. What did you expect?"

Darian sits across from me and rubs his fingers over his jaw. "You're right, Amanda. I dumped this in your lap and I'm sorry."

"Will you be back in the office on Monday?" she asks. Her voice softens, like she feels bad for hounding him. "We need to talk about Flight Risk."

"I'll be in on Monday."

I take a long sip of my watered-down mojito. Amanda's gaze shifts to me, and I can feel the jab before it comes.

"You two have a great time. And beware of the mojitos, Frankie. They do have alcohol in them. They'll sneak up on you if you're not careful."

"She's fun," I say to Darian as soon as Amanda's out of earshot.

"Don't worry about her. She's got a stick up her ass."

"Why is that exactly?"

Darian stands to signal our server, and I lean forward, my arms resting on the table.

"Darian, seriously. Did something happen between you two?"

He heaves a long sigh as he lowers into his chair.

"I'm sorry," I say. "It's none of my—"

"It was a long time ago, Francesca. I already told you part of it…*the girls*? Amanda, well…" He pauses, tracing his finger around the lip of his glass. "She was the one who—she *helped* me." His Adam's apple bobs in his throat and he turns his head away from me. "Let's just say, I owe her a lot."

"Did you have feelings for her? *Do* you have feelings for her?" The words sound brittle as they leave my mouth, and I immediately wish I could take them back.

"No, Francesca, it wasn't like that. I swear to you nothing's happened between us in five years. And nothing's going to. I was a mess back then." He looks down at his fingers now steepled on the table. "Like I said, it was a long time ago. We've both moved on."

"I'm not sure she has," I say gently.

"You're the first girl I've brought around. She might be a little jealous; I don't know. But if she is, it's only because she's used to having my full attention, and lately, she hasn't had it at all." He lifts his head, and his eyes briefly meet mine before he shakes open his sunglasses and slides them on. "She doesn't understand we're just hanging out, having a little extracurricular fun. She'll have me back soon enough."

I think he means to comfort me, but he manages to do the exact opposite. His emotionless words and their easy delivery sting, and all I'm left with is a reminder that this is temporary.

We're temporary.

"Don't let her get to you," Darian says, pushing to his feet. "You ready?"

When I go back to Texas, he'll go back to normal, but I don't think anything will ever be *normal* for me again.

CHAPTER 10

Love Me Two Times

Darian: She met Amanda.

Drew: You introduce her to She Devil and not me? Thanks bro.

Darian: You don't introduce me to all the girls you hang out with.

Drew: This one's different.

Frankie

"So, Ms. Valentine," Darian says, "it's only six and our dinner reservations aren't until nine. What should we do with all this free time?"

His eyes sparkle with mischief and his smile is hard to resist, but our last conversation still smarts like a fresh wound.

I rummage through our suitcase at the foot of the king-size bed. "Actually, I'd like a bath."

He saunters toward me. "I'm up for a bath."

"Rain check?" I ask, pulling out my toiletry bag. "I just need…"

"No, of course. It's okay. Rain check."

I can't believe I just turned down hot bathtub sex. And this bathtub is big enough to get *dirty* in. It's bigger than the one at The Mendón, which I struggle to believe even though I'm sitting in it.

I lie back against the sharp-edged marble and grip the sides to keep my chin above the bubbles. The position I'm in strains my arms and the vanilla scent of the hotel's body wash is cloying.

I laugh at the absurdity. This is the most anticlimactic bath I've ever taken, and it's my fault because I just *had* to take it alone.

You are alone.

I blink the thought away. I'm just…out of my comfort zone. Strange place. Strange man. Strange feelings swirling inside me.

"She doesn't understand we're just hanging out, having a little extracurricular fun. She'll have me back soon enough."

Darian's words affect me on a level I don't understand. He's clearly not interested in her; I have no reason to be jealous.

"Don't let her get to you."

She's not, but *something* is.

My eyes and throat ache. I actually feel like I could cry right now, which is completely ridiculous. It's been ten years, and there's absolutely no indication he'll ever be ready for—

Fuck.

The tub turns into a wave pool, water splashing over the side as I jerk forward. I pull my knees to my chin and fold my arms around them. My heart pounds so loud in my ears, everything else goes silent.

Are you in love with him?
Everything but that.

Wrapped in plush terry cloth, I stand on the balcony overlooking the Atlantic. The full moon casts a pale yellow ribbon across the water, and if I had a pair of earplugs to block out the noise, it would be idyllic.

"How long have I been asleep?" I hear Darian say, chasing his question with a yawn.

"Almost two hours." I walk inside and sit on the edge of the bed. "I was about to wake you."

He kisses my cheek, and then he stands, stretches, and yawns again. "Mojitos," he says, making a face. "The irony of Amanda's warning is not lost on me. I'm gonna grab a shower. There's a dress for you in the wardrobe."

"A dress? Darian…"

"Francesca…" He holds his hands to his temples and blinks his eyes closed. *Mojitos*, he mouths as a reminder. "I skipped the pancakes this morning and I'm paying for it now. So please, please don't…with the dress."

"Can I get you anything? Some aspirin maybe?"

He smiles. "I'll be fine. Just need to wake up."

The dress is burgundy-pink leopard print with a fitted bodice, belted waist, and a full, short skirt. It's gorgeous, and the insta-love I feel for it borders on maternal.

Don't look at the tag, Frankie. Don't look at the—son of a bitch. Doesn't anyone shop at Old Navy anymore?

The fabric is heavy but smooth against my fingers as it slides from the hanger. I carefully pull down the zipper and step into it, letting it balloon around my body while I strap on my sandals. I style my hair in ringlets that hang in layers down my back and paint my eyes a little darker than usual. And, because I plan to make up for all the kissing I missed out on today, I leave my lips bare.

Darian stirs behind me, and I glance at him over my shoulder.

"Feel better?"

"Much, I…" He pauses. "You look…"

"Help me with my dress?"

"I've been dying to see you in this," he says.

He gently tugs at my zipper, then pulls it up so slowly I swear I can hear each tooth catch. I turn around and he takes a step back.

"You're…" His words melt away again and he just stares.

I laugh. "Striking, exquisite, splendid, magnificent…"

"Yes."

The look in his darkening eyes, the intensity, the intent—it steals the air from my lungs. I step around him, crossing the room for our suitcase, and needlessly dig through it while I wait for my breath to return.

"Well, I love it," I say at last, turning to face the mirror. I meet his reflection with a curious smile. "Tell me the truth. *You* picked this out?"

He comes up behind me and places his hands on my waist. "It was all me," he says. "I might have had help with the size, but I picked it. You really like it?"

"I really do." I turn around. "Thank you. But, Darian, this is it, right? No more lavish gifts, okay?"

"Okay," he says. "But only because it makes you uncomfortable. I'd buy you a million dresses if you'd let me."

A warm flush sweeps over my cheeks and a smile breaks between them. "Should we go?" I ask. "We should probably go."

"We should go." Darian pulls a sport coat out of the wardrobe and puts it on.

And then I see him, really see him, somehow for the first time tonight, and I have to find my breath again. He's dressed in a fitted black suit with a light-pink shirt, unbuttoned at the neck, that just happens to go perfectly with my dress. He looks...*wow*, and he smells...*mmm*. Like a beach in the Mediterranean. Not that I've ever been to the Mediterranean, but if I were to go, I bet this is what it'd smell like.

"New cologne?" I ask.

"It's Versace. Do you like it?"

Do I like it? I could lick it off him. "If we don't leave this second, you'll find out."

"Point made. Shall we?"

We have dinner in a small Cuban hideaway a few blocks from our hotel. It's dark but candlelit with a live band and a black and white checkerboard dance floor. We finish our meals, and as the last few dishes are removed Darian pushes back from the table.

"Francesca," he says, standing. He holds out his hand.

Darian warned me there would be dancing, but I guess I thought a full stomach might change his mind. It hasn't, and I find myself being lured from my chair by a firm grip and a sexy smile.

"I'm afraid I'm going to embarrass you," I say.

"Impossible." He pulls me against him, one hand holding mine, the other flat against my back. "All you need to do is hang on."

Easier said than done, I think to myself, but before I can say the words out loud, we're gliding across the dance floor.

The man can dance, and somehow, with him leading me, so can I.

"Where did you learn how to do this?" I ask.

He pulls me into a spin and I follow easily.

"My mom loved to dance," he says, "and she made it her mission to teach me. I've been doing it for as long as I can remember."

The song is beautiful even if I can't understand the Spanish lyrics. Darian lowers his mouth to my ear and translates them for me. It's about a woman who moves on from a failed relationship and a man who can't.

Will that be us one day? I'll eventually move on, and Darian—no. I'll never be the girl he can't overcome.

Wow, Frankie, what's happening to you?

I close my eyes and lay my head against his chest. The tempo is quick, picking up speed as the song progresses. Darian leads me effortlessly, his arms guiding me as he shifts his weight with each deliberate step. Not an inch of the dance floor is spared.

By the time the song ends, Darian's heart is hammering beneath my ear and mine is matching it beat for beat. I step back to suck in a breath, and our gazes lock. His eyes are dark and glistening, his lips parted. He clears his throat, and it makes a deep, raspy sound.

"Francesca…"

"Darian, I think we should…"

"I'm on it."

Darian pays the tab, and then we're out the door, racing toward our hotel. The sidewalks are thick with late-night spring breakers. We weave through them, laughing, as the neon lights of South Beach zoom past us in a blur of color.

"Wait, stop," I say, tugging on Darian's hand. I pull off my shoes and curl my fingers around the straps. "Okay, I'm good."

He smiles. "You sure?"

"I'm sure."

We arrive red-faced and winded. The doorman flashes a knowing grin as we rush inside, and I swear a hundred eyes follow us across the lobby.

"It's like they know," I whisper once we're in the elevator.

Darian laughs. "They can't possibly know what I'm going to do to you once I get you alone."

"We're alone now."

His lips curve into a grin as he drives me against the back wall of the elevator. His fingers trail up my thigh, beneath my dress and just inside my panties.

"You're so fucking wet," he says. His voice is a growl against my neck, and his warm breath tickling my skin makes my body shudder.

My forehead falls against his chest and I moan softly. "Why can't we be in the room already?"

"Fuck, I know."

The elevator stops eight floors too soon. Darian jerks his hand away and I straighten my dress. The doors slide open, and an older couple wearing bathrobes and water shoes steps inside.

"Are you going down?" Darian says through a clenched jaw. "Because we're going up."

The short, copper-haired woman waves a dismissive hand. "We don't mind, dear. We can go up first." She pokes her head in the bag she's carrying and comes back with a tube of lipstick. "You two been here long?" she says. "We just got here today."

The bearded man beside her nods. "We're on our

honeymoon. We eloped. You married?" He glances at my hand. "Don't see a ring."

"Maybe they'll get engaged while they're here," the woman says, her eyes widening. "Or married…on the beach. Wouldn't that be lovely? We got married in Vegas"—she clutches her chest, placing her impossible-to-miss sparkly diamond on full display—"by Elvis."

Darian winces, and it's all I can do to keep from laughing.

I slide my fingers through his. "Congratulations."

The woman paints her lips fire-engine red and then drops the lipstick back in her bag. "Where are you kids from?"

Darian opens his mouth, then shuts it when I squeeze his hand.

"We're from Texas," I say in my best southern drawl. "Here for the big South Beach Bull Ridin' Championship." I nudge Darian's arm. "Buddy Lee here is a real live rodeo clown. Ain't that right, Buddy Lee?"

The elevator dings, and Darian yanks me forward. "It was real nice meetin' y'all," he says as the doors open.

Laughter bursts out of me the second they close. "You have the worst accent ever."

"Yours is pretty fucking hot."

Darian tightens his grip on my hand and pulls me down the hall toward our suite. His feet work in long strides, and I wonder if it would be easier if he just carried me. When we reach our door, he digs the key card out of his pocket and tries it four times without success before I take it from him.

"What the hell is wrong with our key?" he says, lacing his fingers behind his head.

"You can't force it." I gently swipe the card. The green light comes on and I open the door. "See?"

"I didn't force it." He shrugs out of his suit jacket and tosses it over the back of a chair.

"I think you forced it a little, Buddy Lee."

He laughs. "Rodeo clown? Didn't see that one coming."

"Rodeo clowns are hot."

Darian unbuttons his shirt as we move toward the bedroom. "You sayin' I'm hot?"

A giggle climbs up my throat, but I swallow it down when I feel his hands on my waist. He spins me around and pulls me flush against him. His erection is hard against me as he walks me backward the rest of the way.

"I've been waiting to help you out of this dress since the moment I helped you into it," he says, his voice gravelly and deep.

My calves hit the bed and I go for his belt, quickly unfastening it before moving on to his pants.

"Do you have any idea how much I want to fuck you right now?" He reaches behind me and unzips my dress. "How hard I want to fuck you?"

The loud thrumming in my ears is muted by his moans, by his lips against my neck as he brushes the straps from my shoulders. My dress drops to my feet and he turns me around.

"Get on the bed, Francesca," he says. "Knees and elbows on the mattress."

Anticipation and desire flow through me like lava in my veins. I do as he says.

"Now spread your legs." His command is a whisper against my spine. He slips his fingers inside the waistband of my panties, and I feel the cool air kiss my bare skin as they come off. "You're so fucking hot right now," he says, leaning over me. His warm breath tickles my ear as his hand clutches my waist. "You might want to hold on."

Darian slams into me with such force, I'm propelled forward, my arms flying out from under me. I push onto my elbows and grip fistfuls of the bedding for support. He doesn't hold back. He fucks me. Hard. It isn't romantic. It isn't patient or sweet. It's just sex…and I like it.

See? You're not in love with him. You're just attracted to him.

We collapse on the bed, breathless and sated.

Darian works his fingers through my dampened hair. "Are you okay?"

"Of course. Why wouldn't I be?"

"I didn't mean to be so rough. I got caught up in the moment." Holding his hand to my jaw, he leans in and kisses me. "Don't move. I'll be right back."

He returns with a warm, damp washcloth and gently cleans me up before getting into bed. It's a gesture that's the opposite of rough; it's almost…*repentant.*

"Are *you* okay?" I ask him.

"Of course." He smiles. "Why wouldn't I be?"

We both lie down and he pulls me against him, his arms wrapped tightly around me, our legs intertwined. The room is dark but for the faint glow of the alarm clock. I can still make out his face, his pinched features, his wrinkled brow. He looks anxious. And he's watching me like he's afraid I might break.

I promise, Darian, I'm fine.

"What is it about you?" he whispers.

"What do you mean?"

He tucks a lock of hair behind my ear, then closes his eyes. "Nothing. Goodnight, Francesca. Get some sleep."

Get some sleep?

At almost four a.m., it's become clear I'm not getting any sleep. You can't say something like that to a girl—especially *this* girl—and follow it with 'nothing.'

Well, Frankie, Darian just did...three hours and twenty-six minutes ago.

I pull the covers up to my chin and stare at the sliver of light cutting across the ceiling. My mind spins with *maybes* until the throbbing in my head syncs to the pounding in my heart.

Maybe he literally meant nothing.

That's the most likely scenario, I think as I roll on my side to face him. *We're just temporary.*

As if he knows I'm there, Darian inches closer. My whispered name spills from his lips and a smile tugs at mine. He's dreaming about me.

Maybe we're just temporarily temporary...

"Of course I want her to end up with Blane, but every girl across the globe knows she should pick Duckie," I proclaim from the top of my *Pretty in Pink* soapbox.

"But she doesn't love Duckie." Darian sifts through our bowl of popcorn for the perfect piece to throw at me. "She's willing to wait. For him."

I pluck the popcorn out of my hair and throw it back. "Obviously this is a movie, but in the real world, Blane will always be Blane. She needs to give up on him and fall for Duckie."

Darian squints at the midday sun coming through the balcony doors. He climbs off the bed and walks toward them. "I used to be Blane," he says, drawing the drapes closed. The room darkens and it takes a few seconds for my eyes to adjust. I watch Darian's face as he returns to the bed expecting to see a smirk or a grin, but his expression is serious.

"Hold up." I roll onto my stomach with a pillow tucked beneath me. "What do you mean you used to be Blane?"

"I was that asshole in high school." He lies down on the bed, stretching on his side to face me. "My parents enrolled me in private school and it molded me into an arrogant prick." The look he shoots me says, *Hard to believe, I know.* "My mom was always throwing parties and charity events, and she used the same florist for all of them. The owner's sixteen-year-old daughter, Julia, worked there part-time, and my mom became very close to her. She even tried to set us up once, but I refused."

"Julia, Julia?" I say before I can stop myself.

Darian smiles. "Julia, Julia." A long swallow slides down his throat and his gaze falls to the bed. "I wasn't about to be seen with a working girl without a pedigree," he says, pulling at the sheet, twisting it between his fingers. "I totally disgusted my mom. She was convinced it was the private school's influence so she yanked me out and threw me in public school. Julia's school. To say I was pissed would be an understatement." He looks at me then. "And just when I thought things couldn't get any worse, summer came along and Mom got me a job with the florist making deliveries."

"Sounds like you had a good mom."

Darian rolls onto his back, his arms folded beneath his head. "I had a great mom," he says. "She was perfect."

The movie plays softly, like white noise in the background. It's the scene where Andie's father gives her the dress.

"I promise to do better than that," my dad once said to me.

Little did he know, I thought Andie's dad was perfect. I thought my dad was perfect too.

"Jules was impossible not to fall for," Darian says gently. "Believe me, I tried. She was everything I wasn't—kind, funny, good." He laughs. "And she wasn't intimidated by me at all. We both fell, hard and fast, but I was torn between my fucked-up pride and my feelings for her." He turns his head toward me and the corner of his mouth quirks up. "She loved me though, and she waited. Eventually I came to my senses and married her. I'm glad she didn't give up on me. I'm glad she didn't settle for Duckie."

I curl into Darian's side. He closes his hand over mine and holds it against his heart.

"Thank you for sharing that with me," I whisper.

"Andie knows her happiness lies with Blane," he says, "even if he never comes to his senses."

Never?

CHAPTER 11

Light My Fire

Darian: Racquetball Monday?

    Drew: Sounds good. How was SoBe?

Darian: Great. We stayed in bed all day yesterday.

    Drew: Nice. ;-)

Darian: Watching movies.

    Drew: Figures.

Frankie

Two whole days in South Beach, and we never once stepped in the sand or stuck our toes in the water. Not that I minded. A day in bed with Darian at The Ritz-Carlton was a nice alternative. Still, he's determined to make it up to me with a sun-filled day by the pool.

"I'm waiting, Francesca! One more minute and I'm throwing you in!"

"Keep your trunks on, Fox! I'll be right there!"

I exit the house in my new bikini with my sunglasses

low on my nose. Darian blows a whistle through his teeth.

"I have impeccable taste," he says from behind the grill.

The smoky scent fills the patio and makes my stomach rumble. "How are the burgers coming?" I ask. "I'm starving."

"Patience, babe. You can't rush perfection."

It's a beautiful day. The sun is almost directly overhead. It's warm but not quite as humid and sticky as it's been. Darian pulls off his T-shirt and uses it to wipe the sweat from his brow. His chest is golden and glistening.

"Come here and check these out," he says. He pulls his shades out of his back pocket and slides them on.

I smile. "I've seen burgers before."

"Then come here and let me check you out."

My smile blooms to a grin as I walk toward him. He picks up the remote sitting on the counter beside the grill and aims it toward the music system. The Doors come on.

"All Doors, all day, baby," he says, holding out his hand.

I take it and he spins me once before pulling me into his arms, serenading me with "Light My Fire."

It's the first time I've heard him sing, and it does something low in my belly that makes me want to skip lunch and go straight to dessert. I circle my arms around his neck and push up on my toes. "I love your voice."

He bends to me, our noses barely touching, and continues to sing. I stop him with a kiss. His hands slide down the bare skin of my back to grip my ass through the stretchy fabric of my bikini bottoms. He moans against my mouth and my lips part—an open invitation for his tongue. The stubble on his chin chafes my skin in the best possible way, and I'm eager to feel the sensation between my thighs.

"Maybe we should save the burgers for later," I say. "Like tomorrow. Burgers are better for breakfast anyway."

"Oh shit, the burgers." Darian wrenches away from me and turns back to the grill. "You little seductress."

I shrug. "Girl's gotta do what a girl's gotta do."

"John and I got a good thing going on over here," he says, tapping the side of the pit with his spatula. Then he points it at me. "Don't Yoko this band."

"Wouldn't dream of it, Paul," I say over my shoulder as I take off toward the pool. I dip my foot in the cool water and gradually ease in until I'm standing waist-deep, walking on my toes toward a lounger.

"Back Door Man" follows "Light My Fire" and the backyard comes to life with a little bluesy southern sin. So does Darian's foot, tapping away as he sings into his spatula.

"And I thought you were starving," he says over the music. "Breakfast is forever from now and it's"—he scrunches up his nose—"*breakfast*. No one eats burgers in the morning."

"Don't knock it 'til you try it."

"Fine," he says, holding up his makeshift microphone. "Sometime soon I promise we'll have burgers for breakfast. Deal?"

"Deal."

He returns to his *band*. The boy plays a mean air-guitar, and his voice, raspy and growly and just plain sultry, is affecting me in much the same way his fingers did in the elevator of the hotel. I can only imagine what he must have been like onstage, and I'm sure, when I'm back home, alone in my bed, I will imagine it often.

I climb onto the lounger and paddle to the edge nearest the outdoor kitchen to watch my dancing, singing, burger-flipping Adonis.

"I can definitely eat," I mumble to myself. Floating in the pool, watching Darian cook for me while he puts on a mini Doors concert, makes me hungry for a lot of things.

The loud thump of the lid slamming shut interrupts my ogling.

"Now we wait," he says.

I prop myself up on an elbow. "Wait? Why? You're making burgers, not brisket."

"Never question the master," he says, eyeing me over the rim of his sunglasses.

He walks to the far end of the pool and, with a running start, jumps onto the remaining lounger. He surfs halfway to the other side before falling in. When his head pops out of the water, he shakes it hard enough to splash me.

"You are seriously going to hurt yourself," I say, clearing the water droplets from my shades and then putting them back on.

Darian swims toward me. "Are you worried about me?" His smile is a playful smirk.

"I just mean…at your age."

With raised eyebrows, he submerges the side of my float and I roll into his arms. "Are you calling me old?"

"I'd never," I say with a teasing grin.

I laugh and splash and wiggle as he carries me to the deep end, but as hard as I try, I'm no match for him as he throws me into the water. By the time I make it back to the other side, he's hijacked my float. I shoot him a threatening look.

"Don't even think about it," he says.

I don't. Instead I climb onto his pretend surfboard and paddle to him. He reaches for my hand. We float beside each other with laced fingers as Morrison sings to us beneath the Miami sun.

I tilt my head to Darian. "I'm so happy I came."

And it's going to hurt like hell to leave.

He smiles. "Me too, Francesca."

"Oh, baby. Hold on. Let me help you," Darian says in the early morning as he tries to untangle me from the bedding. "Didn't you use sunscreen?"

"Yes I used sunscreen." *Once.* The sight of my lobster-tinted arms makes me queasy. My skin's on fire and everything aches. "I guess it wore off in the pool."

"I should have said something. That coastal breeze can be deceptive." He balls up the comforter and tosses it on the floor, then loosely covers me with a sheet. "Just try not to move." His voice rings from the bathroom. "I'll take care of you."

I notice the sheet marks embedded in my arm and sigh. "I look like I just woke up from a nap in an incinerator."

Darian clears his throat to suppress a laugh as he sits on the edge of the bed. "Here, take these," he says, pulling back the sheet I'm trying to hide under. He hands me a couple ibuprofen and a glass of water. "Francesca, you could be green and covered in scales and you'd still be beautiful."

I blush, but who can tell?

Darian reaches for the hem of my shirt and I freeze with fear.

207

"I've got aloe," he says, pointing to the bottle on the nightstand. "I promise not to attack you."

I curl my lip. "I hate aloe."

"You need aloe." With careful hands, he smooths the sticky green gunk over my burn, beginning with my forehead and ending with my toes. "Can you roll over?"

I do, and he gets my back.

He tosses the bottle on the bed and fans the sheet over me. "It's not so bad when it's dry."

I shiver, but aside from the initial chill, it makes me feel better.

He's so sweet, I think to myself as he lies down beside me and combs the tacky strands of hair away from my face.

But then he slides his hand in his pocket and, with a smug smile, pulls out a remote. He presses a button and the room fills with "Blister in the Sun."

"Really?"

"I'm sorry. That was mean," he says, turning the volume down a notch.

He carefully wraps his arm around me and I snuggle into him. Just as sleep begins to pull at me, the Violent Femmes are replaced with Johnny Cash's "Ring of Fire."

I elbow Darian in the gut.

He laughs. "Are you hungry?"

I ignore him.

"I'll feed you."

I perk up.

Welcome back, sweet Darian.

Darian makes it so easy to get swept up in the fantasy of being here, I tend to ignore the reality of going home. But it still gnaws at me—like a little voice in the back of my mind warning me not to get attached. And standing here in the guest room closet with my gaze fixed on my duffel, I realize just how attached I am.

My dad used to say, "Get out while the gettin's good." But the last time the 'gettin' was good' was the day I left Austin.

"I want to move your things upstairs," Darian says, the sudden sound of his voice jerking me from my thoughts. "I was going to do it yesterday, but I got distracted with your sunburn."

I step over my bag and lean against the doorframe with my arms crossed. "It's okay. I don't mind coming downstairs. It's not like I'm going to be here that much longer anyway." The words spill from my lips before I can stop them, and the look on Darian's face makes me wish I could take them back.

He sags against the wall and rakes a hand through his hair. "You're leaving soon?"

"Not right this second, but I can't stay forever. Besides, you have to work this week, and I should at least pretend to."

"Do you want me to take off? Is that it?" He paces back and forth in front of the door. "I will if—"

"That's not what I'm saying."

"It hasn't even been a full week."

"It will be tomorrow." My eyes are drawn to his feet, to the heels of his Chucks kicking at the wall behind him.

"Do you *want* to go?"

"No." My voice splinters. "I don't."

"Good." He clears his throat. "Go take your shower. I have a few things to take care of down here and then I'll be up to smother you in more aloe."

His smile is seductive, and I wonder if maybe he said chocolate and I just heard aloe. Crossing my fingers.

After grabbing a few things from my bag, I head upstairs for a lukewarm shower and then slip into a baggy T-shirt and a pair of boy shorts. When I step out of the bathroom, I notice my clothes are stacked in folded piles on Darian's bed. He's at his desk, a small secretary in the corner of the room, plugging in my laptop.

"You can work in here this week. The entire property is set up with wireless, so really you can work anywhere, but if you'd like an actual workspace, you can use this," he says, never lifting his head. "I got you some notepads and pens. A stapler, paper clips…can you think of anything else you might need? I can hook up a landline if you want. Oh, you'll need a mouse." He turns toward the door. "I think I have an extra one in my—"

"Darian, wait. This is fine. Thank you."

"It's absurd for your stuff to be down there when you're up here," he says. "I meant well, but I don't know what I was thinking." He moves to his bed, collects my clothes, and carries them to his closet. "You only had a few things left in the bathroom. I put them on the dresser."

Part of me wants to do cartwheels through the backyard, but the other part of me wants to hide in the closet right along with my clothes. I know it's just stuff. And I know it's only for a few more days, but the gesture feels…

"You're set up to work, and everything you need will be right here. There's no reason not to stay a little longer."

Confusing. I think we're back to confusing.

"Now lose your clothes and hop on the bed," Darian

210

says, holding up a bottle of cocoa butter.

I feel like I'm teetering on a tightrope and I'm not sure which way I'm going to fall, only that I will.

"No aloe?" I ask.

He smiles. "No aloe."

Then hold on tighter, Frankie.

Darian's doing everything he can to make me stay. He wants me here, and I don't want to be anywhere else.

What's so confusing about that?

I take off my shirt, quickly crossing my arms over my bare chest. I lie down on top of the covers, wearing nothing but my underwear.

Darian climbs on the bed and straddles my thighs. He sets the bottle of cocoa butter on the nightstand and pumps a little into his hand.

"The red's fading," he says, gently rubbing the lotion into my forehead and cheeks. He continues down my neck, paying special attention to my shoulders. The corner of his mouth quirks up as he peels my arms from my chest. "No hiding."

No hiding.

I laugh as he spreads lotion over my completely sun-deprived breasts.

"Sorry, Francesca, I can't help myself. Coincidentally, the fun parts are all burn-free."

The morning sneaks up on me, and I'm pulled from perfect sleep by Ellie Goulding belting out "Burn" through Darian's alarm clock. It's still dark. I can't see him, but I can feel him chuckling beside me.

"It wasn't me this time, I swear." His arm slides

around my waist and he carefully pulls me against him.

"Are you saying Mr. Classic Rock keeps his alarm preset to a pop station?"

"It's the only thing awful enough to make me want to get out of bed."

I laugh. "At least it isn't Kenny G."

He buries his face in my hair and presses a smile against my healing shoulder. "How are you feeling?"

"Much better," I say. "But can you do something about Ellie?"

He leans away from me, his hand flailing behind him until the song is silenced. "Ten more minutes."

I roll over and curl into the hollow of his chest. I can still smell the lingering scent of soap on his skin from yesterday's shower. His stubble scratches my forehead as he kisses it, and he's warm. His body against mine is like my own personal furnace. Waking up with him is even better than falling asleep with him, and though my head is telling me it's time to go, my heart begs for more mornings like this.

"I can't bail on Amanda today," he says. "God I want to, but I can't."

"I know. I'd never ask you to." I find his hand and twine our fingers. "I have stuff to do too. Real world and all."

We lie just like that for another ten perfect minutes until the morning Miami traffic chimes in to ruin it.

Darian makes a grunting noise as he pulls away from me. "I'm gonna hit the shower. Go back to sleep."

His bed feels vast and empty without him, much less appealing than it was only minutes ago. I kick off the covers and sit on the edge of the mattress, my hand fumbling clumsily for the lamp switch. Darian's Pantera T-shirt is on the floor by my foot. I pull it over my head and then dig through his drawers until I find where he put my underwear.

The house is dark and unfamiliar this early in the morning as I pad down the stairs and make my way to the kitchen. The sun is just beginning to rise and the moon is in its final hour, illuminating the sleepy backyard in wan light.

I turn on the Keurig and rummage through the freezer for Gloria's premade breakfast tacos. I heat two in the microwave, and I'm wrapping the second one in foil when Darian finds me. He's dressed in slim-fit light gray pants and a deep purple dress shirt.

"You look nice," I say over my shoulder as he walks toward me.

His eyes roll up and down my body in a way I will never tire of. "Mmm, so do you." He turns me around to face him, slips his hands beneath the hem of my T-shirt—his T-shirt—and cages me against the counter. His lips meet mine in an eager but brief kiss that ends in a lazy smile. "What's all this?"

"I thought you might be hungry."

He unwraps the taco I'm holding and takes a bite. "Thank you. I'm starving," he says, a hand over his mouth as he swallows.

The Keurig gurgles to life, and I fill his travel mug with fresh coffee. "I'm not sure how much milk…"

"None actually," he says. "Café con leche is a little rich for me this early. Please don't tell Gloria."

A frown pulls at my face. "We've spent weeks together now. How did I not know that?"

"Always on different schedules, I guess," he says, spooning a little sugar into his cup. "I don't drink coffee all the time, but when I do, just a little sugar, no cream."

I smile. "Sugar, no cream. Got it."

"I'm not placing an order," he says, laughing. "I just wanted you to know something insignificant about me."

"Nothing about you is insignificant," I say aloud even though I only meant to think it. I turn abruptly to the refrigerator and take out a Diet Coke.

"I like being on the same schedule as you," he says. "But you don't have to get up with me. The sun isn't even up yet."

"I don't mind." I pop open my soda, take a long pull, and then set the bottle on the counter. "When's Gloria coming back?"

"Not until I ask her to," he says. "I told her to take some time off—unless you want her here?"

"I don't mind her here at all, but I'm totally fine on my own."

Darian screws the lid closed on his travel mug and picks up his second taco. "I should get going. Call me if you need anything, okay?" He gives me a kiss on the cheek.

"Okay." I follow him as far as the family room and lean against the sofa with my arms crossed. "Have a good day, dear."

I grimace. *Really, Frankie?*

Darian turns, and it's happiness, not amusement, I find in his smile. "You too."

Frankie: I like him, Jane.

> Jane: You more than like him. You're in love with him.

Frankie: I'm not in love with him.

> Jane: Are you sure about that?

214

"Damn, Francesca. It smells amazing in here," Darian calls from the family room.

I set my pen on the mess of paperwork in front of me and rotate my barstool toward his voice. He appears in the kitchen, carrying flowers and a bottle of wine.

A smile spreads over my face. "Hot date?"

"The hottest," he says, striding purposefully toward me. He sets the wine and flowers on the counter and draws me into a slow, mind-numbing kiss. "I missed you today."

"I missed you too."

My legs circle his waist and my fingers tangle in his hair, pulling him back to me. His mouth opens in a smile against my lips and I slip my tongue inside. He leans closer, a gruff moan vibrating from his throat, and dinner is all but forgotten.

By me anyway.

Darian pulls back and his eyes cut to the stove. "I think something might be burning."

The smell of scorched tomatoes wafts through the air and I bolt from the barstool. The sauce is bubbling over the side.

"Oh no!" I turn off the flame and grab the wooden spoon off the counter to test the bottom of the pan. "Thank God."

Just the splatter that leaked onto the burner is burned; the sauce is fine. I smile in relief and then look up to find Darian watching me with an amused smirk.

"It's your fault," I say. "You distracted me."

"If I remember correctly, it was your tongue working its way into my mouth."

"Semantics."

He comes up behind me, snakes his arms around my waist, and rests his chin on my shoulder. I dip the spoon in the sauce and give him a taste.

"I thought you couldn't cook," he says.

"I don't cook very often, but I can. My dad cooked some, and I spent a lot of time at the diner as a kid. Much of it in the kitchen."

"I'd say it paid off. This sauce is fantastic. Spaghetti?"

I nod.

He steals the spoon from me and takes another bite. "So what did you do today besides slave over the stove?"

I shoot a glance at the stack of papers on the other side of the island. "I started working on an Easter brunch for an old client."

"Consulting?"

I smile. "I quit for a while, but I miss it."

"Good for you." Darian starts toward my spot at the bar. "Can I see?"

"Sure. I don't have much. Just some break-the-ice party game I'm toying with." I open the cabinet beneath the stove, looking for a spaghetti pot but find sheet pans and baking dishes instead. "Where's your—"

"Try the one on the right." He sits on the barstool, hunched over my notes, his chin resting on the back of his hand.

"My client has kind of an uptight family, and most of them don't drink. We have to come up with creative ways to get everyone to loosen up." I take the spaghetti pot to the sink and turn on the water. "Booze is best, but when that fails, give them games."

"How do you play?"

As soon as the pot fills, I set it on the stove to boil and walk over to him. "Those are prompts," I say of the list he's holding, "and they go inside plastic Easter eggs to be drawn and answered at random."

Darian sits back in his chair and studies the page. His stern expression makes me anxious, especially since this is the first consulting project I've attempted in almost a year. I lean over the counter, my elbows propped on the granite.

"Huh," he says.

"Is it lame? I was just brainstorming. I might—"

"Not at all." His eyes trail his index finger down the page. "Favorite color…last thing that made you laugh…books or TV—that's obvious…" He stops and a smile tugs at his lips. "Here's one," he says, glancing over at me. "Favorite movie."

My cheeks heat. Now it's *Pretty in Pink*, but I'm not about to admit it. "*Dirty Dancing*," I say, then wince at my lack of originality.

Darian grins. "I actually like *Dirty Dancing*. It's one of the only chick flicks Drew can get me to watch."

"Wait…Drew makes you watch chick flicks with him?"

"Drew thinks chick flicks and romance novels give him an edge with the ladies. It started as research, but now he's a die-hard fan."

"So this works for him? This misguided insight into the female psyche?"

Darian cocks his head. "I don't know that I'd call it misguided. He's rarely free on a Saturday night, if you know what I mean." His lips curl into a devilish grin. "So what about me? Do you think I've learned anything by association?" Before I can answer, he slides off the barstool and circles back to the stove. "Water's boiling. You ready to eat?"

"I've got this," I say, opening a package of spaghetti. "You do the wine. And don't leave me hanging. What's your favorite movie?" My hand juts out in front of me, stopping him. "Wait, don't tell me. I saw a lightsaber in your office."

He grins, and I know I've got him.

"*Star Wars*," I say, dumping the pasta in the boiling water.

I love that he's as unoriginal as I am. Every girl's favorite movie is *Dirty Dancing*, and every boy's is *Star Wars*—or so I hear.

"Not just any Star Wars. *The Empire Strikes Back*."

"Please. Same thing."

The cork makes a faint pop as he opens the wine. He begins to pour, then stops and sets the bottle down. "Did you just say, 'same thing'?" His pupils stretch wide and he points to the door. "Get out. Get out of my house until you've learned your lesson."

"I think your buns are wound a little tight there, Princess Leia." I grab the bottle and pour my own glass of wine.

I'm not going anywhere.

Yet.

The next morning, it's Miley Cyrus who drives us from the bed.

"Ellie's one thing," I tell Darian while pulling my T-shirt over a pair of shorts. "Miley's another. I was kidding yesterday, but if I wake up to Kenny G tomorrow I'm confiscating your clock."

He shoots me a mock glare as he passes me for the

bathroom. "Shouldn't you be making breakfast or something?"

I laugh. "Hungry for anything in particular?"

"Francesca," he says. "I was teasing. You don't have to cook for me."

"I like cooking for you. It's cooking for myself that gets old."

Darian turns around in the doorway and leans against the frame. "Well, when you put it that way," he says, grinning. "Something sweet? Your Easter project has me craving Peeps."

"I don't think I can top Peeps, but I'll see what I can do."

"This is nice," he says.

"What's nice?"

"Waking up with you."

I smile. "Yeah, it is."

I head downstairs into a very quiet, very dark kitchen. The sun hasn't even begun to rise. I flip on the light and the Keurig, then stand in the pantry with my arms crossed.

Something sweet. Hmm…

What's sweet that doesn't have to be made from scratch?

The only thing that stands out to me is a loaf of bread.

When's the last time you had cinnamon toast, Darian?

After rummaging through rows of spices, I finally find the cinnamon hiding behind several cans of misplaced peas on what appears to be the small appliance shelf.

When's the last time you had cinnamon?

And directly behind that, I find a pink Minnie Mouse PEZ dispenser.

Oh my God. It's so cute. Jacob would flip if it were Mickey.

I pick it up and blow off the dust. It's filthy. *What is that, mud?* "I think you need a bath."

"What are you doing?"

"Jesus, Darian," I say, my heart thumping in my ears as I spin around. "You scared the shit out of me." I hold up the PEZ dispenser, a wide smile spreading over my lips. "Check this out. I know you wanted Peeps, but look! PEZ! Did you even know you had this?"

Darian's phone vibrates in his pocket. He slips his hand inside and the vibrating stops.

"It's a little gross right now," I say as I examine it, "but if you have an old toothbrush I can…" I quit talking, and my smile slides off my face as my eyes meet Darian's hard stare. Then it hits me.

It's Anabel's.

I look from Darian to the toy and then back again. My body freezes in place, my grip tightening around the grenade in my hand.

"I'm sorry—I didn't mean…"

Darian blinks, then clears his throat. "Sorry for what? I don't even know where it came from." His phone vibrates again. He ignores it. "Just throw it away. If you're into PEZ, I'll get you a new one." He smiles thinly. "Clean with edible candy."

I don't move. My eyes begin to water. It's hers; I'm sure of it.

Then why would he keep it in there?

"Francesca, throw it away." His voice is stern this time and it makes me flinch.

"Okay," I whisper. I uncurl my fingers, and the toy falls in the waste bin. "I was…um…thinking of making cinnamon—"

"Actually, I'm not that hungry," Darian says, stepping into the pantry. He bends to kiss me. It's quick. "I'm going to go. I've got a meeting I should prepare for."

"Okay," I say again.

He adjusts his tie and then grabs his suit jacket from the island. "I shouldn't be late."

As soon as I hear the door to the garage close behind him, the tears I was holding back spill over. I slide down the wall of the pantry until I'm on my butt, and then I close my eyes and lean my head against a shelf. Anabel's sweet cherub face flashes in my mind, just before my father comes into view.

"Frankie, why do you have that, honey?"

I looked in the mirror. Dad's reflection stood in the doorway of my bedroom holding a cup of coffee. "Have what?"

"That." He nodded toward the newspaper clipping sitting beside me on the dresser. "A picture of that girl. The one from the crash."

My heart rate spiked. I didn't mean to leave it out.

I shrugged. "I don't know." I put on my pink, shimmery lip gloss, the only makeup I was allowed to wear, and smacked my lips together. "I found it in my school stuff. Thought I'd put it in my scrapbook."

Dad sighed. "I don't think that's a good idea, Frankie. You're finally doing better. What if the nightmares come back?"

They never left.

"It's not a big deal, but if it makes you feel better, I'll just throw it away." I felt this strange sense of guilt, like I was doing something wrong, but the relief in Dad's reflection told me I wasn't. I picked up the newspaper clipping and dropped it in the trash can beside my dresser. "Better?" I asked, turning around.

He smiled. "Better."

But it wasn't, not for me anyway, and as soon as he was gone, I took the picture of Anabel out of the garbage and hid it away.

Dad wore worry like a second skin that year, and I blamed my doctor. She convinced him that I'd linked the crash to my mother's death. She even had a name for it— *Grief Transference* or *Grief Displacement. Grief Something.*

It wasn't any of those things.

The crash was tragic. I was young. End of story.

I hated that woman. She made my dad anxious over nothing. The day I noticed that the bags under his eyes matched my own was the day I miraculously healed. The nightmares "stopped," and we never spoke of them again.

I dry my eyes on the hem of my shirt and get up off the floor. The same sense of guilt I felt all those years ago returns. I retrieve Minnie from the waste bin and put her back on the shelf she came from. Right behind the cinnamon. Right where Darian wanted her.

"Francesca?" Darian calls to me from downstairs and the apprehension I've felt all day swells to nervous worry. The tension rolling off him this morning was practically palpable, and I haven't spoken to him since.

"Upstairs!"

I considered calling him, but I couldn't bring myself to do it.

"Have you been up here all day?"

He pulls off his tie as he walks into the room. He comes straight to me, leans over the small desk I'm using, and kisses me. It's a much different kiss than the one he left me with this morning.

"I've been up here for most of it." I close my laptop and push back in my chair. "How was your day?"

"Better now that I'm home," he says, unbuttoning his

shirt as he takes off toward the closet. "Are you done?" He's acting so normal it's hard to believe this morning even happened.

Maybe it didn't. Maybe he was telling you the truth.

"All done."

He crosses from the closet to the bathroom, wearing jeans and a Rolling Stones T-shirt. "Good because I have a surprise for you."

My smile is hesitant. "A surprise? Wait…what kind of surprise?"

Darian cocks his head. "It's dinner. Am I allowed to surprise you with dinner?"

"Dinner's allowed." I peer down at my haggard appearance. "I need a few minutes though." *Maybe more.* "Are we staying in or going out?"

"Staying in," he says. "Take your time. I'll be setting up."

After a quick shower and a change of clothes, I head downstairs. The blazing fire in the courtyard catches my eye as I circle the banister at the bottom of the staircase. I find Darian outside sitting on the wicker sofa, cursing a…*hanger?*

"What's this?"

He looks up at me, a smile chasing away his scowl. "Hot dogs and s'mores," he says, holding up the hanger. "God willing."

I take the hanger from him and easily straighten it. Darian shakes his head.

"You gotta bend it first," I say with a shrug. "Years of practice." I set the hanger on the cushion next to him.

"Are you cool with this?" he asks. "I hope I didn't set your expectations too high with the word *surprise.*"

"This is the best surprise. My dad…" I flinch at the word, the memory of this morning flashing in my mind.

"Your dad *what?*" Darian asks. He reaches for my hand and pulls me onto his lap.

"My dad used to do this for me." My eyes begin to blur. "Now Jane and I do it for Jacob."

"You talked to her lately? I know you must miss her."

"We've been texting. She's a worrier and too intuitive for her own good." *Too intuitive for* my *own good.* "It's better if I don't actually talk to her until I get home."

Darian's jaw clenches. "Speaking of home, I know you must miss that too." He leans to the side and pulls the ever-present remote out of the pocket of his jeans.

I make a face. *Really?*

He laughs. With the press of a button, he takes me home to my backyard in Texas as a cacophony of cicadas and whip-poor-wills flood the courtyard. "I spent the last two days trying to think of ways to convince you to stay, but then it occurred to me you might just be homesick."

My throat tightens and I close my eyes, unaware of the few tears that dot my cheeks until he wipes them away.

"Although in retrospect," he says, "this might have had the opposite effect."

"No. It's perfect."

We sit quietly for a moment, just listening, and then Darian lifts his gaze to the sky.

"Francesca…what the hell is that whistling noise?"

A laugh bursts out of me. "Whip-poor-wills? They're birds. I love that whistling noise. It's haunting, isn't it?"

"Creepy is more like it." He takes my hands in his and glides his thumbs across my knuckles. "I want to take you away this weekend. Someplace without scary birds. Will you stay a little longer?" When I don't answer right away, he adds, "Someplace important to me."

I nod. "I'll stay."

CHAPTER 12

Blue Sunday

Drew: Can't make it today. New client coming in.

    Darian: I'm backed up anyway.

Drew: I bet you are.

    Darian: Fuck off.

Drew: Jeez Dare. Lighten up.

    Darian: Sorry.

Drew: So how long is she staying? I'm getting restless.

    Darian: No luck with the ladies?

Drew: None that like to fish at the crack of dawn.

Frankie

"Are you ready?" Darian shouts from the bottom of the staircase. "Car's out front. Grab your scarf…unless you want to use one of the communal scarves in the glove compartment." His laughter hangs in the air until the door closes behind him.

Jackass.

A silk scarf hardly goes with a faded University of Texas T-shirt and khaki shorts. I rummage through Darian's closet until I arrive at an Aerosmith trucker cap.

But this does.

"I take it back. Fuck the scarf," Darian says as I sit in the passenger seat. "You look pretty hot in a Backwoods Barbie kind of way."

Batting my eyelashes, I take his hand and place it at the hem of my shorts. "How long's the drive?" I ask in the southern drawl he likes so much.

His fingers walk up my inner thigh, just far enough to brush the edge of my panties. I hold my breath as he gently tugs at the elastic around the leg, then squeal when he yanks his finger free and it pops back into place.

"You're a bit of a road hazard," he says in his own terrible accent. He starts the engine and his come-fuck-me car purrs to life. "The drive is about two and a half hours, but if we get hungry we can stop for a bite in Key Largo. Pick some music."

"Key Largo? We're going to the Keys?" I drum my feet in quick succession on the floorboard of his car. "Which one?"

His smile is a flash on his lips. "Anabel Key," he says softly.

My chest tightens. "Anabel?"

"It's my island. Well, kind of." He laughs. "It's not as impressive as it sounds. I say island, but it's actually more of a rock."

Hearing him say her name for the first time sends a sharp pain to the back of my throat.

Darian shifts into gear and we head down the long palm tree-lined driveway.

"Where is it?" I ask. "I mean, how do you get to it?"

"It's off Marathon," he says as we wait for the gate to open. "I have a boat parked at the marina."

We turn onto the main road, and a few miles pass in silence before he speaks again. "It's named after my daughter, Annie, but I guess you probably figured that out already. I bought it shortly after moving here. I've never taken anyone before. Not even Drew."

"And you're taking me." My words are barely a whisper, but I know he hears them.

"I want to share it with you."

I turn toward my window and stare at the passing landscape through blurry eyes. The emotions I'm feeling are both perplexing and conflicting. This island is a product of Darian's deepest pain, and he wants to share it with me. *Why me?*

Is it because of what happened in the pantry?

Darian squeezes my shoulder. "Are you okay?"

"Am *I* okay?" I turn in my seat to face him. "Why would you ask me that?" My voice breaks on a small gasp and my hand flies to my mouth. I push back the threat of tears with an awkward laugh. "I'm so embarrassed," I say. "I shouldn't be reacting like this in front of you. I'm such a—"

"Human?" Darian says. "You're a compassionate, loving human. And that's one of the reasons I wanted to bring you. I can just be myself. I can just *be* with you."

He's quiet a moment, his hand resting on my shoulder, his fingers playing with my ponytail. "That's not something I get from anyone else." He laughs then. "And maybe I should have told you where I was taking you before I strapped you in my car and set off down the road. I've had ten years to get used to this trip, Francesca. You've had ten minutes."

My hands curl into fists. "Just the fact that you want to share this with me makes me happier than you could possibly know, but it sucks because you shouldn't *have it* to share with me. You shouldn't *have it* at all. This island shouldn't exist for you, but it does, and it's so fucking unfair."

I bite down on my lip when I realize the car has stopped and we're parked on the side of the road. Darian has a white-knuckled grip on the wheel.

"I'm sorry," I whisper. "I can't believe I said all that."

"Thank you," he says.

"For what?"

"For being the only person in ten years who isn't afraid to talk to me. It *does* suck. It is *fucking* unfair. And, Christ, that's so much better to hear than *God has a plan* and *Everything happens for a fucking reason.*" He draws in a deep breath and blows out a long exhale. "Enough of this. We're going to have fun this weekend, okay?"

I nod. "Will you tell me about her sometime? Annie?"

"I will," Darian says with a sincere smile. He takes his sunglasses from the console and slides them on. "I promise."

Frankie: We're going away for the weekend and there won't be cell/Wi-Fi.

> Jane: Where is he taking you? The moon?

Frankie: The Keys. He has an island.

> Jane: Of course he does.

Frankie: He's never taken anyone before. I'm the first.

Jane: Wow Frankie. That's big.

Frankie: I know.

Jane: Maybe he's falling for U 2. :-)

Anxious to get to the island, we drive straight through Key Largo and grab snacks and groceries from a market in Marathon. Thirty minutes later, we're at the marina boarding his boat. He sits in the captain's chair, and I sit nearby on the bench seat, transfixed as I watch him man the wheel.

"She's nice," I say as we pull away from the dock. "She looks new."

His eyes light up at the mention of her. "I just got her a few months ago." He grins proudly, his dimple breaking through. "She's my *other* baby," he says, waving goodbye to the Maserati parked in front of the marina. "She's fun. We can ski."

"I noticed you haven't named her," I say.

Darian laughs. "I've been leaning toward my *Come-Fuck-Me Boat*, but that seems a little cliché at this point."

We've barely made any headway, and already Darian looks as if ten years have melted from his face. And with each passing break, he seems to lose another.

"It won't be long," he says as the boat picks up speed.

I lean against the white leather cushion and tilt my head back, smiling as the late afternoon sun and sea spray kiss my cheeks. The ride is short, maybe fifteen minutes. I relax to the sound of the engine as the boat carves its way through the gulf.

Darian's voice brings me back. "There it is."

A giant grin replaces my smile as the island comes into view. The *rock*, as he referred to it, is small. A couple of acres, tops. But it's private, remote, and I can easily see why he was drawn to it.

"Welcome to my hideaway."

The boat sways in the bumpy current as we dock, and as I try to stand, the wind whips my hat backward until it catches on my ponytail.

"Take my hand," Darian says, his footing sturdy from experience. He helps me off the boat. "Another gust like that and I'll have to fish you out of the water."

We walk along the planked pathway toward the house. Nestled in the wild, untamed landscape, the octagon-shaped bungalow is a bright and cheerful turquoise, trimmed in white. It's cute, rustic, and true to form, not what I expected.

We cross a small deck with an old wooden rocking chair and a pair of empty bird feeders. Darian unlocks the front door and we enter through the living room. The interior is cozy and charming and reminds me of my cabin. The walls and floors are paneled in what appears to be old barn wood and are sparsely covered in patterned rugs and seascape paintings. On the right, a cornflower blue island with two aluminum barstools separates the living area from the open kitchen. I lean against the side of the bar as Darian unpacks our groceries.

"I love it," I say. "You continue to surprise me."

"The outside's even better. Speaking of, I forgot charcoal. Come with me and I'll show you. Fingers crossed there's a bag out there."

I follow him to the back deck, which is considerably larger than the front deck and has an outdoor grill and dining area.

"Yes! We're in luck," he says with animated enthusiasm.

I can't blame him. I guess popping into a convenience store isn't very convenient when you're on a private island.

"How do you feel about dolphin?" Darian asks, pulling the bag of charcoal from its hiding place.

My nostrils flare. "Dolphin?"

He laughs. "You're way too easy. Not Flipper, the mammal. Mahimahi, the fish…" He waits. "Dolphin*fish*?"

I exhale. "Mahi I can do. Flipper? I'd have to pass."

Darian fires up the pit and I decide to explore a little farther from the house. A sandy footpath through the heavily wooded terrain leads me to a small private beach. With my flip-flops dangling from my fingers, I push my toes through the untouched sand. Unspoiled and idyllic. That's really the only way I can describe it. I hold my arms in front of me, framing the view with my hands. A perfect picture of blue on top of blue—so similar in color, I have to squint to separate the ocean from the sky. The surf rolls in, stealing the sand from beneath my feet. I step back and grin—a teeth-baring, face-stretching grin.

The fact I'm literally stranded in this paradise with him makes me giddy. Okay, maybe not *literally* stranded, but a girl can dream. It's not like I can swim back to the mainland, so if he could just lose the boat keys or if the gas tank could just mysteriously drain or—

"You're a vision, Francesca."

His voice catches me by surprise and I spin around.

"This is extraordinary," I say. "I'm so glad you brought me."

Never take me home.

"Me too."

He reaches for my hand, and we stroll along the small stretch of sand to a weather-beaten log at the far end of the beach. It reminds me of *the bench* behind my cabin. We sit, facing the setting sun, and I regard it with newfound appreciation as Darian drapes his arm over my shoulder.

"I don't know how you ever leave," I say.

"I think it'll be harder this time."

I inch closer to him on the log and rest my head against his arm. Pastels paint the clouds like cotton candy floating over the ocean, and we're quiet for long minutes, just watching them drift by. The wind is gentler on this side of the island, but I can still hear it behind us, high above in the swaying palms.

Darian steals his arm from my shoulder and leans forward, fingers steepled, elbows on his knees. "Annie loved the beach," he whispers after a short span of silence. "I imagine she would have really liked this place."

My heart stills at the mention of her name, and I turn my body sideways on the log. Darian keeps his gaze fixed on his fingers but wears a small smile that grows despite the brittle edge to his voice.

"She was beautiful," he says softly, "and she loved me unconditionally." He sits taller, his legs extended in front of him. A muffled cough serves to clear his throat and leaves us both with glassy eyes.

"I know all kids love their parents unconditionally, but with her, I could do no wrong. And it was the same for me." His smile breaks into a laugh. "Jules used to get so frustrated, especially during Annie's terrible twos, but I just found her…enchanting." Darian rubs his eyes with the hem of his shirt and then blows out a breath. "Thank you for putting the PEZ dispenser back."

"Darian…"

He shakes his head.

"You're welcome."

"Come on," he says, squeezing my hand, "I'm sure the fire's ready by now."

After dinner, Darian takes me for a walk around the property. The moon is bright enough that we don't need a flashlight, so we just pick one of the many trails that circle the house.

Sounds of life filter through the brush, and I hold Darian's hand a little tighter. "And you think *my* place is scary?"

"At least I don't have harbingers of death here."

"Harbingers of death? Are you talking about whip-poor-wills?"

He shrugs.

"They're better than"—I motion to the trees—"whatever you have lurking out there."

Darian stops walking and crosses his arms. "Raccoons? You're comparing cute, little, furry raccoons to those devil birds?"

"Devil birds?" I clutch my stomach in laughter. "You make it sound as if they have beady red eyes and horns."

"They don't?"

"They're ethereal."

"Exactly. Like demons." He takes my hand again. "Come on. I promise to protect you from the evil coons."

The long, winding trail makes the tiny island seem deceptively larger. We take a right here and a left there, and I try to memorize landmarks so I can get around on my own. It doesn't matter though; with the beach only steps away, it would be hard to get lost.

We come to a small clearing and I stop.

Darian flashes me a proud smile as he walks on. "It's beautiful, isn't it?" He lies on his back on the moonlit ground beneath a blanket of stars. "This is my favorite part of the island," he says. "It's why I bought it." He pats the patch of sand next to him. "It's peaceful."

"Aside from the evil coons," I tease.

"Yes, aside from that."

I lie down beside him, resting my head on his shoulder. We point out the few constellations we know and make up several more. I gasp when a shooting star dashes across the sky, but before I can make a wish, I see another one.

"Just watch," Darian says. "Once they get going, they don't stop."

"The island of unlimited wishes," I say.

Darian laughs. "Good luck with that."

"What?" I nudge his side. "You don't believe in making wishes?"

"It hasn't worked for me yet," he says.

"Maybe you should try again."

"Maybe I should."

The next morning, we set off for the beach. Darian takes me to a spot on the right side of the shoreline where a flat rock emerges from the whitecaps. He sits in the surf and leans against the rock, bending his knees and spreading them wide enough to accommodate me.

"I take it you've done this before." I laugh. "The

rock, I mean. Not the girl between your legs."

I rest my back against his chest and bury my toes in the wet sand. The water is warm, and the clement ocean air mingles with his scent.

"A time or two," Darian says with a smile in his voice. "But it's better with the girl between my legs."

I tilt my grin toward him. "Well, girl or no girl, it's beautiful. I'd be here all the time. It's the perfect place to be alone and just think."

"That's the thing," he says. "When I'm here, I *don't* think. It's like the second I get behind the wheel of my boat, everything else fades away. There's no yesterday, no tomorrow. I get to be in the present." He's quiet for a moment and then, "That's why I've never brought Drew. He's seen me at my worst. This place is my escape and I worry that if I brought him here…"

"He'd taint it somehow."

"Yeah," he says. "But not intentionally. I don't want you to think—I mean, he's a great guy…"

"I get it. Even though he's in your *present* life and your *future* life, he's still part of the past you come here to escape."

Darian leans forward and drops his chin to my shoulder. "It's so freeing. Being able to talk to someone who understands. Who I don't have to explain myself to."

"Do you really feel like you have to explain yourself to Drew?"

He blows out a sigh. "I feel like I do, but I know I don't. Does that make sense?"

"To me it does, but it might not to him. I think you should try talking to him about it. Tell him what you told me." A soft laugh vibrates against my shoulder. "What? Did I say something wrong?"

"No. I'm laughing because what you said is exactly

right. Drew doesn't understand why I keep this place from him because I've never bothered to tell him." Darian smooths his hands up and down my arms. "I'm so fucking glad you didn't go home."

I turn my head to look at him over my shoulder. "What would you be doing right now if I wasn't here?"

"Fishing, probably." A slow, sexy smile unfurls on his face as he lowers his mouth to my ear. "But I think I like this better."

Desire flickers to life inside me. "Mmm. Me too."

He pulls my earlobe between his teeth and nibbles it gently, sending tremors all the way to my sand covered toes.

"I mean, I like to fish," I say, "but…oh God, that feels good."

"Francesca…"

"Mmm hmm?"

"No more talking."

I nod.

He digs his fingers into my hips and pulls me back, his erection like steel against my spine. "Turn around," he says, his voice deep and gravelly in my ear, "and spread those beautiful legs over me."

The desire inside me escalates to a full-blown inferno. I circle my body and straddle him, my fingers tangling in his hair as a smile dances on my lips.

Darian's eyes, shining like emeralds beneath the cloudless sky, bore into mine for long seconds before he leans in and brushes his nose against mine. "Yes," he whispers. "I definitely like this better."

I grab his face in my hands and our mouths crash together. His lips part, and I breach them with my tongue. God, how I love kissing him. I could kiss him for hours. I could kiss him until…

He slips his finger inside the leg of my bikini bottoms. *Okay. I love that too.*

"Ever been fucked on the beach in the middle of the day?" he whispers against my mouth. His hands move to my waist and he flips me onto my back. "Because you're about to be."

My body dissolves like warm sugar beneath him. He pulls off my bottoms and unclasps my top. Then he's inside me, driving me up the spongy sand.

I close my eyes. "God, Darian…"

His thrusts sync with the waves crashing over us. It's rhythmic. Almost hypnotic. His weight, combined with the friction of the sand against my skin, ignites my nerve endings. My orgasm is instant. I come hard, my eyes snapping open to the mid-morning sun, its rays like fireworks as Darian explodes inside me.

"Christ, I love fucking you," he says, giving me one last bruising kiss before lifting off of me. He pulls up his shorts as I feel around for my swimsuit.

"Oh no."

A laugh bursts from his throat, and I realize I've lost it. "Don't worry; we'll get you another one."

"It's not that," I say, jumping to my feet. "You gave me that bikini. It was a gift."

"Wait, Francesca. Don't…"

I take off through the surf, not heeding Darian's warning as it fades in the background. I only make it a few dozen feet before I tumble off a sandbar, but a long, muscular arm brings me back.

"I tried to stop you," he says, pulling me toward him.

The corner of my mouth quirks up. "Not hard enough."

Even on the sandbar, I'm barely above water. Darian lifts me up and I tie my legs around his waist.

"No. Running. Away." He stresses each word with the touch of his forehead to mine.

I'm not the one running, I think as I catch sight of my suit drifting toward the horizon. I let out a *hmmmph* and then turn back to Darian, whose eyes are locked on me.

He grins. "Good thing you won't be needing that."

Turns out, actual sex on the beach is just as tranquilizing as the cocktail. We turn in early and crash hard, but it appears I'm the only one who's slept in; Darian's side of the bed is cool and empty.

I kick off the covers and sit up against the headboard with my legs drawn and folded in front of me. The sun bursts through the window in blinding light and I shield my eyes.

Jeez, how late did I sleep?

I turn toward the alarm clock. A yawn rips from my throat and then settles into a six-year-old's grin when I see the Easter basket sitting on the nightstand.

It's Easter? I'm so turned around, I didn't even realize it was Sunday.

The basket is filled to the brim with a rainbow of plastic eggs. I pull a pink one from the top, open it, and find a small strip of paper inside that says, *Chocolate.*

Then I see the note.

YOUR PARTY GAME GAVE ME AN IDEA.

FOLLOW THE TRAIL TO THE CLEARING.

BRING THE BASKET, AND DON'T PEEK.

"Oops."

It's late morning when I step outside and everything is still fresh with dew. Darian drew a simple map on the back of his note, but in the light of day, the trails aren't that hard to navigate. I remember the flame tree where I need to make a left and the red maple where I need to make a right. The walk takes me roughly ten minutes, and if I wasn't carrying a basket, I probably could've made it in five.

Darian's shirtless and sprawled out on layers of blankets and pillows when I finally reach the clearing. His fingers are linked over his stomach and his eyes are closed. I think I caught him sleeping. A week ago, my mind would be brimming with salacious thoughts, but right now, all I want to do is curl up beside him.

I try to be stealthy as I cross the sandy ground, but the shuffling of plastic eggs gives me away. His head jerks in my direction, and he sits up.

"Good morning," he says, rubbing the sleep from his eyes. He stretches his legs out in front of him and then glances at his watch. "Or should I say afternoon?"

"It's only eleven thirty." I kick off my flip-flops and sit across from him. "Happy Easter, by the way, and thanks for this," I say, holding up the basket. "Whatever it is." I notice a cooler sitting behind him and a small storage tub just beyond that. I cock my head. "What is all this?"

His grin is elusive. "Thought we could do something…Easter-themed." He gestures to the cooler. "And I brought brunch."

"I have a confession. I accidentally opened an egg before I saw your note."

He pulls his knees in. "What did it say?"

"Chocolate." I smile. "And if you're planning on stuffing me full of confections all day, I'd be wise to skip brunch."

A hearty laugh bellows out of him and he rolls back into a pile of pillows.

My eyes narrow. "What am I missing?"

"Sounds like you're missing brunch," he says, lifting onto his elbows.

"You really made me brunch?"

"*Made* is a strong word. I have fruit and muffins. And mimosas. At least have a mimosa with me."

"I can do a mimosa," I say. "I'll save the muffin for later."

A smile slides over Darian's face as he digs in the cooler for champagne and orange juice. He's much more careful when getting into the tub. He lifts the lid just enough to pull out a pair of plastic champagne flutes. Whatever else is in there is meant to stay hidden.

"You're being very secretive," I say when he hands me my drink. I take a sip and then set it in the sand. "Your note said something about a game?"

"And you're being impatient, Francesca. Why are you in such a hurry?"

"I'm not in a hurry. I'm just curious."

"You're just curious because you think it involves chocolate."

I feign a frown. "It doesn't?"

"I think my idea of chocolate and your idea of chocolate may differ a little."

He waggles his eyebrows, and I shake my head as realization sets in.

"This is going to be kinky, isn't it?" I blow out an exaggerated sigh. "Oh well. Chocolate's chocolate. How do we play?"

Darian takes a long drink of his mimosa and sets his cup beside mine in the sand. "I do appreciate your enthusiasm," he says, reaching for the basket. He glances up at the sky. "And I suppose it wasn't much later than this when I had you naked in the sand yesterday."

"That's a very valid point."

He picks an egg from the basket and rolls it around in his hand. After a long, deliberate pause, he pops it open and pulls out a small piece of paper. "Ice," he says, grinning.

"Ice?" My shoulders fall. "Not ice *cream?*"

"Lie down, Francesca," he says. "Pull up your shirt and use it to cover your eyes."

I give him a pointed look. "I think I liked this game better when I thought I was going to lick chocolate off you," I say, lying back. I pull my tank over my eyes and try to ignore my bare breasts pointing toward the sky. I skipped a bra this morning, and the jury is still out as to whether or not that was a good decision.

I hear Darian rummage through the cooler, for ice I suppose, and I wait patiently until—"Ahh!"—he places a pile of it on my belly. It's so cold, my whole body clenches.

"Sorry, babe. I thought you were ready," he says. His voice is laced with humor.

"And I thought the eggs held yummy surprises, not torture devices."

"Torture devices?" He laughs. "I think ice *is* a yummy surprise."

"For you maybe."

"We'll see about that."

He unfastens my shorts and slides them down my legs along with my panties. I'm completely naked with my eyes covered and my ankles bound. For someone who usually spends Easter working doubles at the diner, this is definitely a change.

He spreads the ice over my chest, my navel, my—

"Shit, that's cold!"

It's a bitter, bone-chilling kind of cold and easily supports my original assessment of it being a torture device. My skin is frozen gooseflesh, and the little bit of ice melting from the sun dribbles down my sides in rivulets. They're acutely cold and ticklish, and when I begin to wiggle, Darian lowers himself on top of me.

"Try to stay still," he whispers.

He crushes the ice between us, grinding against it, liquefying it with the heat radiating from his body. The sensation of hot and cold is arousing in a way that completely takes my mind off chocolate. Need for *more* pools low in my belly and I go from wiggling to writhing.

"Darian…" His name is a moan followed by a giggle, then a grin. "The ice is a yummy surprise."

"Not a torture device?"

"Only the best kind." My voice doesn't even sound like my own.

He moves down my body, his lips and tongue trailing over my cold, wet skin. I fight the denim binding my ankles with no success.

"Let me help you," he says. His fingers slip inside my shorts, but instead of pulling them off, he pulls them up. "Your turn."

"My what?" I lift onto my elbows and adjust my shirt. "What do you mean my turn?"

Darian pushes the basket toward me. "Your turn," he says again. His smile is mischievous.

I'm beginning to get the *game* part of the game.

"Okay," I say. "You asked for it." I close my eyes and blindly choose an egg. It's pink, and hope flares in my chest that I drew chocolate again.

Close enough.

"Whipped cream," I say, arching my brows. "Not very original, but I'll see what I can do."

Darian pokes through the cooler until he comes to a can of Reddi-wip.

I slip him a curious glance. "You came prepared."

"You have no idea." He lies on his back. "Okay, Francesca, do your worst."

"You might as well remove everything before you get comfortable," I say.

"Everything?"

"Everything."

Darian kicks his cargo shorts to his feet but makes a show of stripping out of his Easter bunny boxers.

Of course.

"Sexy," I say.

"Thanks, but I was going for *eggs-cellent*."

I blink. "Oh Lord."

He links his fingers behind his head and lies stretched across the blankets like it's the most natural thing in the world. His eyes are shut and his smile borders on a smirk.

Kneeling beside him, I give the can of Reddi-wip a fervent shake. "All set?"

"All set."

"Open wide," I say in a singsong voice.

His lips curve into a half-smile, and then he slowly opens his mouth like he's visiting a dentist. Giggles burst out of me.

"This isn't supposed to be funny," he says.

"I know, I know." I blow out a breath. "Okay, I got this."

Holding the dispenser steady, I pump whipped cream onto his tongue. The sight of him—eyes closed, mouth open and filled with white foam—is beyond amusing, but I try to power through it.

"Mmm." I lean over him, touch my lips to his, and drag my tongue through the cream. "Mmm," I say again and then collapse against his chest in another fit of giggles.

Darian's eyes snap open. "What's so funny?"

"You. This." I laugh harder. "I don't know if I can be serious."

He gives me a playful glare.

"But I'm determined to try," I say, fighting a grin. "Close your eyes."

This time, I straddle him. I dispense a thick trail of whipped cream down his torso and then follow it with my hands, smearing it over his skin. Darian's cock grows hard and shifts between my legs. When I feel more laughter bubbling inside me, I stop and wait for it to pass.

"Really?" Darian says.

"I'm sorry. I can't help it."

He sits up with me still straddling him and makes a *tsk-tsk* sound with his tongue. "You only have yourself to blame."

"For what?" The words barely leave my lips before I'm flat on my back, looking up at him. "Did not see that coming."

He lifts my shirt to my neck, and I squeal and squirm beneath him.

"I bet you didn't see this coming either," he says.

"See what—ew." My face pulls into a grimace as Darian rubs the sticky cream all over my bare chest and stomach. I laugh again. "I hope you know this is the polar opposite of sexy."

He stops moving and pushes up on his elbows. "What would Francesca find sexy?" His sugar-coated lips touch mine briefly, then curve into a smile as he lifts his head. "My turn."

"Of course it is."

He puts his shorts back on and sits beside the basket. "The beach might have been a better location for this now that I think about it," he says, scraping the last of the drying whipped cream from his chest.

I pull my shirt down as I sit up and then lean against my hands. "I don't mind getting a little dirty."

"Let's test that theory."

Darian digs in the basket and pulls out a yellow egg. He shakes it and then rolls it around in his hand like he did the first time. His lips purse when he reads the piece of paper inside. "Feathers. Nope." He picks another egg, lime green this time. "Candle wax. Don't know what I was thinking with that one. Pass." And another—blue. "Handcuffs. Hmm, maybe later." And another—purple. His face brightens. "This'll work," he says. "Lady's choice."

"And what, pray tell, does *lady's choice* mean?"

"It means just what it says—it's your choice," Darian says, smiling. "Your wish is my command."

"I can pick anything?"

"Anything."

Hmm…

I take a long sip of my warm mimosa.

"Well, Francesca? What will it be?" He taps the lid of the plastic bin behind him. "We have all sorts of fun stuff in here," he says. "Feel free to take a look before making your decision."

I smile.

No need.

"Do I have to pick something from the tub?"

"Not if you don't want to," he says.

"I don't have to pick from the cooler either?"

He eyes me suspiciously. "You don't have to pick anything. You can just make a request if you want." A slow grin builds on his face. "An unfulfilled fantasy perhaps?"

I finish off my drink and toss the empty cup in the sand.

"Don't tell me. You can't take the torture anymore and you just want to attack me," he says.

"No," I say, drawing out the word. I smile nervously as I crawl toward him. "I don't want to attack you. I don't want you to attack me."

The air in my lungs feels heavy, like it's weighing me down. I sit back on my heels, Darian watching me curiously.

"I just…" *God, this is harder than I thought it would be.* "I just want to be with you. Without ice or feathers or—"

"Chocolate?"

I unbutton my shorts. "Or chocolate."

"You surprise me, Francesca. I figured you might be getting bored with all this endless fucking we do."

"That's just it. I don't want you to fuck me." I unzip the zipper. "You're right; we fuck all the time, and it's great. *Really* great. But you picked lady's choice, and this *lady*"—I smile on the last word as I pull off my tank top—"wants you to make love to her"—and throw it at him—"right here, in this beautiful clearing."

Darian lowers his head just as my shirt hits his chin and falls to his lap. He rubs the back of his neck, and a deep, weighted sigh gusts out of him. Without looking up, he tosses it back to me. "Please put that on."

I grab my shirt and hold it over my chest. "What's wrong?"

"That's not—I thought we…" He pushes to his feet.

"It doesn't matter. The answer's no. It will always be no."

My mouth falls open. "What are you talking about? I'm not asking for anything we haven't done before."

"Yes, Francesca, you are," he says, his voice growing louder. He paces across the blankets, shoves a hand through his hair, and then paces back. "Are you trying to tell me that every time I was gentle or slow, you thought we were *making love?*"

"Darian, that's not—"

The veins cord in his neck. "Goddammit, Francesca, I don't know what I need to do to get through to you. This will never happen. *We* will never happen!"

His shrill voice echoes loudly in the small clearing and I jerk back, swallowing a gasp. It takes a moment before the shock begins to fade.

Breathe, Frankie.

My eyes burn, my throat...

"Francesca," he says, calmer now, "we talked about this."

A few tears trickle down my cheeks, and then they all seem to come at once.

Darian's jaw clenches. "What do you think this is?"

I don't know. I don't know what any of this is.

I realize I'm still hugging my shirt. I pull it over my head, fasten my shorts, and push clumsily to my feet. Darian crosses the blankets to get to me, and his hand against my cheek makes my heart ache. I close my eyes.

Oh God, what's happening?

"Please don't do this," he says. "We have something really good going here." His hand falls away. "Please don't ruin it."

"I haven't—I didn't..." My throat thickens with fresh tears. "Darian, I'm not—I think I just..." I stumble backward and knock over the basket. "I'm not feeling so hot." Plastic eggs of every color spill onto the ground. "I think it's the heat."

I lose my footing and crush several of them with my bare feet. Jagged pieces of plastic slice through my skin, but I barely feel a thing.

I look at Darian. His eyes are wide and aimed at my feet.

"Francesca, wait. You're bleeding," he says. "Let me help you."

"No, please. Just let me go."

CHAPTER 13

When the Music's Over

Drew: Just scored 4 courtside Heat tickets! Gonna ask that hot little receptionist we just hired.

Drew: Bring your mythical girlfriend. Or are you still hiding her?

Drew: Hello? Courtside!

Drew: WTF?

Drew: Where are you?

Drew: She Devil is an impenetrable fortress but sweet Gloria can't resist me. The island? Really?

Drew: You suck, you know that? For 10 yrs you refuse to take me.

Drew: Motherfucker. Just friends, my ass.

Frankie

I'm curled in a ball on the cold tile floor. Scalding-hot water rains down on me, melting the caked sand from my feet in chunks. Somehow I managed to get away with only a few minor cuts, plus one slightly stubborn gash, which continues to bleed even under a constant stream of water. Eventually, the bleeding stops.

I get out of the shower and put on a pair of yoga pants and a white tee. I use toilet paper to bandage the cut and then cover my foot with a sock.

Now that I'm away from Darian and free to cry without judgment, I can't. It's like the tears that have been building for the last hour are stuck. My brain can't process what happened, and my heart doesn't want it to. I just want to sleep this off, and since the sun has no immediate plans to set, I toss back a couple Tylenol PM and wash them down with a handful of water from the sink.

Darian's sitting on the edge of the bed when I exit the bathroom, his gaze fixed on a white plastic box on his lap. He doesn't notice me come in, and I stand there, watching him for a moment before I make myself known.

"Shower's all yours," I say, combing my fingers through my towel-dried hair.

He holds up the box. "I have a first aid kit. Just want to take a look at your foot."

His voice is kind, and I'm in no mood to argue. I lie down on his side of the bed, the side closest to where he sits, and hold up my foot. He carefully pulls off my sock, but I wince when he tries to take off the paper.

"Francesca…" He makes a guttural sound in his throat. "The paper's stuck to your cut. Why didn't you ask me…" His question fades, and he gets up from the bed. "It's okay. I promise I'll be gentle." He disappears into the bathroom and returns with a warm washcloth that he holds against my foot. The paper dissolves, and he dabs the area until it's clean. "I was worried you were going to need stitches," he says. "This will be a little cool. It's just antiseptic; it won't sting." He smooths the cream over my cut and it instantly feels better. "It's definitely not as bad as I thought. Does it hurt?"

I shake my head.

Darian places a bandage over the cut and covers it with my sock. "I don't have a lot of comfort-type food here because I usually grill, but—"

"I'm not hungry."

"Francesca, you have to be. You haven't eaten today."

I hug his pillow beneath my cheek. "Please, Darian, just let me sleep for a little while."

"Okay," he says, conceding, but at least a minute passes before he stands. "Get some rest." He leaves the room and the door closes behind him.

I sleep hard and undisturbed for a full eight hours, but it's still only one a.m. when I wake. The scent of frying bacon wafting in from the kitchen sends my angry stomach into fits. I haven't had a thing to eat since dinner on Saturday.

I find Darian at the stove with a large cup of coffee in his hand and a dish towel slung over his shoulder. A small, rueful smile pulls at his lips as he turns around. He sets the cup on the counter and reaches for the towel to wipe his hands.

"Hey," he says, coming around the small island as I sit on one of the barstools. "How is it?"

"Better, thank you."

Darian crouches down beside my foot. "If you want to get it checked out…"

"It's fine, I promise. It doesn't even hurt."

When he stands, he's close to me, really close. I can smell the fresh scent of soap on his skin, even over the bacon. He slips his hands in the pockets of a pair of pajama pants I've never seen him wear. His shirt is a plain white V-neck. Something about it, something about *him*, just feels off. Everything feels off. I hate that this is where we are. And to think, if he had just gone with *handcuffs*, none of this would be happening.

"So, food," he says, returning to the kitchen. He takes a Diet Coke out of the refrigerator, pops it open, and hands it to me across the island. "I figured you'd be waking up, so I dug around and found biscuits and bacon in the freezer. How do you feel about breakfast? We had eggs and cheese so I thought I could make sandwiches." He doesn't wait for me to answer. "And please don't say you aren't hungry; your stomach was growling in your sleep."

"You checked on me?" My voice sounds small.

"I sat with you," he says and then quickly turns his attention back to the bacon. "Shouldn't be much longer." The oven beeps. He puts in the biscuits and sets the timer. "Everything else is ready."

I feel like I'm in such a precarious place with him. The lines between us have always been blurred, but lately, they've been nonexistent. Yesterday a line was drawn, and I don't even know why.

"Thank you for cooking," I say over my rumbling stomach. "I am pretty hungry."

He smiles. "Of course."

Darian attempts small talk while we wait for the biscuits, but I mostly stay quiet, nodding when I think I should, shrugging occasionally.

"I was thinking we could take the boat out today," he says, sitting beside me at the island. "Cruise around, maybe anchor somewhere and swim?"

My empty stomach suddenly feels heavy. "Um…we could do that."

"Did you bring another swimsuit? Because if you didn't—"

"I have one."

"Francesca, about yesterday," he says, turning toward me on the barstool, "what you said caught me off guard."

I look up at him, and his eyes briefly meet mine before dropping to his hands wrapped around his coffee mug.

"You say you're the overreactor," he continues, "but yesterday...I guess I just misunderstood. I did misunderstand, right?"

"Darian, it's not that you—"

"Because I thought we were on the same page." He lifts the mug to his lips and holds it there for a second, then sets it back down without drinking any. "I don't mean to lead you on, but that's exactly what I'm doing, isn't it? I care about you, Francesca. I like making you happy, but that's as far as this can go. I *need* to know you understand that."

"Darian, I do, but—"

The buzz of the timer cuts me off, and I slump over the bar, heaving a long sigh as he takes the biscuits out of the oven. One o'clock in the morning is obviously not the time to discuss anything serious when he's wired on coffee and I'm starving.

Darian sets my plate in front of me and then downs his sandwich in a couple of bites while standing over the sink.

"You don't have to wait for me; you should get some sleep," I say, my eyes darting to the cup of coffee on the counter. "If that's possible."

He shrugs. "I'll be fine. Are you coming back to bed?"

"I think I'm going to read for a while."

I don't miss the slight downturn of his lips or the way his brows pull into a subtle frown. His disappointment shouldn't bother me, but it does.

"Okay," he says, walking toward me.

He leans in like he's going to kiss me, but I pull back just enough to deter him. I can tell my rejection stings, which only makes me feel worse. He squeezes my shoulder instead.

"Don't stay up all night. We have a big day ahead of us."

We anchor in an empty cove, walled on three sides by jagged cliffs. The water is a deep cerulean blue, a stark contrast to the periwinkle sky. Clouds are few and far between and stretch like white taffy above us. The beauty of this place makes it easy to ignore the elephant in the room.

"Nice, huh?" Darian calls from behind me. "I mean, they should be. They've never been used."

I turn around. "Why do you have skis if you always come alone?"

"Drew," he says. "He gave them to me as a housewarming gift, but I'm pretty sure they were a bribe."

I smile. "So you'd bring him."

Darian lays the skis across the rear of the boat and takes a seat at the helm. "I'll bring him eventually." He peeks over the rim of his sunglasses at my foot. "So what do you think?"

"I don't think I should risk it," I say. "I'm not much of a skier anyway. I like it better when I can keep my legs closed. Together I mean. On my knees." I hide my face in my hands. "Like on a kneeboard."

Darian laughs. "Why don't we just hang out today? And tomorrow, if you're up to it, we'll go into Marathon for a kneeboard or a tube."

A lump forms in my throat. He says *tomorrow* like it's nothing, but to me it feels so far away.

"Sounds like fun."

"And I can teach you how to drive the boat," he says. "Matter of fact, come here."

My gaze cuts to the open water. "Maybe we should think about this. I'll probably crash into a whale or something."

"Nonsense."

Darian pats his lap and my chest tightens. The thought of being *that* close to him makes me anxious. I never did go back to bed last night. I stayed on the couch with a book and pretended to read.

A small smile touches his lips as I take hesitant steps in his direction.

"I promise, Francesca. It's easier than you think."

If only that's what I was nervous about.

I sit with him behind the wheel and focus my attention on the switches and gauges on the dash panel, but as soon as I feel his hands on my skin, my focus falters.

"You need sunscreen," he says, pulling the hair off my back. "Your shoulders are pink."

He digs the bottle of SPF 30 out of the bag by his feet and pops the lid. My head falls forward as he works the cool, satiny cream into my skin. His touch draws out an accidental moan, and I stiffen beneath his fingers.

"I can think of a few more places that could use sunscreen," he whispers against my neck.

Nervous laughter bubbles out of me. I climb off his

lap and move away from him, my arms wrapping protectively around my waist as I warm my face in the sun.

"I shouldn't have said that," Darian says from behind me.

My lips pull in a tight smile, and I turn around. "I think we need to talk about yesterday."

"I thought we did talk about yesterday."

"No, *you* talked about yesterday. *We* didn't talk about anything." I slip my hands in the pockets of my shorts and press my back against the wall behind me. "Darian," I say softly, "what you did in that clearing goes way beyond overreacting. You were *cruel*. You *yelled* at me."

He takes off his sunglasses and sets them on top of the console. Then he leans forward with his fingers linked, forearms resting on his thighs.

"In my whole life, no one has ever screamed at me like that," I say, my voice turning brittle. "Even at the diner, and I'm not a very good waitress. Darian, the fact that it was *you*—"

"Francesca…"

"Can you not see how much that *hurt* me? You didn't even apologize."

He sits up. "Of course I apologized."

"No, Darian, you didn't."

"I'm sorry then. But it was just a stupid misunderstanding. It happens." Darian shoves out of his chair and moves to the rear of the boat. "Why do we have to make a big deal out of it?"

"Because it *is* a big deal. It's a big deal to *me*."

He stands with his legs planted wide, his arms crossed. "Yell at me."

"What?"

"Yell at me," he says again. "Even the score so we

can move past this. Be *cruel*. Say what's on your mind. Come on, Francesca."

My heart sinks. "I don't want to yell at you."

"Why not?"

"Because I'm hurt, Darian, not angry."

"What if it were Jane?" he says. "What if Jane had overreacted?"

"What does Jane have to do with this?"

"Just humor me, Francesca."

I look out over the gulf and watch the birds circling in the distance. "Jane would never talk to me that way."

"Let's say she did. Would you be *hurt*?"

My gaze darts back to Darian. I move away from the wall and take a step toward him, my arms at my sides, my hands clenched into fists. "If Jane screamed at me the way you did yesterday, I'd be pissed. I'd tell her to fuck off."

"Then be pissed at *me*," he says, his face twisting in a scowl. "Tell *me* to fuck off."

"I can't!"

"Why not? What's the fucking difference?" He links his fingers behind his head and turns away from me. "Why be pissed at Jane and not me?"

"Because I'm not in love with Jane!"

Oh God.

My hand catches a sharp gasp as it leaves my lips. I spin away from Darian and brace myself against the fiberglass wall.

Jane's right. I'm in love with him.

The wind starts up and the boat begins to sway. A large osprey flies overhead and casts an ominous shadow. It chirps loudly, breaking the short silence that settled in.

"The water's getting choppy," Darian says. "I didn't check the weather. I don't want to get caught out here if it storms."

I sink into the closest seat and keep my eyes trained on the bird as it circles above us.

It was such a beautiful day, and then the sun just disappeared.

Darian secures the skis, then moves to the helm. "I've missed a lot of work that I should get back to," he says over his shoulder. "And I know you have stuff to catch up on."

I nod, but I don't think he sees me.

"I'd like to get out of here by seven tomorrow if you can be ready," he says.

I nod at that too.

The drive back to Miami is unbearably tense. Darian doesn't speak to me once, nor does he turn on the radio. Two and a half hours is a long time to be punished by that level of silence. I stay curled against the door for most of it, pretending I'm asleep.

We get to Darian's place at a quarter past ten. He parks in the forecourt, directly in front of the house. I lift my head as he cuts the engine.

"We're here." His voice is quiet. He keeps his eyes and hands on the wheel and makes no immediate move to get out of the car.

A trace of hope flickers in my chest. I take off my seatbelt and turn toward him, but he still doesn't acknowledge me.

"Will you please say something?" I ask.

"What do you want me to say, Francesca?"

"Anything, Darian. Everything." I hug my shoulders, resting my cheek on the back of my hand. "Something."

He says nothing.

"You can't seriously be mad at me. It's not like I planned this. You aren't some asshole I'm fucking. You're a genuinely good guy—maybe not right this second but usually. Of course I was going to fall for you."

Darian reclines his seat back and crosses his arms over his chest. "Yes, Francesca, I can be mad at you," he says. "I'm fucking pissed. I was up-front with you. I told you from day one, nothing could come of this. And what did you say? You said, 'We're both adults,' and that I wouldn't have to worry about you."

My nails dig into my palms. "And what did *you* say, Darian? You said we were *friends*."

"We are friends!"

"No, we're not. You buy me expensive gifts, you take me on dates, you cook for me, bring me flowers—that's not what friends do. What the hell was I supposed to think? I even called you out on it. I told you it was confusing. The very next day, you took me on a romantic getaway to South Beach."

Darian opens his mouth to speak, but I cut him off. "I'm not blaming you. It's not like I woke up this morning and thought, *Darian's saying one thing and doing another.* I knew you were sending me mixed signals, but I only paid attention to the ones that suited me. I'm a masochist, Darian, not an idiot. So be mad at me if it makes you feel better, but you're gonna have to get in line." I draw a shaky breath and reach for the door handle. "I'll take a cab to the airport and book a flight when I get there."

"Wait." Darian reaches for my hand, and I swear my heart stops when his fingers close around it. "I talked you into coming. You were hesitant, and I…" His words fall away as his thumb sweeps over my knuckles. "And you hate flying. I'll have a plane ready by one."

I nod, my eyes filling with tears behind the dark lenses of my sunglasses.

"Francesca…" He squeezes my hand once, then lets it go. "Let me know when you're ready."

I grab my clothes from Darian's closet and carelessly throw them on his bed.

What did you expect, Frankie?

I empty the drawer he gave me and then clear my stuff out of his bathroom.

Did you think you were just gonna laugh it off and go back to the way things were?

I shove everything in my duffel.

Pretend it never happened and never speak of it again?

I fold his Doors T-shirt and leave it on his dresser. Then I pick it up and stuff it in my bag. Then I put it back on his dresser.

Or did you think he'd be in love with you too?

I take one last agonizing look around. It's all so very normal. The same faint tick of the library clock sounds through the bedroom door. Birds tweet from the same branch outside the window. The late morning sun warms the same area of carpet and casts the same yellow glow on the walls. Everything is exactly as it was before me and will be this way long after I'm gone.

"Darian?" I call his name as I descend the staircase, my duffel strapped across my chest, my laptop bag hanging from my shoulder. I'm met with more of his silence…

And the addition of a scribbled note on the console table.

I HAD AN EMERGENCY AT WORK.
I'M SORRY I COULDN'T STAY.

CJ WILL BE HERE AT NOON
TO TAKE YOU TO THE AIRPORT.

HAVE A SAFE FLIGHT.

DF

My heart drops like lead to the pit of my stomach. He isn't even going to tell me goodbye.

"Hello, milady. Your chariot awaits," CJ says as I slide into the backseat of the familiar Mercedes SUV.

"Hello, CJ."

Despite my desire to sleep, I stay awake for the drive.

"Traffic is at its best this time of day," CJ tells me.

His eyes meet mine in the rearview mirror and I manage a smile.

Rural becomes urban, and homes become buildings as we close in on the airport. Anxiety builds inside me at every turn, and by the time we pull onto the tarmac, I'm ready to crack. My stomach is a tangled mess of nerves and it has nothing to do with flying, only flying *away*.

"We're here," CJ says as he puts the car in park.

I turn to look out my window and I see a small jet, dark blue and silver with burgundy trim.

Of course.

It's like this whole trip has turned into a bad movie playing in reverse. The same driver, the same car, the same plane.

So I take the *same* seat by the window because why not?

God, this sucks.

My finger hovers over Jane's number for a while before I press Call, and any semblance of calm I possessed crumbles the second she picks up. My voice breaks as soon as I say her name, and then I completely fall apart.

"Frankie? What's wrong? Are you okay?"

"I'm coming home," I say, choking out the words. "You were right about me. Wrong about him."

There's silence on the line, then a sigh.

"Oh, Frankie. *Fuck*. I'm so sorry."

"I thought things were changing. I thought…" I wipe my eyes beneath the lenses of my sunglasses. "No. He said *friends*, and I should have listened."

"You aren't friends," Jane says. "You never were."

"Then why did he insist on calling us that?"

"I don't know, sweetie, but my guess is…he *had* to."

I stare out the window as CJ's SUV rolls out of sight. "Why do I feel like this? It hasn't even been that long."

"It doesn't matter how long it's been," she says. "Love happens when it happens. Some people fall in love; some people start out that way."

And some people refuse to love at all.

CHAPTER 14

Love Street

Darian

A sigh of relief gusts out of me when I pull into Drew's driveway and notice his car's missing. God bless him for having a real job that he actually goes to, unlike me. Amanda can be trying at times, but she deserves a goddamn medal for the way she covers for my sorry ass.

I cut the engine and grab my phone from the console. Francesca's nonexistent texts and voice mails sting like a fresh wound doused in alcohol. My own absurdity makes me laugh. *Why the fuck would she call me?*

She wouldn't. You made sure of it.

I glance at the bottle of Macallan 18 in the passenger seat. "Actually, dousing a fresh wound in alcohol sounds like a damn good idea," I mumble as I scroll through my phone.

I find a string of missed texts from Drew, and I think it's safe to say I'm on his shit list. His last text in particular sends a two-fold stab of guilt to my chest.

Drew: Motherfucker. Just friends, my ass.

Yeah, well, not anymore.

Darian: Hanging out at your place. We'll talk tonight. Bring steaks.

After the accident, Drew's place became my sanctuary. I'd lived in a hotel for months. Room service and On Demand movies had replaced family dinners and bedtime stories with my daughter. It was the worst kind of lonely, and it was self-inflicted. I'd pushed everyone away. Gloria was patient for a while and gave me space, but Drew wouldn't let up. He'd show up at my hotel at six o'clock every goddamn day with a six-pack of beer and takeout. It'd taken me two weeks to realize he wasn't going away, so I started coming here—earlier and earlier each time until it was just expected I'd be here when he came in from work.

I step inside and lock the door behind me. The familiarity of this place goes a long way to propel me from my funk. Leather, dark wood, stainless steel—despite his penchant for chick flicks, or maybe because of it, Drew's place is *almost* masculine. He prefers remote controls to knickknacks and Kandinsky to Monet, but he burns fucking *man* candles. I hated the damn things when I was here all the time, but right now, the lingering scent of vanilla bourbon is a welcome change from honeysuckle.

I walk straight through, out the back door and across the yard, then plop my ass in one of the two Adirondacks on the dock. I slip on my sunglasses and stare across the sun-drenched canal as I untwist the cap off my bottle of scotch. I welcome the burn of that first shot as it slides down my throat and the numbness that builds with every one that follows. The noise in my head begins to dissipate and I relax for the first time in days. Tension slips from my shoulders at the sounds of seagulls crying overhead, the cover on Drew's boat flapping in the wind, and…

Drew's voice as he comes up behind me on the dock. "Hey, man, what happened?" he asks, the wood creaking loudly beneath his feet.

Fuck me.

"Nothing happened. She went home." I glance over my shoulder at him.

He's Mr. Professional in dress pants and a button-down while I'm Mr. Slacker in board shorts and a tank. He takes a long pull of water from the bottle he's carrying; I take a long pull of scotch.

"I needed to get out of the house. That cool, or are you still pissed?"

Drew drags the second Adirondack across the wooden slats of the dock and my face twists in a grimace at the sound.

"I'm over it," he says, stopping to study me. He finishes off the last of his water and tosses the empty bottle over my head. "You look like hell. No fun kicking you while you're down."

"Thanks." I take another swig of my scotch. "Why are you here? Don't you have a day job?"

He laughs. "Don't you?"

"Touché."

He sits down with his ankle crossed over his knee, his fingers steepled and resting on his calf. "My best friend texts me that he's hiding out at my place when he's supposed to be doing the dirty with his smokin'-hot, extracurricular, twenty-something *friend*. I'm a grief counselor. You're obviously grieving. I *am* working."

"I'm not fucking grieving," I say as I pass him the bottle.

He takes a long look at the label and then shakes his head. "Whatever, man."

"It was time for her to go and I didn't want to drag it out. I hired her a car and a plane. I'm not a *total* asshole."

He chokes on a swallow. "You didn't even take her to the airport? Shit, Dare, what happened?"

"What do you think happened?" I hold out my hand.

He tosses back another shot, then hands me the bottle. "Why won't you just admit you're in love with her?"

My jaw clenches. "Give up, Drew. It's the other way around."

"Jesus, Darian. You *are* an asshole. Let me guess. She fessed up and you sent her packing?"

Let's not forget the part where I yelled at her.

I take a drink. "I didn't send her packing—exactly. Like I said, it was just time. Things were about to get complicated."

"About to?" Drew says with a laugh. "Do you hear yourself? Things got complicated the moment you met her. You haven't so much as looked at a girl in five years. Then all of a sudden you're besties with one? When did you fall for her, Dare? Was it love at first sight or did it happen after you fucked her?"

My fist strikes the arm of the Adirondack a little harder than I intend. "I didn't fall for her," I say bitterly. "I've been in love once in my life, and you fucking know it."

"You wanna know what I know?" Drew says, bending toward me. "I know I've kept my mouth shut for far too long. It's been ten years, man. Ten fucking years. If you want to throw away all the good shit that happens to you that's your prerogative, but don't sit there acting so fucking oblivious. Your actions affect other people—

innocent people. Open your goddamn eyes."

I put the bottle to my lips and slowly tip it back, dousing my anger before it detonates. Drew doesn't deserve it.

She didn't deserve it either.

"I didn't get to meet the lovely Francesca," Drew says as he sinks back in his chair, "but even I knew she was in love with you. She had to be."

"How so?" My voice is quiet.

"Because she followed you here. She *stayed* with you here despite that bullshit friend thing you laid on her. Girls hate that, by the way."

"It isn't bullshit."

"It's just a word, Darian. A label. Let it go because it *is* bullshit." He smooths his hand over his cropped hair. "Whether you want to admit it or not, what you had was a relationship, not a friendship. Can't you see what's going on here? You're so full of guilt over Julia you had to label this thing with Francesca just so you could rationalize it."

"That's ridiculous."

"Is it? Can you honestly look back on the past few weeks and mean that? Casual sex, fuck buddies, *friends with benefits*—whatever you want to call it entails late-night booty calls and occasionally hanging out. Not"—he waves his hand in front of me—"whatever it is you two were doing. You chased her home from Austin. You took her to SoBe. Dare, you took her to your fucking island." His arm falls limp. "It's okay if you have feelings for this girl. You're allowed to move on. Julia—"

"That's enough, Drew."

"Would have wanted you to."

"Enough!" I shout, my hand clenched tight around the neck of the bottle. "She's gone. They're both gone.

Let it go." I take a long, numbing swig.

"Okay, you win. Waving the white flag." Drew stands, pries what's left of the Macallan from my grip, and lets out a pained sigh. "What a waste," he says, hugging the bottle to his chest. "All right. Get off your stubborn ass and ride with me to the store. We're gonna need more scotch."

The blanket I drag over my eyes does little to dull the sharp pain slicing through my skull. We polished off the scotch rather early and then I went to beer. No wonder I feel like hell. My empty stomach churns at the memory, and I carefully sit up on Drew's couch, squinting as my eyes adjust to the light.

My headache dampens my senses, but the faint smell of food cooking lures me to the kitchen. I go straight for the ibuprofen Drew keeps in the cabinet above his sink and toss it back with a handful of water. Then I see the bacon. *God bless him.* Drew's famous BLT is worth every bit of the hangover I have to endure to get it.

"I don't deserve you," I say as the door to his garage swings open.

"No, probably not." Drew comes in carrying a twelve pack of bottled water and tosses one to me over the island. "How are you feeling?" he asks, sounding fucking sprightly.

"Worse than you from the looks of it." My voice comes out rough and gravelly. I open the bottle and take a long pull before speaking again. "You seen my phone?"

Drew sets the water on the counter and then picks up a package of sourdough. He loads two slices in the toaster. "I skipped the beer last night," he says, grinning, "and your phone's on top of the fridge."

"Uh…why?"

"Because as much as I want you to call Francesca and put an end to this bullshit, last night was not the time, and you, my friend, were adamant."

Oh God, I remember.

I was desperate. I just wanted to hear her voice. Even if all she had to say to me was *Fuck off.*

My head falls back. "You are a good man," I say, reaching for my phone.

The weight of Drew's stare is heavy as I glance at the screen. No new messages. I try to keep my expression neutral, but I'm not sure I succeed. Her absence is pervasive. I feel it in my bones.

What did you expect?

The bread pops out of the toaster and Drew goes back to building my sandwich. "Why don't you call her now?" he says. "It's almost noon, and you seem sober enough."

I slide my phone in my pocket and lean against the fridge with my arms and ankles crossed. "I don't want to call her." I sound petulant.

Drew smirks over his shoulder as he opens a jar of mayonnaise. "You sure wanted to last night."

"I also wanted to buy a yacht and move to Zimbabwe last night."

"Yes, yes, you did," he says, bent over the counter, laughing. "And you were adamant about that too." He pushes my plate toward me on the island. "But eat first. You can sail to Africa later."

I take a huge bite of my BLT and my eyes roll back in my head as the salty bacon and requisite Brie attack my hangover. "Why aren't you eating?"

Drew snickers. "You might not remember, but I made a pretty big breakfast last night. Then you passed out, and I ate for two."

"I remember you taking too fucking long." I wolf down the rest of my sandwich and carry my empty plate to the sink. "Shouldn't you be at work? Did you get fired and forget to tell me?"

"I thought we could do some fishing."

His smile is suspicious and I know better than to trust it.

"Good try," I say, digging my keys out of my pocket.

"What? You're leaving?"

"It's past noon; you never fish this late. So just spit it out so I can go home and enjoy my hangover in peace."

Wearing a stiff smile, he links his fingers behind his head and casts his gaze at the ceiling.

"I'm not calling her," I say. "You need to let this go."

"I can't let this go." Drew drags his hand down his face and then turns to me.

His eyes are heavy and red, and I can *feel* the pain they've held for me all these years. I wonder what it's like to stand by while your best friend withers away, knowing there's not a fucking thing you can do about it.

"You've been given a second chance," he says. "It may be nothing or it may be everything, but I can't just sit here and watch you waste it."

"Yesterday you said it was my prerogative."

"And yesterday you were being a douche." He shrugs. "But last night…when you talked about her, even when you complained about her…*you came alive.* You've made some fantastic mistakes over the years, but pushing her away might be your biggest one yet."

My hand closes in a tight fist around my keys. "That's far from my biggest mistake."

"Dare, come on," he says. "It was an accident. One of these days, you're going to have to accept that."

I grab my sunglasses off the counter and slide them on. "Annie would have been fourteen tomorrow," I say, my voice thick but quiet. I draw in a deep breath. "Fourteen. Is that dating age? Probably not to Julia." I let out a small, hollow laugh. "She'd have said eighteen, I'm sure. Maybe thirty."

"Jesus. I'm sorry, man. I forgot."

"Don't be. I forgot too. I mean, I knew it was coming, but then"—I shake my head—"I got preoccupied."

Drew's hand closes on my shoulder and I turn around.

"I tried to make her fit, Drew, but I can't. I can't have them both."

"You're right," he says gently. "You can't have them both. So let yourself be happy with the one you can."

It was the band's manager, Rick, who first told me the plane had gone down. He couldn't be sure it was our flight, but he was confident my family and I weren't on it. It appeared Global Records had saved our lives that day.

I'd been cruising down the interstate with our demo cranked at full volume so I hadn't heard my phone blowing up on the passenger seat. It was the blinking blue light that finally caught my attention. I turned down the music and glanced at the screen. I'd missed seven calls from Rick. I answered on the eighth.

"Oh thank God," he said.

I remember thinking his voice sounded strange, like

he was both panicked and relieved at the same time.

I don't remember anything else.

My mom used to say the best memories were often the most painful in times of loss, and I went to great lengths to bury mine. Anyone who says you can't avoid grief doesn't know how to do it properly. The trick is to stay focused; one false move and everything goes to shit. The label was my focus. Francesca was my one false move. I brought her into my life without thinking it through, and now I can't think of anything else. I shouldn't be thinking of her at all. I shouldn't be missing her, especially today.

It's been almost twenty-four hours since I left Drew's, and every single one of them has felt endless. I can't concentrate enough to work and I can't relax enough to sleep. I lay in bed most of the night just waiting for the sun to rise, but it's nearing ten a.m. and I'm still here.

At fifteen past eleven, the strong scent of garlic seeps through the air-conditioning vents in my room. It isn't the first time Gloria's lured me to the kitchen with food, but it is the first time I'm annoyed by it. I specifically remember telling her not to worry about me until Francesca went home, and she has no way of knowing—

"Drew told her." His name elicits an eye-roll as I pick my jeans and T-shirt up off the floor and put them on. "Drew, Drew, Drew."

"You look pitiful, *mijo*," Gloria says to me as I enter the kitchen. She's standing over the stove, wearing the same vintage floral apron she's worn since I was a child. It used to be red, but it has since faded to an orangey pink.

"I feel pitiful. Thanks for noticing." I give her a quick kiss on her cheek. "What are you doing?"

"Making you homemade tomato soup," she says.

"What does it look like I'm doing?"

"I mean, what are you doing *here*?"

"Oh, that. I talk to Drew." She holds up a spoonful for me to taste.

"Needs citrus," I say, reaching around her for the fruit bowl. I grab a lemon and quarter it on the cutting board by the sink. "Did you call Drew or did Drew call you?"

"Does it matter?"

"No, I suppose not." I heave a sigh. "I'm fine, by the way. I appreciate your concern, but I'm fine."

"Is that so? A minute ago, you were pitiful." She wipes her hands on her apron as she turns around. "Now go sit so you can eat."

I watch Gloria move around the kitchen with effortless grace. She ladles soup into two large bowls, tops them with a squeeze of lemon, and then pulls a tray of grilled cheese sandwich triangles out of the warmer. A smile breaks across my face as she slides the tray toward me.

"You cut off the crusts."

"Just like your mama used to."

She rounds the island with a bowl of soup in each hand, and I take them from her before helping her onto a barstool.

"Sometimes there is nothing we can do to help the people we love so we do what we can to make them smile," she says as she adjusts herself in her seat. "Your mama said that to me after I lost my Theodore. *Dios mío.* That was a long time ago. I was still working for your grandma."

"You worked for Gram?"

"*Sí.* It wasn't until you were born that I came to work for your parents." She pulls off a piece of her sandwich and dips it in her soup. "I have known you your whole life, *mijo*, and I mostly stay out of your business…"

"But…"

"But"—she smiles—"I have something to say. If you don't want to talk, that's fine, but I want you to listen."

I begin to protest but decide it's pointless and swallow a spoonful of soup instead.

"I think you should talk to her," she says, then pops the piece of dipped grilled cheese in her mouth.

My head falls back. "I've already been over this with Drew. I'm not calling Francesca."

"I'm not talking about Ms. Frankie." She pulls off another piece. "I'm talking about Ms. Julia."

The little bit I've eaten settles in the pit of my stomach like a pile of bricks. I pick up my spoon, swirl it around my bowl, and then set it back on my plate. "Julia."

"I was nineteen when I found out my Theodore wasn't coming home from Vietnam, and I still talk to him almost every single day. You should try it. He gives me peace."

"What do you talk about?"

"Everything, *mijo*. The weather, politics, *you*. When I'm sad, he makes me smile, and my smile makes him happy." Her small hand wraps around mine and holds it tight. "Theodore was my first love, but that doesn't mean he was my only. If I were to find love again, I know he'd be happy for me."

"How do you know?"

She nudges my arm with her elbow. "I told you, *mijo*. We talk."

"Talk to Julia," Gloria said.

I don't think she meant talk to Julia *at the cemetery*, yet here I am.

When Julia's mom proposed headstones and cemetery space, I didn't argue. It was something she said she needed, and I wasn't about to deny her.

There's nothing to bury, I screamed in my head, but my voice stayed silent.

I showed up for the funeral because it was expected of me, but I haven't been back since. Not until today.

And now that I'm here, I feel even more pitiful than I did at home.

What do you say to the people you loved most in the world, the people you abandoned because they were just too hard to think about?

How's it going? Sorry I haven't dropped by in the last ten years?

I stuff my hands in my pockets, fists closed tight and nails digging into my palms.

Been keeping pretty busy. You know how it is.

My shoulders sag in a way they haven't since I was seven years old. My eyes are so heavy with shame, they can only look down. I wonder what my family thinks of me right now, showing up after all this time.

"I *am* sorry." Saying it out loud feels foreign and painful in my ears, but saying it out loud *to them* is gutting. "I miss you guys so much, and just thinking about you, it's…impossible. I don't do it. I *can't* do it. It's my fucking fault you're gone."

A wave of nausea washes over me, pitching my body forward until I'm hunched over, clutching my stomach. "Drew says it's survivor's guilt, but you know the truth. *I* put you on that plane—*me*—because I didn't want to let Annie down." My voice breaks and I can feel the tears welling inside me, stinging my throat, the backs of my eyes. I bite the inside of my cheek, trying to stop it, but it's no use, and as soon as my gaze locks on my little girl's name, I begin to crumble.

"God, Annie." I crouch down to her headstone, arms folded over the top, forehead resting on the beveled edge. "It's Daddy, honey." The tears I couldn't hold back spill down the surface of her memorial, cutting through layers of dirt and grime. "It's your birthday."

With my hand clenched in a fist, I try to scrub it off, but if anything, I make it worse.

Next time I'll bring something to clean it with, I think idly.

But there probably won't be a next time. I don't think I can do this again.

"You'd be starting high school this year. Can you believe that? My sweet girl, all grown-up."

I picture Annie as a teenaged Julia, with the same wild brunette curls and big brown eyes. She looked so much like her mother at four; I'm sure she would've at fourteen. I used to joke, if it weren't for her dimple, no one would believe she was mine. It was the only physical trait I gave her, and it was always visible, just like mine used to be.

"I wanted to teach you how to play guitar. I used to tell your mom we'd have our own band one day."

Jules would roll those big brown eyes of hers every time I brought up the idea, but on Annie's fourth birthday, she gave her a pink guitar.

"That would've been something, huh? We could have opened for Daddy's other band. Your mom thought that was silly. She'd say, 'No one wants to see you open for yourself,' but I think we'd have been a hit."

"Think of a name yet?" Julia asked as she put the last plate in the dishwasher.

276

"Sucks that The Doors is taken. What do you think about The Windows?"

She spun around. "Oh God, you're serious, aren't you?"

"You don't like it?" I shrugged. "I've got ten years. I'll come up with something."

"Ten years? You're delusional. No way Annie's going to be in a rock band with her daddy when she could be out with boys."

I arched my brows at her. "You're going to let her date at fourteen?"

"Now that I think about it, The Windows does have a nice ring to it."

A small smile pulls at my lips as the memory fades. "I think we were both delusional. I'm sure you would've had a boyfriend by now, and I would've hated him. Dads are supposed to, you know."

I push to my feet and dry my eyes on my shirtsleeve.

"Your mom wasn't allowed to date until she was seventeen, but since we were together all the time anyway, your grandma caved. Our first date was at a botanical garden not far from here. I wanted to surround her with flowers that were still growing and not stuck in vases in the back of our delivery van."

I turn toward my wife's headstone. "Do you remember that, Jules? I promised I'd marry you and build you a house in a field of flowers."

Reality was a two-story walk-up in Coral Terrace. It wasn't much, but it was ours. We talked about moving, and when things with the band started to take off, it became a possibility. But then we booked a tour, and...

"I know how much you hated me being gone all the time, and Annie was so young. If I could go back, I swear, I'd quit the band and live there forever with the two of you in that tiny apartment." I drop to my knees in front of her headstone. "Why did you get on that plane, Jules?"

A sharp pain stabs my chest at the sight of her name—the name her mother started and I completed—etched forever in a dusty slab of granite.

Julia March Fox.

I tear my gaze away and stare straight ahead, past the nameless, faceless graves that don't belong to me. Past the chain-link fence on the other side of the cemetery. Past the line of palm trees that border the street. Then I look up as pinks, purples, and oranges absorb the baby-blue sky and I know it will be dark soon.

"Do we have to leave right now? And miss the sunset? Annie's having so much fun building sand castles, and it's romantic."

"Who am I to stand in the way of sand castles and romance?" I pointed a finger at my wife. "But she's going straight to bed when we get home. And so are you."

"Mr. Fox, what do you have in mind?"

"Well, Mrs. Fox, I thought I'd bend you over our bed and fuck you so hard, you'll—ouch! You hit me!"

Julia's hands flew to her hips. "Stop teasing me!"

"Then tell me what you want."

"No."

"Say it."

"You'll laugh at me."

"Oh please, Jules," I begged. "It's so fucking cute when you say it."

"Fine. I want you to make love to me." Her face turned crimson. "Now stop laughing!"

"I can't help it. You turn bright red every time. Say it again."

"Make love to me."

"One more time."

"Make love to me, Darian."

"I miss you so fucking much. Why did you listen to me? Why did you get on that fucking plane?" I drag my hand down my face. "You didn't want to go. Why didn't you refuse? Not once in our whole relationship had you ever backed down from me. I loved that about you. So why the hell did you choose *that* day to finally do it?

"Every morning for years I'd wake up, expecting to find you lying next to me. But it's not you anymore, Jules; it's...*her.*"

My confession knocks the wind out of me and I fall forward, gasping for air. I close my eyes and breathe through the pain. Deep, palliative breaths.

Inhale.

"Baby, I met someone."

Exhale.

Other than the faint sound of a lawn mower buzzing in the distance, the cemetery is peaceful and quiet.

Inhale.

And when the wind blows, there's something sweet in the air, like jasmine or...*honeysuckle.*

Exhale.

"She's different from you in so many ways, but she has your quick wit and determination." I push off the ground and sit back on my heels. "And she can definitely put me in my place, as I remember you doing often.

"She loves me, Jules. She's beautiful and strong and *she loves me* and I let her go." An angry, hollow groan rips from my throat. "She was just supposed to be a distraction, someone to take my mind off you, but I fucking fell in love with her. And, God, now I miss her like I miss you."

"Then you should get her back."

My heart stops at the sound of her voice. A voice so similar to Julia's, it takes me a minute to digest that it isn't *her* but her mother, who's standing behind me.

Evelyn.

I buckle and my body collapses in a ball on the grass, trembling from sobs that make no sound.

"Shh…there, there," she whispers, kneeling beside me. Her arms wrap around me with a familiarity I haven't felt in years. "My sweet, sweet boy. How I've missed you."

She holds me close to her, rocking me as she smooths her hand over my back.

"This girl, this woman you speak of—she sounds pretty special. Do you really think so little of my Julia? Do you honestly believe she wouldn't have wanted you to move on? Be happy?"

Bravery pushes through her brittle voice. She's trying to be strong for me, and even though I know I don't deserve it, I need it. I need *her*. I slowly lift my head, and she tucks it into the crook of her neck. She smells exactly the same, like flowers and cinnamon. It's comforting, and I don't deserve that either.

"I miss them so much."

"I know, baby. I do too. But you can't stop living because they're gone. You've been lucky enough to find love twice? Are you really just going to let it slip away?"

"It was my fault. If I'd…"

"Hush now. I never want to hear you say that again. You didn't cause that plane to go down. You didn't take them from me. God did that, not you. But you, my love, you broke my heart. I shouldn't have had to mourn you too. I come here almost every day, hoping against hope you'll show. I guess today is my lucky day. On Annie's birthday no less."

"I'm sorry…I was so lost…I…"

Evelyn's arms tighten around me. "No more

apologies, baby. I think you've done enough of that today. Everyone has to grieve in their own way. I know how hard it has been for me. I can only imagine how hard it's been for you. I'm just happy you're here now."

I look up at her. Her straight, chin-length hair is almost completely silver, and her beautiful brown eyes—identical to Julia's and Annie's—are framed by a new set of wrinkles. But it's her smile that stands out to me; it hasn't changed.

All the pain I've caused her, and her smile for me is the same.

"Why are you being so nice to me?"

"Oh, my boy," she says with a resigned laugh. "I've known you since you were sixteen years old. I know you did what you had to for your own survival, and I accepted it because, well, what choice did I have? But don't think for a second that you were out of my life. I was just out of yours for a little while." She presses a kiss to my temple. "What's her name?"

"Francesca."

"Francesca. That's a beautiful name," she says. "And you love her?"

"Yes, I love her. I love her and it's killing me to be away from her."

"Does Francesca live here in Miami?"

"Texas."

"Texas," she says. She combs her fingers through my hair, fussing with it until every strand is back in place. "Sounds to me like you have a plane to catch."

"I can't. I hurt her. She deserves better. And *Julia*..." I turn to face her headstone. "*She* deserves better."

"Julia's gone. And, Darian, honey, you're the very best there is. Julia knew it, and I know it. Francesca will too." She cups my chin in her small hand and draws my gaze back to her. "You had a horrific thing happen to you. Just be honest with her. And patient. She'll come around." Her eyes are warm as they rake over me. "How could she not?"

She uses my shoulders to push herself up, then holds out her hand. "You go fix this mess you've made with Francesca, and then you come see me. Do you hear me? Darian Thomas Fox, I swear to God, if you disappear on me again, I'll stalk you like the crazy lady you know me to be." Her shoulders sag in a sigh. "I've never lost sight of you, sweetheart. All these years, I've kept up with you. Kept tabs. But staying away from you has been the worst kind of torture. Please don't make me do that anymore."

"I promise you, I won't."

I can't.

I stand up, forcing a heavy swallow down my throat as I take in my mother-in-law. I did what I thought I had to do to survive, but it doesn't make it right, does it?

"I love you so much," I say to her, "and I am…I'm so—"

"Shh," she says, squeezing my hand. "I love you too."

Evelyn's right; I have a plane to catch, but it's too late to charter one. So I do the one thing I swore I'd never do. I drive to Miami International and buy a one-way ticket for a commercial flight.

I refuse to wait another second. I miss her that goddamn much. For the first time in ten years, my mind's at peace, quiet, but for one thought: *go to her.*

But once I get to the terminal, it's all I can do to keep it quiet. It remembers being here, and it remembers the agony that followed. It's telling me how stupid I am. It's asking me what I'm thinking. It wants to know how I can board a flight to see *her* in the very same airport I last saw *them.*

It's just a place.

I draw in deep breaths.

It's just a building with walls.

My ears swallow the noises around me until they all blend together in a single shrill ring. Sweat begins to bead on my forehead.

It's just this place. It's this building, these walls.

A chill shoots up my spine, causing my damp skin to prickle. I rub my arms to warm them and close my eyes.

Once I'm on the plane, I'll be fine.

Memories of that day begin to circle like sharks, smiling at me with razor-sharp teeth, mocking me before dragging me under.

"Bye, Annie, honey. You be a good girl for Mommy, okay?"

"I will, Daddy."

Panic tears away every last stitch of calm, and I know I need to move.

Stand, Fox. Just stand up.

I push out of my chair, my eyes darting around the busy terminal.

Move, dammit!

My feet are as heavy as lead as I drag them away from the gate. It's like trudging through quicksand, each step more grueling than the last. I don't make it far before they stop, leaving me stranded in the middle of the busy concourse with tingling limbs and a roiling stomach. The room begins to spin, and then everything goes dark.

"Sir, are you okay?"

"It's this place," I say.

"What place, sir?"

I pull myself together just enough to get out of the goddamn airport, and twenty long-as-fuck minutes later, I'm getting into my car. The pressure in my head eases to a dull thud, and I sit there with my door cracked, enjoying the stale air of the valet parking garage until a tap on the passenger window urges me on. I shift into drive and roll away from the curb.

Get me the fuck home.

I exit the airport and travel south toward my neighborhood, but as soon as I reach the interchange, my heart takes control of the wheel.

A nervous laugh bursts from my throat as the runway lights of Miami International fade in the rearview mirror.

I head east on the Dolphin Expressway and barrel north on 95.

Out of Miami.

Out of my past.

And straight to her.

CHAPTER 15

Love Her Madly

Drew: Making sure you're alive. Call me.

Drew: Where are you? And where the hell is Gloria? Please don't make me resort to calling She Devil.

Drew: Guess what I learned today? Amanda responds to expensive chocolate.

Drew: And you might want to call her. She's not very happy with you right now.

> Darian: Sorry. I've been driving. In Tallahassee, headed to Texas.

> Darian: And I don't want to get into it with you, if you don't mind.

Drew: :-)

Darian: I'm going to be out a while longer.

> Amanda: Are you kidding me? Do you have any idea what's going on with Flight Risk?

Darian: Riley filled me in. It's being taken care of. Take it off your plate.

> Amanda: I saw Drew. He told me Princess Jailbait went back to Texas.

Darian: She did and that's where I'm headed.

> Amanda: I knew you were due for a breakdown.

Darian: Already had it and I'm fine. Thanks for your concern.

> Amanda: So this is serious?

Darian: Potentially.

> Amanda: You handle FR. I'll handle the rest.

Darian: Thanks, Amanda.

> Amanda: She's a lucky girl.

Frankie

The NyQuil I took wears off, and like an addict after a fix, I trudge to the kitchen for more. I've been over my welcome-home cold for a couple of days now, but NyQuil is the only thing that allows me to sleep. I should probably just leave the stupid bottle on my nightstand so I don't have to keep getting up. But then I might never get up.

I toss back the shot just as my phone vibrates on the counter. A nervous chill sweeps over me. At three a.m., my mind immediately goes to Jane, but as I yank my phone free from the charger, I find it's Darian's face, not Jane's, displayed on the screen. My heart launches into full-blown panic.

Why is he calling me?

Why is he calling me so late?

I don't answer. I *can't* answer.

Seconds later, I get a text.

Darian: I'm in your driveway.

My gaze shoots to the window, but with the light on in my kitchen, all I see is my slack-jawed reflection staring back at me. I flip the switch and look again.

Shit.

Darian's in my driveway—bent forward with his arms wrapped around the wheel, his hunched silhouette illuminated. The sight of him knocks the wind out of me.

I stare, dumbstruck, not sure what I should do. Other than cracking his door, he hasn't moved.

These past few days have been hell. I've been sick. I've been drunk. I've cried until I've run out of tears. I've slept through whole days and spent whole nights staring out this window. Having your heart broken is no fucking joke, but it's true what they say: every day, it *does* get a little easier.

Unless the cause of your heartbreak shows up at your house at three in the morning just when you're starting to get it together. I want to lock the door and pretend this isn't happening. I want to run to him and pretend everything's okay.

What is he even doing here?

I take a deep, steadying breath and open the door. The bracing chill from an early spring cold front hugs me with frozen arms. I welcome it; it's numbing, and right now, numbing is good.

Darian's gaze locks on me as he climbs out of the car.

"Why are you here?" I ask.

His breath hits the air in clouds of white vapor. He shivers as he walks toward me, his arms wrapped tightly around his torso. He gets to my bottom step and stops. He doesn't complain about the cold, nor does he ask to come inside.

"I saw your light on," he says.

"That's not what I asked."

"I needed to see you. I was going to wait until morning, but…"

"But you were freezing?"

"I knew you were up."

A blistery gust of wind slices through the railing. The bitter cold fills my lungs and my cough threatens to return.

"Get your stuff and come in."

He holds up a white plastic drugstore bag. "This is all I have."

I give him a single nod, and he climbs the steps. He stops just short of the door and lifts a hand to my face like he's going to touch me but decides against it.

"I'm sorry," he says. "I don't know what else to say but I'm sorry."

I'm sorry too.

"Not out here." I wave him in.

Darian's body goes rigid the second he enters my kitchen, and my cheeks heat from embarrassment.

"It's not as bad as it looks," I say. "I've been sick."

He turns on the overhead light, and I turn it off behind him; the moonlight coming through the window is bad enough. I sink into the closest chair at the table and watch as his eyes trail over the mess I've made of my life in the last four days—the scattered contents of my duffel, the empty wine bottles on the counter, the overflowing trash bin.

"Francesca…" My name comes out as a sigh and only makes me feel worse. Darian sits in the chair across from me but keeps his eyes downturned.

"You weren't supposed to see this." I peer down at my guys-suck pajama pants and the mystery stain on my tank. "You weren't supposed to see *me* like this."

He swallows hard. "I'm in no position to judge."

Then why aren't you looking at me?

"And you don't need to worry about me either," I say. "I'm *fine*."

He eyes the half-empty bottle of NyQuil sitting on the counter beside the sink. "You said you're sick?"

I shrug. "I haven't been feeling well. But I'm *fine*."

His gaze lingers on the NyQuil, but mine falls on him. He looks so different. His eyes are bloodshot and his sexy stubble is on its way to a full-grown beard. He's dressed in jeans and a plain white T-shirt—no band, no logo, no tour dates gracing the back. Despite everything that's happened, it makes my chest ache to see him this way, so…unlike himself.

"Why are you here, Darian? I know you didn't drive over a thousand miles just to tell me you're sorry."

He glances down at his thumb sliding back and forth across the edge of the table. "I know I should have called before showing up in the middle of the night, but I thought you'd tell me not to come."

"You would have been right."

"God, baby, I'm so sorry," he says, lifting his gaze.

Now he decides to look at me, just as my eyes begin to water.

I shove out of my chair and move to the sink. "Yes, I

know. You've said that already. And please don't call me *baby*. I'm not your baby; I'm not your anything."

I crack the window and draw in a sharp breath of cold air. My body is exhausted and the NyQuil is kicking in. I'm emotional, to say the least, and it wouldn't take much to make me a sobbing mess.

"You warned me. I was the one who fell in love and broke our agreement." A tear spills down my cheek and I brush it away. "You're far from innocent in all this, but I can't fault you for not loving me back."

"Francesca, there's so much I need to say to you."

The legs of his chair scrape against the linoleum as he pushes out of it. I watch his reflection advance toward me in the glass. He cups his hands over my shoulders, and I duck away from him, moving a safe distance across the kitchen.

"You didn't even tell me goodbye." My voice splinters and I can feel my resolve splintering right along with it. "I think that was the worst part. You just discarded me like I wasn't even worth a wave or a handshake."

He leans forward, gripping the edge of the counter. "I know."

"Darian, it's really late…or really early. Like I said, I haven't been feeling well. The only reason I was up was to take something to help me sleep, and that's what I need to be doing."

We both look up at the same time, our eyes catching in the window.

"I can't do this right now."

"Okay," he says gently. "I don't want to upset you any more than I already have." He turns around to look at me. "I understand if you want me to find somewhere else to stay tonight."

The thought of him being here, with only a wall to separate us…it's unbearable. But the thought of him leaving is worse.

"It's fine," I say, moving to the linen closet. "You can have the sofa." I grab an extra pillow and blanket. "It's not very comfortable, but it's better than your car."

"Thank you, Francesca." He sits on the edge of my couch, hunched forward with his head in his hands. "I hate that I hurt you," he whispers as I turn toward my room.

"I know," I whisper back.

I wake up expecting the same onslaught of tears that have greeted me every morning, but today it seems I've been spared. Having Darian here gives me the tiniest flutter of false hope. I'm not foolish enough to think this will end well. I know he will leave and the agony of that loss will hit me tenfold, but right now, my heart feels just a little less broken.

Darian's back is to me as I step into the kitchen. He's standing over the sink in a pair of loose-fitting basketball shorts and a white tee. His jeans are spread out in front of him and he's scrubbing them with a dishcloth.

I stand there a moment and stare. *God, how I've missed him.*

"Spill something?" I ask as I slide into a chair.

The sound of my voice startles him and his head whips around.

"Grass stains," he says, hanging the rag on the faucet. He grabs a paper towel to dry his hands and then tosses it in the waste bin—the emptied waste bin.

I glance around my kitchen. It's clean. My duffel is zipped closed and parked near the back door. My counters are clutter-free. I stretch my arms across my bare table and notice even the wine rings are missing.

I'm both embarrassed and grateful he did this for me.

"Thank you for picking up," I say. "I'm not usually so messy, but I wasn't expecting…company."

His lips curve slightly. "Couldn't sleep. Figured I'd do something to help out." He takes a white paper bag out of the oven and sets it on the table with a couple of plates. "Sucks trying to do stuff when you're sick."

Or when you're heartbroken.

The savory scent rising from the bag teases my stomach. I pull it open and peek inside. "Tacos?"

"From that food truck next to Rose's." He thumbs the neck of his shirt. "Needed to get a few things and thought you might be hungry."

"I'm starving. I haven't…"

Eaten, I think, as I pull out a taco and set it on a plate. *But Darian already knows that because this is what he does. This is how he takes care of me, and he's done it this whole time.*

Warmth spreads through me at the realization.

I sit back in my chair and slowly lift my eyes to his. "Darian, why didn't you bring anything? And why didn't you fly?"

"Last-minute decision," he says, turning back to the sink to inspect his jeans. He turns on the faucet and runs water over the knees.

"There's an old toothbrush in the junk drawer on your right," I tell him. "How did you manage to get grass stains on—"

My question's interrupted by Jane's face lighting up my phone. It vibrates across the table and I grab it just before it slides off the edge.

"If that's Jane," Darian says, "you might want to answer. She's been calling all morning."

A long sigh heaves from my throat as I get up from the chair. "Yeah, I should probably talk to her before she calls in a SWAT team."

I wouldn't say I've been avoiding her exactly, but I have been putting her off. I can't blame her for being worried. It's not like I've been the picture of health and stability this week.

I've been...*blah*. And there's nothing you can do to cheer up *blah*, so I spared her the effort.

I grab my sweater hanging by the door and shrug into it. The biting wind slams into me as I step outside, rendering the flimsy fabric useless. I huddle in the corner of my patio and dial Jane back.

"It's about time," she says, picking up on the first ring. "You know you freak me out when you don't answer."

"I didn't mean to freak you out. I slept in this morning."

"Morning? It's one thirty."

"I was up late," I say as my teeth begin to chatter.

"Then I hope you got plenty of rest because I just bought both Magic Mikes, oh, and get this, I found *Pole Dance 101* on Amazon. We're gonna need margaritas. I know that doesn't exactly go with pizza, but I don't think we want to be sloshing red wine around your—"

"Jane—"

"Duh. We don't have poles. Red wine it is then."

Ugh. It's Saturday. I told her she could come over. I drag my fingers through my hair, pulling it into a clump at my neck. "Pizza and strippers sound heavenly, but we're going to have to reschedule."

"Oh no you don't. Dammit, Frankie. I knew you were

going to flake on me."

"I'm not flaking," I say, stepping away from the wall with my phone wedged between my ear and shoulder. I run my hands up and down my thinly covered arms trying to warm them. "He's here."

"Darian?"

"Yes Darian. Who else?"

I hear her sliding glass door open and close followed by the squeak of the rusted lawn chair she refuses to part with.

"Did you know he was coming?" Her voice stutters in the cold. "How long has he been there?"

I cup my hand over my mouth as if Darian might hear me through the wall. "No. He just showed up. *At three this morning.* Jane, it's weird. He drove."

"Why did he drive? And what does he want?"

"He said it was a last-minute decision, and I don't know what he wants. We haven't gotten that far yet." I move back to my corner. "I think he feels bad. It's not like we parted on good terms."

She blows out a loud exhale. "Frankie, you understand this whole friends-with-benefits thing can't continue, right?"

"Yes."

"I'm serious. You could really get hurt. You've *already* gotten hurt."

"I know."

"It's freaking cold out here," she says through her own set of chattering teeth. "Text me with updates, and don't forget I'm going to Houston for that writers' retreat on Monday, but I'll have my phone on the whole time. God I hope it's warmer there. Call me if you need anything. Call me if you *don't* need anything. Just call me, okay?"

"I will. I promise." My frozen lips curve into a smile as I reach for the door handle. "Have fun, and don't forget to pack your condoms."

Jane laughs. "Please. They stay packed. I love you, Frankie."

"Love you too."

I hang up my sweater when I step inside the kitchen and then shiver from the lack of warmth it managed to provide. After spending two weeks in the Sunshine State, this weather is just plain cruel.

Darian's sitting at the table in the chair across from mine. He pops open a can of Diet Coke, pours it over ice, and slides it toward my plate. My mouth waters. Real food *and* a Diet Coke. I haven't had either lately.

"Everything okay with Jane?" he asks as I drop into my chair.

"My late night awarded me a pass." I hold up my soda before taking a sip. "Thanks for this."

We eat in heavy silence—heavy by way of Darian's stare that never seems to leave me. I know he's here to talk; I just don't know what he wants to talk about, and to be honest, I'm a little scared to find out. If all he wanted to do was apologize a phone call would have sufficed.

I'm worried it's more than that. I'm worried he wants to go back to the way things were—you know, before I opened my big mouth and spilled my feelings all over his boat.

I wish it were that simple.

I push my glass aside and trace my finger around the water ring it left on my newly polished table—around and around as I try to figure out a way to get this over with.

Say your piece, make nice, and go home...so I can start this whole miserable process all over again.

I look up at him. "Are you going to tell me why

you're here?"

"I miss you, Francesca," he says without hesitation. He leans forward and rests his forearms on the table. His fingers inch toward mine. "I fucking miss you, and I'm sorry…"

My gaze drops to his hands and my heart aches with longing. I want nothing more than to feel the warmth of his skin, the strength of his grip, the familiar comfort of his thumb as it grazes my knuckles. But I can't. I can't let myself feel *him* because when he lets go, I'll shatter.

I grab our empty plates instead.

"Darian, I miss you too, but I'm going to have to *keep* missing you." I set our dishes on the counter and pull open my junk drawer. With trembling fingers, I dig for the toothbrush and then stretch his jeans taut across the sink. "I'm sorry I fell for you, but I did and I can't be your *friend* anymore." The sentence hurts. I blink back tears as I turn on the faucet and focus on the task at hand.

"You wanted to know how I got the grass stains…" Darian's voice sounds fragile and quiet, as if we're suddenly in a library. "I went to the cemetery. Before I came here, that's where I was."

My hands stop moving and I lift my blurry gaze to the window.

"I've been there exactly twice," he says as he edges up to the sink. He takes the brush and jeans from my stalled fingers and resumes what I barely managed to start. He's silent for a moment while he works, but then his hand stills, closing tight around the brush. "And both times, I ruined a perfectly good pair of jeans." His smile is mirthless. He wipes his eyes with his forearm, then returns to the stain.

The image my mind conjures is heartrending. I move

to the side, a hand held to my mouth as I watch Darian work the brush with gentle strokes. The soap lathers to a thick foam, and he rinses it beneath the faucet. The stubborn stain doesn't even have the decency to fade.

"The first time was right after the funeral," he says. "I kneeled before Julia's headstone and promised her there would never be anyone else." His gaze burns through the window. He splays his fingers and the brush falls from his hand. "The second time was two days ago—when I broke that promise. I told her I was in love with you." He turns to me then, and a long, slow swallow rolls down his throat. "I love you, Francesca."

He loves me.

My heart swells with the words and then crashes to the pit of my stomach.

But he wishes he didn't.

The tears I managed to quell burst free, sliding down my face in a solid sheet.

"I tried to fight it," he says. "God knows I tried. You left and I thought my only choice was to get over you...but I can't."

He scrubs his hand over his face, leaving behind damp cheeks and thick, wet lashes. His eyes search mine, and the desperate look he gives me causes my breath to catch. My fingers itch to touch him and my arms long to wrap around him, but I don't do either. I just stand and stare, unable to move or speak.

"I'm sorry," he says. "This isn't how I wanted this conversation to go." He rakes a hand through his hair. "I didn't mean to dump all this on you. I wanted to tell you I fucked up and to please forgive me and that I hope like hell you still love me because I love you."

Aside from the running water, the room goes completely silent.

"I don't know what I'm supposed to say." I hug my arms to my chest. "I can't imagine what that must have been like for you, but you really hurt me, Darian."

"I know," he says, "and I'm going to fix it. Please, Francesca, let me fix it. At least let me try."

"How?"

"Come with me to Austin tomorrow, just for one night. There's something I want to show you."

"Austin." The word falls from my mouth.

Where we began…

I feel light-headed. "This is a lot, Darian," I say, gripping the counter for support, "and *so* not what I thought you were going to tell me." I turn off the faucet. "I'm a little overwhelmed. Actually, I'm a lot overwhelmed. I need to clear my head and just…*think*."

Darian nods. "I understand. Do you want me to go?"

"No," I say quickly, turning toward my bedroom door. *I don't want you to go.* "You don't have to go. Just give me some time."

Frankie: He told me he loves me.

Jane: I knew it! What did you say?

Frankie: Not a lot. I'm scared. What if he still isn't ready?

Jane: What if he is?

I sink low in my claw-foot tub as honeysuckle-scented bubbles rise to my chin. My knees are bent, my feet perched on the lip of the porcelain. The faint glow of the afternoon sun filters through sheer white curtains, bathing the room in dim light. The effect is calming, and I begin to relax for the first time in days.

I lie there for maybe an hour as the water cools and the dim light turns gray. I'm about to get out when my phone vibrates with a text.

> Darian: I heard a song on my way here that made me think of you. It's called Flight. Ironic, huh? Can we erase every stupid thing I've said since I got here and pretend I led with this?
>
> Frankie: Darian…
>
> Darian: I know. I'm not playing fair. Just listen.

Seconds later, the link appears on my screen and I click on it. A soft piano intro fills my small bathroom and I lie back in the lukewarm water, close my eyes, and let the melody envelop me. The lyrics are both a confession and a promise, and I listen to them again and again until my skin prunes.

Darian's telling me he loves me.

He's telling me I'm his lifeline.

He's telling me…*he's ready*.

> Frankie: I'll go with you to Austin.

CHAPTER 16

Waiting For The Sun

Amanda: Checking in. Thanks for handling Flight Risk.

Darian: No problem. I have a meeting in the morning with the Kellerman Group.

Amanda: I thought we decided to wait on that.

Darian: I'm moving forward.

Amanda: I knew it! Riley owes me $20.

Frankie

Darian lost his entire world the day that plane went down. How could a person ever move on from something like that? I don't think I could. I didn't think he did. Yet ten years later, here he is. Ready to move on...with *me*.

I just don't know if *I'm* ready.

"You okay?" Darian asks, glancing at me from the driver's seat. "You seem...far away."

You know the saying *sometimes love isn't enough*? I used

to think it was such bullshit. *Love is everything.*

But now I'm starting to get it.

"I'm fine," I say. "Just in a daze I guess."

Because I do love him, and it might not be enough.

A slight frown pulls at his lips as he turns back to the road. "Thank you for doing this."

I nod, then tuck my feet beneath me on the seat and rest my head against the window.

Is my love for him stronger than my fear of losing him?

I push the question from my mind and focus on the blur of bluebonnets lining I-35. It looks like spring has finally sprung in the Hill Country, and with the sun no longer battling a cold front, it's a perfect day.

"Are they always this thick?" Darian asks as he moves into the right-hand lane. "The wildflowers?"

"It's all the rain we've had." I glance at him and then back out my window. "It's been a wet month."

Usually there'd be a mix of colors made up of Indian Blankets, Mexican Hats, and Winecups, but this stretch of highway is nothing but blue.

We exit the interstate and head west on Cesar Chavez. Without the festival traffic, Austin feels like a ghost town. The streets are empty by comparison and we make almost every light.

Darian takes a left at San Jacinto, then immediately veers into the turn lane.

My head jerks to the side. "The Four Seasons?"

"You won't need your bag," he says with a small smile. "We're not staying; we're just…visiting."

We roll up to the curb and he puts the car in park. A valet opens my door.

"So this is like a do-over?" I ask.

I step onto the sidewalk as Darian makes his way around the car. He's dressed in the indigo-washed jeans and short-sleeved white button-down he bought on our way into Austin. I'm used to seeing him dressed down in concert T-shirts or dressed up in the occasional suit. This is a nice change. He looks handsome.

"A do-over implies the need to do something a second time because the first time was a failure," he says. "I've made a lot of mistakes, Francesca, but approaching you that day wasn't one of them."

A flush creeps up my neck and I spin toward the door, walking ahead as Darian falls in step behind me. I feel the tips of his fingers graze my back and then withdraw as we cross the threshold. I slow my pace until he's beside me. He keeps his hand close but doesn't touch me again. I'm tempted to stop so he's forced to touch me, but I don't know if I'm ready for that either.

"Someone to Watch Over Me" drifts softly from the Steinway in the corner as we cross the vacant lobby toward the lounge. It's as quiet in the hotel as it was on the streets outside. South By blew in like a hurricane but only left calm in its wake.

We choose the first table we come to. Darian pulls out my chair and then takes the one on the opposite side. A smile tugs at his lips as he turns his head back to the lobby. We have a perfect view of the front desk, and I don't think it's a coincidence.

"What about the antipasto platter?" Darian asks as he skims the menu. "Something light since we're having a big dinner?"

"Where's dinner?" I ask, shrugging out of my sweater.

"I was thinking French."

Not a do-over but a repeat. A walk down memory lane.

My chest warms. "French sounds perfect."

"Mr. Fox, I thought that was you." The voice comes from behind me and gives me a start.

"Mr. Harper." Darian stands with his hand extended. *Mr. who?*

Our guest firmly grips Darian's hand and then turns to me.

Oh.

"And, Ms. Valentine, what a pleasure." His face brightens as his eyes flicker between us. "Are you staying with us tonight?"

"Not this time," Darian says. "This date's a bit...location specific."

Mr. Harper chuckles. "Next time then. And thank you again for the tickets. My wife is beside herself."

Tickets?

"My pleasure. Glad I could help."

"I'll leave you kids alone," Mr. Harper says. "Enjoy your time in Austin."

The hotel manager walks away and I shoot Darian a look. "Tickets?"

"I may have bribed him a little," he says, drawing out the *I*.

"Bribed him?"

"Bribed...traded..." He purses his lips. "I had something he wanted, and he had something I wanted."

I lean forward with my forearms pressed against the edge of the table, hands folded at my chest. "What did he have that you wanted?"

Darian smiles. "In a sense...you."

My brows furrow.

"This might be easier to explain if I start at the beginning," he says, turning his gaze to the front desk. "I brought you back here, Francesca, because this is where my life changed course. That day, you gave me a gift.

"The panel I'd given had just wrapped up and I was headed through the lobby when I heard you. In a sea of people…I heard *you*."

My hand flies to my face. "Oh God, was I that loud?"

Darian shakes his head. "No, you weren't…not yet anyway. I followed the sound of your voice until I found you pressed against the front desk. You were arguing with the clerk, but I couldn't make out what you were saying. I could just tell you were frustrated and I remember thinking…it was cute."

"Cute?"

He shrugs. "I watched you for a minute. I was about to walk away when you flung your head back and said— no, *shouted*—that you were *kaput*. Everything just stopped. I was rooted in place, and all I could do was stare. Eventually you caught me staring, but I still couldn't take my eyes off you."

I remember that moment so clearly. The way my skin tingled and the hairs on the back of my neck stood on end. I knew someone was watching me. Darian was watching me. I *felt* him.

"The day I lost my family was the worst day of my life," he says, "and thank Christ I don't remember much of it. What I do remember was pure *agony*. I'd never considered what that word actually meant. To someone who hasn't experienced it, agony is just a synonym for *pain*." The muscles in his jaw clench, followed by my stomach. "Pain has levels. It even has a fucking scale. Agony has no levels, no scale."

Darian's eyes close, and mine lower to his hand, balling into a fist on the table. I reach for it, slide my fingers through his, and squeeze it as tight as I can.

"I'm sorry," he says. He looks at me and then at our joined hands. His eyes are like glass.

"Don't be sorry. Not for this."

His thumb brushes against my knuckles, sending a

chill up my arm.

"There were some good memories from that day too," he says. "Memories I'd forgotten." His expression softens. "And you brought them back."

"Me? How?"

"It was that word…*kaput*." Darian smiles, and the rare sight of his dimple lowers my defenses even further. "I swear every week my mother had a new word, and that week—that *day*—it was *kaput*. She said it like it was a word she used often, but I'd never heard her say it before. I remember thinking, *God, this crazy woman. I love her so much.*" His gaze falls to the table. He picks up a sugar packet and flicks it between his fingers. "Her force-fed vocabulary lessons used to annoy the hell out of me, but as I got older I learned to appreciate them.

"That day I asked her, 'Is that your new word this week?'

"She smiled and told me it was. Then she said, 'It's a great word, but nobody ever uses it.'" He pauses. "But you did."

"I did," I say, thinking back on the moment. "And I never do. It's not something I normally say."

Darian's eyes meet mine and his smile tightens. "I wish I could remember all the words she tried to teach me. At least I remember that one, thanks to you. It was a beautiful moment that got lost in a horrible day…and you gave it back to me."

We barely touch the antipasto platter. Darian's confession is too big for our small table, and we hurry to leave it. He drives us to The Mendón where we check into the same rooms we had before. And aside from getting in and out of his car, he never lets go of my hand.

The walk to our floor is silent. I'm lost in my thoughts, my mind reeling with questions I need answers for—hard questions I can't bring myself to ask. So I don't say anything until we're standing in front of my door, and even then, I opt to ask an easy one.

"What if I had said no?"

Darian's still holding my hand. His gaze is aimed at my face, but he isn't looking at me so much as *through* me. He's lost in his thoughts too. My voice catches him off guard and it takes a moment for my words to register.

"Said no?"

"When you offered me a room. What if I had said no?"

He shoves his free hand in his pocket and rocks back on his heels. "I was prepared to wait with you. I was even prepared to have my driver take you home, but I was selfish and didn't want to do either." He pauses, then says, "There's just something about you, Francesca." His gaze falls to our threaded fingers and he holds my hand a little tighter. "I wish I could explain it. I wish I could *understand* it. What started out as wanting to do right by my mother turned into wanting something for me. You. I wanted *you* for me even though I didn't know it yet." He shakes his head. "I'm not making any sense, am I?"

"No, you're…I get it…"

I feel my defenses peeling away in layers. I'm trying to stay strong. Think clearly. Rationally. But Darian's words cloud the air like a thick mist and I can't see past my own heart.

A jagged swallow grazes my throat. "I should go." I pull my hand free, then slip it inside my purse and take out my key card. "Oh, my bag…"

"Already inside," he says, staring down at his empty fingers. "Take your time. Our reservations aren't until seven." He bends to kiss my forehead, then stops.

"It's okay," I whisper.

Is it okay?

The feel of his lips is so faint, I wonder if they touch my skin at all.

"See you soon, Francesca," he says and then turns toward his door.

My chest tightens as if the walls of the corridor are closing in. "Darian?"

He stops and smiles at me over his shoulder.

I shake my head. "Never mind. I'll see you soon."

We sit at a small corner table beneath a bronze farmhouse chandelier. The restaurant is full, but the level of noise is considerably lower than it was during South By.

Darian asks if I'd like the same Bordeaux we had that night in my room—the night we were together for the first time. My mind burns with the memory, but I pass. Today has been intense and my emotions are all over the place. The last thing I need is alcohol clouding my judgment.

When the waiter arrives, Darian hands him the wine list and orders sparkling water instead. Then we're alone, and our table falls quiet. Darian unfolds his napkin and then folds it again. A hesitant smile pulls at the corners of his lips and a flush comes over his face.

I cock my head. "What is it?"

His eyes lift to mine and his smile widens. "I was just remembering the last time we were here. How much I wanted to kiss you." He unfolds his napkin once more and drapes it across his lap. "I almost did; I was so close."

"Why didn't you? You had to have known I wanted you to."

The waiter delivers a bottle of San Pellegrino and says he'll return for our orders. Darian pours the water, and I close my hand around my glass to give it something to do.

"I was going to...I was so nervous I was clutching the tablecloth beneath the table. I didn't even know I was doing it. When I moved closer to you, I felt it pull." He winces. "We were seconds away from a disaster. I took it as a sign."

"It would have been worth it."

"I wasn't so sure." His pinkie slides against mine, and they curl together. "I was afraid of scaring you off. I think yanking everything off the table might have done it."

I let go of my glass for his hand. "Like I scared you off? Attacking you in front of my room?" I squeeze my eyes closed, pressing my lips together. "I wish *I'd* been given a sign."

Darian laughs. "I still can't believe you thought I rejected you. I was so...*enamored*. But I was also terrified—of hurting you, of falling for you..." His grip tightens. "And I managed to do both."

Darian's quick to take my hand the second we leave the restaurant, and I'm quick to let him. I know I should slow down and put some space between us, but I can't help wondering if my time with him is fleeting.

At some point, he's going to go home and we'll have

nothing but space between us.

With our fingers meshed together, he keeps me close as we wander toward the hotel. We opt for Fifth Street over Sixth, which is fairly quiet on a Sunday night. Darian's quiet too. Halfway between Neches and Trinity, he stops, as if his feet are suddenly cemented to the sidewalk, and it's obvious something's weighing on him.

"You can tell me," I say. "Whatever it is, you can tell me."

A warm gust of wind whips through my hair, blowing it in my face. Darian steps in front of me and tucks the loose strands behind my ear.

"I was falling in love with you," he says. "Already. I could feel it, and it scared the hell out of me." His hand skims my neck and then disappears in the pocket of his jeans. "That's why I didn't go that night."

I'm quiet for a moment as memories from that night resurface. I'd considered everything from *he regretted asking me* to *he got tied up with work and forgot.* I even wondered if it was the sex. *Was I terrible? Or did he get what he wanted and no longer have a use for me?*

Those thoughts were quickly discounted. Darian wasn't like that; I was sure of it.

When he showed up at my cabin, I ruled out that it had anything to do with me at all.

But it did.

"I need to sit down." I don't realize I've spoken out loud until we're climbing the steps to a loading dock.

We sit on the edge, in front of an old warehouse with graffitied sheets of plywood covering the windows.

"I woke up that morning in your bed, and I knew. I didn't want to be anywhere else, but I *needed* to be...somewhere, *anywhere*...else. I guess I just panicked." Darian turns his body toward mine, my hand sandwiched between both of his. "I never meant to bail on you. It wasn't something I planned. It just...happened. Riley found me at the hotel bar and got me back to my room."

I pull my hand free and play with the buttons on my sweater. "I heard your voice when I got back. I almost knocked."

"I'm glad you didn't. I wouldn't have wanted you to see me like that. I was a mess." He leans forward, his elbows propped on his knees, his head lowered. "I loved my wife, and I made a promise the day I married her, one I vowed to keep even after her death. My feelings for you were a direct betrayal of that promise...at least, that's how I saw it at the time."

My breath hardens in my lungs. "Do you see it that way now?"

"No," he says, turning his gaze to me. "I still have guilt. I think I'll always have guilt. But I understand she's gone, and no matter what I do, I can't stay away from you. And I...can't change how I feel about you.

"When I woke up that next morning, I knew what I'd done, but I didn't know to what extent. I had no idea they'd put you on that stage. I figured you'd be pissed at me—angry but not embarrassed. Please believe me, Francesca. If I had known..."

"I believe you. But I wasn't just embarrassed; I was hurt."

"I know that now, but then..."

Darian's words are lost in a rush of voices spilling out of a nearby bar. When the noise tapers, I hop down from the loading dock and stand in front of him with my hands on his knees.

"It doesn't matter," I say, looking up at him. "I forgive you, Darian. For all of it."

He nods once, a swallow bobbing in his throat, as he

pushes off the dock and gathers me in his arms. "Thank you," he says, his voice barely above a whisper.

I rest my head against his chest and close my eyes. For just a moment, nothing stands between us.

There's no yesterday, no tomorrow. I get to be in the present.

But unlike Darian, I don't want to *stay* in the present. I want *tomorrow* too.

I pull away. "We should probably get back."

He nods again and takes my hand. We walk to our hotel in silence, neither of us saying a word until we're standing in front of my door.

"This is me," I say stupidly.

Darian smiles. "So it is."

"Look, I want to ask you in, but…"

"It's okay. You're not ready, and to be honest, I'm not sure I am either."

"I'm scared," I whisper.

"I know." He squeezes my hand a final time, then lets it go. "I am too."

I pull my lip between my teeth as I dig my key card out of my back pocket. "What time should I be ready in the morning?"

"Ten. I have a thing I need to take care of, but I'll be back by then."

"What kind of thing?"

"A work thing. It won't take long." He shuffles his feet. "I'll tell you about it tomorrow."

"Okay," I say, the key cutting into my palm.

"Okay."

"Well, goodnight."

"Goodnight."

Neither of us turns for our doors. Our feet stay grounded, eyes locked.

A quiet laugh rumbles from Darian's chest and he

runs a hand through his hair. "This is fucking killing me."

He takes a step forward, closing the small gap between us. My back presses against the door; his chest presses against me.

"Tell me not to kiss you." He watches me, stares at me. Then his eyes fall closed and his long fingers slide into my hair. "Tell me, Francesca, and I swear I'll go."

I don't say anything. I refuse. I bury my voice deep inside me. I'm scared if I try to speak the wrong words will come out—*Don't kiss me, Darian.* Fear rules my heart the way guilt rules his, and I'll be damned if I let it take this moment from me. I want him to kiss me. I *need* him to.

"Kiss me, Darian."

He bends slightly until his forehead touches mine and then holds it there. "Francesca."

The whisper finds my mouth before his lips do. I inhale my name as my arms ring around his neck. I pull him closer.

The kiss is soft, reverent. Our lips brush together, opening, closing. I part mine just enough to encourage him, and then I feel his tongue sweep into my mouth. I feel him in every nerve. Every cell. He kisses me like he can't believe I'm letting him, like maybe I'll ask him to stop. I won't stop him.

I can't stop him.

And when I feel his movements slow, his body pulling back, I ache. I ache for a loss that hasn't even happened yet. He could kiss me forever and it wouldn't be long enough. I don't want it to end, but I *need* it to end.

"I love you," he says.

I taste the words more than hear them. He touches his lips to my forehead, then turns and walks away.

I go to bed with Darian's kiss wrapped around me like a blanket. I didn't have a sip of wine, but I feel its warmth. As the hours press on, my euphoric buzz melts into trepidation that keeps me up most of the night.

Where do we go from here?

The question I've been avoiding haunts me until the early morning hours. I finally give up and watch the sunrise on the terrace while contemplating its answer.

Nowhere. He lives in Miami and you live here.

Darian picks me up in front of the hotel just before ten a.m. My stomach growls as I buckle myself into his car. He shifts into drive and gives me an apologetic look as he veers onto the street.

"You're hungry," he says as we slow to a stop at the light. "I ordered breakfast, but maybe I should have sent up room service again."

"I'm a big girl. I could have grabbed something if I wanted." I take a sip of my Diet Coke, nearly choking on it when his words register. "What do you mean you ordered breakfast? Where are we going?"

His fingers dance across the wheel. "It's a surprise."

Darian's wearing a suit, and I'm in a pair of cutoff denim shorts and a *Keep Austin Weird* T-shirt.

"I'm not really dressed to dine with the likes of you," I say, arching my brows at him. "Couldn't we just hit up Whataburger on the way home?"

"I promise you're fine. It'll just be the two of us."

"Okay, so like a picnic."

He tilts his head from side to side. "Yeah, I guess you could call it that."

The drive is short and within minutes we're pulling up

to the curb in front of a high-rise. Darian puts the car in park and cuts the engine.

Stepping onto the sidewalk, I lift my gaze to the building we're standing in front of. It's so tall I have to crane my neck just to see the top of it. Covered in reflective glass, it's like one giant mirror, and at this early hour, the glare is blinding.

I squint, turning away from it to face Darian as he rounds the front of the car. "Where are we?"

His smile is as brilliant as the sun. He doesn't answer, but wherever we are, he's excited to be here.

"We're having a picnic in an office building?"

He holds his hand out to me. "Come on."

We enter a lobby where we're greeted by a twenty-something receptionist with short, spiky blue hair and dark burgundy lips. She's dressed in a semi-conservative business suit that only partially covers the music-staff tattoo vining around her leg.

"Welcome back, Mr. Fox," she says before turning to me. "Welcome, Ms. Valentine."

"Francesca, this is Ms. Carlisle."

I shake her hand. For such a tiny little thing, she has a scary-firm grip. "Pleasure to meet you."

"Likewise." She turns back to Darian. "Mr. Fox, your food should be here in about thirty minutes. If there's anything else I can do for you, please don't hesitate to ask."

Darian's grip tightens around my hand as he pulls me to the bank of elevators in the back of the lobby. He presses a button and then brings me in front of him, slipping his arms around my waist. I melt against him. Aside from last night's kiss, this is the closest we've been in days.

And who knows how long it will last?

The elevator doors slide open and we step inside. Darian flashes a key card in front of the digital reader on the control panel, and as soon as the doors close we begin to rise.

"Is this where your meeting was?" I ask, arms crossed as I lean back against the mirrored wall.

He shrugs out of his suit coat. "It was."

"Is it…over?"

"It's over."

"Then why are we eating here?"

Darian's mouth twitches as he rolls up his sleeves. "I like the view."

"You're up to something," I say and then take a sip of my soda.

"And you're paranoid."

I don't care where we eat—or *what* for that matter—but every place he's taken me since we rolled into Austin has been intentional. He's definitely up to something.

The elevator stops on the fifty-sixth floor and the doors slide open to a second smaller lobby. It's a little run-down, and except for a dated desk and a pair of rolling chairs, it's empty.

"Where are we?" I ask a second time, but I let my question go as I take in the room. The carpet is clean but worn and the paint could use some attention. A sign hanging on the opposite wall reads *E.B. Brent & Company*, and to my right are floor-to-ceiling windows, which capture the view Darian mentioned. I stand in front of it, my eyes sweeping over the eclectic mix of buildings set in the Texas hills.

"Nice, right?" Darian says.

"The view? Definitely. But the rest looks… abandoned. Who were you meeting? A drug dealer?"

Darian laughs. "Come on. It's not so bad. And I don't

typically get to pick where meetings are held outside of Miami." He slides his hands in his pockets and leans against the wall beside the elevator. "Why do you care so much?"

I set my can on the desk. "Keeps my mind off my growling stomach," I say with a shrug. "So what did you order?"

"Something I promised you."

"Hmm…" I sit backward in one of the chairs, my legs folded on the seat. "Wait, are we having burgers for breakfast?"

Darian nods. "And waffles."

A huge smile spreads over my lips. "Oh my God, Darian. You remembered."

"I remember everything you tell me," he says, taking the empty chair beside me.

Heat builds in my chest and climbs to my cheeks. I pull my bottom lip between my teeth to keep from grinning. "Thank you."

"You're welcome."

Grabbing the edge of the desk, I turn myself to face the window. The sky is a soft baby blue, dotted with cotton-ball clouds, the city *where we began* stretched beneath it. My face soaks up the little bit of sun that manages to penetrate the tinted glass while my eyes soak up the view.

"You've got to admit," Darian says, "a place like this? It's all about the view."

"I know, and I was teasing. This place is great." I slowly spin in my chair, my eyes trailing around the room before returning to the window. "It's just a shame they let it go. All it needs is a little TLC."

"Some new furniture," he says. "Carpet."

I reach for my Diet Coke and take a sip, my gaze

317

lingering on the wall behind the desk. "Paint."

"Agreed. Paint's a must." Darian rolls his chair closer to mine and leans forward, his lips hovering at my ear. "So do you think you could help me?" he says. "I could hire somebody but—"

"Help you?" I jerk back to look at him, my soda splashing over the rim of the can. "Oh, wow…Darian…did you *buy* this place? Was your meeting with a realtor?"

He shrugs and a grin breaks across his face. "Welcome to Fox Independent's Austin branch."

"That's so great! When did you decide this?" I set my can on the desk and grab his hands. "And why didn't you tell me?"

"Amanda and I have been talking about it for a while," he says, "but I just recently decided to bite the bullet."

I let go of his hands and straighten in my chair. "How recent?"

"Friday."

"Darian, is this…" I suck in a breath. "Did you do this for me?"

"No. I did it for me."

"Thank God." A nervous laugh bubbles out of me. "The last thing you need to be doing is making business decisions with your…" I jut my chin toward his crotch.

He laughs. "I didn't. I made it with this."

My eyes lift to his hand, closed over his heart. I expect a joke. Some corny punch line, but there's nothing but the unexplainable pull that's always been between us. I'm powerless against it.

A thoughtful look settles on his face. "I don't want you to freak out. An expansion was going to happen sooner or later."

I should be freaking out, shouldn't I? But I'm not. I'm too damn happy. *He wants tomorrow too.*

Darian leans forward, piercing me with his olive gaze. "I'm really excited about this. It's about time we had an Austin presence, and just because you inspired me to do it sooner rather than later doesn't mean it was a bad move. I know what I'm doing. I promise."

"I believe you," I say. "I just don't want you to jump into something you haven't thought through."

I don't want you to make a mistake because of me.

"I've thought it through. Okay?"

"Okay."

Darian's face brightens, his pensive expression falling away. "So? What do you think?"

"I think it's great. I'm so proud of you, and…"

"And?"

I can't help but grin. "And it means you'll be in Texas more."

He sits back in his chair, his eyes searching mine as if he's looking for answers to questions he's yet to ask.

I know the feeling.

"Actually," Darian says, smiling tightly, "I'm hoping it means *you'll* be in Texas more."

Me?

My eyes narrow. "I don't understand."

"Francesca…" He reaches for my hand. "I have a proposition for you."

To Be Continued…

ACKNOWLEDGMENTS

Some books take a village. This one took a universe.

First, I want to thank the pros that turned my jumbled mess into something resembling a book. To Jovana, my editor and formatter; to Rach, my meticulous proofreader; to Robin, my very patient cover designer; and to Marianna, who painted said cover. Marianna, this painting is the number one reason I chose to self-publish. I might have been willing to compromise on some things, but my cover was never one of them.

To Steve, AKA SID, AKA my first beta. Sometimes I go back and glance at those initial pages I sent you and cringe. You must love me A LOT. Thank you for enduring the torture and for guiding me with grace.

To my first betas: Amanda, Emma G., Frederique, Beth, Crystal, Leama, and Lili. You guys are badass. So much has changed (including the genre), but the central story is still there. Your input really helped shape it into what it is today. Thank you so much for hanging in there with me.

To my final betas: Jennifer, Josiane, Lisa, and Nadine. Thank you for your honesty, encouragement, and excitement, and for giving me as much peace of mind as possible at this stage. I desperately needed all of it.

To Dee for being my go-to Miami guru. Thank you for answering all my questions—even during your vacation—and offering insight I didn't even think to ask.

To Ally for killing off eighty-eight innocent characters when you suggested a plane crash. Killer piece of advice. Literally.

To Jeannine for lighting a fire under my ass. You gave me the push I needed when I was at a standstill and advice at the end that helped me wrap everything up. I admire you as a writer and as a person, and I'm so happy I got to know you last year. Anytime you need a roommate, I'm your girl.

To Donna for keeping me sane. You may not know this, but your enthusiasm and encouragement got me through some trying days. I'll have a case of PG ready when you visit. I may even share it with you. **inserts our gif here**

To Heather B. for stepping in when you did. Your advice got me out of a horrible rut. You've been an awesome support and a great friend. I love our new CP relationship, although I feel like you may be getting the short end of the stick.

To my FB group, Books, Boys, and Booze. You guys have been amazing, and if it wasn't for FB being a butt, I wouldn't have you. I never intended to start a group so early—I never intended to start a group at all—but it seemed like the best (and potentially only) way to keep in contact with my favorite peeps. Not only did you step in and support me, you made this release more than I ever thought it could be. We're just a big bunch of book-lovin', boy-crazy procrastinators, and I love "wasting" time with you. ♥

To everyone who pushed this book, especially these repeat offenders: S. Ann, Sarah, Heather R., Irene, Paige, Nicky, Billy, Lynn, Deanna PinkLady, Malene with Bad & Dirty Books, Nadine with Let's Chat Books, Jessica with Chatterbooks Book Blog, Vanilla & Spice Books, and Biblio Belles. Thank you for your continued support and for all the posts, shares, retweets, comments, likes, emails, beta-reads, and that one crazy AF autograph request. ;-)

To Maryse for so many things. Your blog has truly been a home away from home, a place I can go and just be R. When I first found you, I bought and read almost every five-star book you'd reviewed. Then I went through your four stars. It wasn't until I'd exhausted that list that I decided to write my own. You rekindled my love of reading (which gave me the desire to write), but even more than that, you introduced me to these crazies: Fabi, Nay, Ela, Grey, Leslie, Tessa, Anna, Amy, Paula, Jan, Jean, Tasha, Melinda, Michelle, Lisa, bev, D.G., Cheryl, and Kooloo. Thank you all so much for your support and friendship over the past two years and for teaching me more about this industry than I ever could have learned otherwise. I adore all of you and I respect your opinions. Even when you're wrong. :-P

To Fabi for being one of the best betas I've ever worked with. You have and incredible knack for cutting through the crap. You were able to encourage and redirect me simultaneously—and there were a few places where I really needed that redirection. I could always take you at your word, and when you said you loved something, I had no doubt you did. You have been an immeasurable help to me and a genuine friend. I'm sorry I spread all those rumors about you streaking in my backyard.

To Renee for being my savior. You came in at the 11th hour, picked me up, and carried me across the finish line. I don't know how I would have made it without you. 2017 was not kind to you, and the holidays were especially tough. I know the sacrifice you made for me. As I write this, you are poring over a week's worth of emails and questions and reviewing highlights from three different manuscripts. It's still the holidays. There are a million things you should be doing, but instead you're doing this. I'm so grateful. Your help has been vital to me, and your patience is otherworldly. I can't wait to work with you on book two. I promise to be less crazy. **crosses fingers behind back**

To Erica for being a true friend, as well as my sounding board, my cocktail taster, and my therapist. You went through hell last year with Hurricane Harvey and you still managed to put out three books *while* being there for me amid all my craziness. I'm so proud of you and inspired by you. I love you to the moon and back. You're more than just a friend to me. You're family.

To Ashley. Can you believe it's only been two years? We clicked the second we met, and you instantly became my person. I didn't realize it at the time, but everything fell into place for me that day. Who knew beta-reading *your* book would change *my* life? Keep in mind, before you, Rojay was alive and well and Frankie was cryin' in di rain… Oy to the vey. That feels like foreverago. You have always been my biggest cheerleader, teacher, supporter, and confidante. You give me the best advice, and then you wait patiently for me to take it. I always do…eventually. By the time you read this, I will have popped the cork on the Waiting for the Sun wine you sent me for my birthday and drank it from the Darian Fox glass you sent me for Christmas. I wish you could have been here to share it with me, but we'll make up for it soon with a bottle of bubbly because *that* time has come. I love you and I miss you and I can't wait to see you.

To Emma. I'm not gonna cry. I'm not gonna cry. I'm not—dammit! When the hell did I become such an emotional sap? I'm going to skip over all the fangirl/stalker stuff that brought us together and jump ahead about six books. You went from being my role model to my mentor to my BFF. You've taught me so much, and it has been an honor and a privilege to learn from you. You think the scales are tipped in your favor, but they aren't. Not even close. Our relationship has come a long way, but you're still my favorite writer and I'm still your biggest fan. I just don't stalk you all that much anymore, despite what FB thinks. I'll rectify that next month when I'm crashing on your couch, eating all your babka. I love you more than Josh Duhamel and LP combined. XOXOXO.

To Briana and Stephan for their boundless patience. For the past three years, I've been a crazy person. Hard to believe, I know. These two put up with me—or survived me, I should say. I love you both. Briana, this book has been a true testament that if you put your mind to it, you can accomplish anything. Figure out what it is you want and go get it. Life is too short and the world is too small to let it pass you by.

And finally, to you, the readers. If you picked up my little labor of love, thank you. It means so much that you'd take a chance on a newbie like me. This story has been a part of my life for years (YEARSSSSS, my husband would say), and I'm so happy to finally be able to share it with you.

ABOUT THE AUTHOR

Robin Hill spends 75% of her day writing, 30% reading, and a good 25% hanging out with her husband whilst simultaneously stalking random people online. She's terrible at math. She loves wine. Coincidence? Maybe.

She also loves to cook, eat cheeseburgers, listen to The Doors, and watch Jeopardy. She hates flying and blue cheese, and she's not too keen on treadmills. She believes in aliens but not ghosts. And she dream casts Josh Duhamel in every book she reads.

Robin hides out at her Texas Hill Country compound with her husband and their little poodle princess, Alice Malice.

Waiting for the Sun is her first novel. Part two, Riders on the Storm, is coming soon. For updates, sign up for her newsletter, join her Facebook reader's group, Robin Hill's Books, Boys, & Booze, or stalk her online:

Website: http://smarturl.it/robinhillwrites

Facebook: http://smarturl.it/robinhillfacebook

Twitter: http://smarturl.it/robinhilltwitter

Instagram: http://smarturl.it/robinhillinstagram

Goodreads: http://smarturl.it/robinhillgoodreads

Amazon: http://smarturl.it/amazonrobinhill

Made in the USA
San Bernardino, CA
26 January 2018